Our Extended Universe

By

Dane Johns

Our Extended Universe

Copyright © 2023 Dane Johns

Paperback: 978-1-0880-0863-8

Ebook: 978-1-0880-1989-4

First Edition May 2023

Edited by Evan Fisher

Cover & Layout by Sarah Baldwin

Honey Gold Records / Heavy Hands Press

Printed by Lightning Source in the USA.

www.danecjohns.com

For **Stacy**

& all the stars in her sky.

"If you don't have anxiety, the way I would describe it is like there's an edgy improv group in your brain and it just needs like a one-word suggestion to spin countless scenarios that no one is comfortable with."

-Aparna Nancherla, comedian.

Our Extended Universe

A Big, Beautiful, Complicated Mess

MAY

Come to find out.

Erin & The Mission (Not Quite) Accomplished
Chapter One

On the morning of my Great Triumph, I wait for Blaide at our usual table in our usual place. It's comforting how Cole Brews never changes. The espresso machine whirrs behind the counter while the scent of cinnamon and coffee beans sway together to the sardonic melancholy of Phoebe Bridgers. Harrison, Cole's younger (and cuter) brother, works the counter in full hipster barista glory. He's got the whole cuffed-jeans, flannel shirt with sleeves rolled back to show off his colorful tattoos, high & tight thing going on. He catches me watching him and sends a little smile my way. I look away so fast I'm lucky I don't need a neck brace (or the self-duplicating medical bills associated with said neck brace).

Thankfully, my phone buzzes on the table before this line of thinking gets out of hand. Madison: "I think you should rethink this. Re: Breaking Up with Blaide."

Madison always texts in bursts of three, so I wait to respond.

Madison: "Just with tonight and everything…do you really think it's a good idea to add more stress?"

Madison: "I mean, and I don't say this to be a jerk, but remember what happened last time?"

I click the screen dark and put my phone face down.

She has a point though. Remember the funeral?

Shut up. Your reign is over.

Tonight's the night. I win. You lose.

We'll see about that.

"Hey, you look nice." Blaide swoops in across from me.

"Thank you," I say, just barely stopping myself from complimenting him back. Best to keep my game face on. Operation Break Up W/ Blaide Then Kick Ass Tonight is in full effect. He does look good though. Even with the bedhead factor taken into account, his dark blonde hair still hits the perfect balance of elegantly disheveled.

"You already order?" Blaide asks right as Harrison brings over a steaming Snoopy mug. Outdated cartoon mugs are (of course) the main reason I love this place.

"Vanilla Latte." Harrison announces as he sets it down.

"Thank you." I watch Harrison as he leans over me. Warmth passes through my cheeks before I even take a sip.

Okay, well, the mugs are *another* reason why I love this place.

"What about you?" Harrison juts his chin at Blaide. The two of them were in the same graduating class last year and are unspoken rivals.

"I'll need a minute." Blaide's thick black eyebrows slant together as he studies the menu that hasn't changed since my sophomore year.

"Just let me know." Harrison flips his order pad closed and walks away.

"So how was band practice last night?" Let's ease into this with a little light conversation. Blaide's not a bad guy. He's just not the right one for me anymore.

"Really great," Blaide says without looking away from the menu. "I showed them, 'Nobody's Girl,' the new song I've been working on. You remember. I played it for you last week."

"Mhmmm." I take a sip of my drink. Writing music is how Blaide deals with his anxiety, which is great. Most of his songs are about his ex-girlfriend from two years ago though, so not *that* great.

"The guys really liked it," Blaide continues. "Jackson thought we could make it the lead single after we hit the studio next month."

"Awesome." Another sip.

"I'll be right back." Blaide puts the menu down and leans across the table to kiss my cheek. I let it happen. The sweet nip of his cologne lingers in the air after he leaves. You know, Madison may have had a point about waiting until after tonight.

Ah, there's my girl. Welcome back.

Nope. I'm doing this. This is going to happen.

Sure.

Blaide soon returns with a SpongeBob mug. A waft of steam follows after him. He sets the mug down and reaches for my hand on the table. "How're you feeling about tonight? It's so cool that you get to deliver the commencement speech. Did you watch that video I sent you of Greta Gerwig speaking at Vassar?" Blaide asks as though I'm not the one who sent him the video in the first place, which he left on Read, and only sent back to me a week later after he saw the hype a few scattered clips had gotten online.

I pull my hand back to take a drink, burning the tip of my tongue. "Blaide, listen, I—"

"It was really cool," Blaide interrupts. "You just have to give yourself permission to *be* yourself, you know?"

My feet bounce beneath the table. SpongeBob's long nose is pointing towards the door. I turn Blaide's mug so it's facing the window instead. Okay. Here's where I do it. Five mighty words: *I want to break up.* Just like I practiced at home, then in Fiona (the name of my Ford Focus, thank you) on the way over. Clean. Definitive. Not: *I think we should break up.* Not: *Maybe we should see other people.* Just: *I want to break up.* Here it goes: "I want..." I start as Blaide's phone starts humming in his pocket.

"Sorry, babe, it's Jackson. I better take this." Blaide pushes up from the table and walks away.

My phone buzzes again. I clench my hands into fists then release them. Keep your mind on the mission here, Erin. You don't need another text from Madison bringing you down.

Stay focused.

Stay...

Bzzz. Bzzz.

Focused.

Come on, we both know you're going to check it.

Screw you. I'm the pinnacle of self-control over here.

Bzzz. Bzzz.

I scan the room while Blaide paces out front.

It could be a minute.

Bzzz. Bzzz.

Oh well, a quick distraction won't hurt anything.

I snatch my phone off the table.

Big deal, it's just a couple instant messages and a new notification from DN-YAY. Likely just another second cousin on my dad's side that I've never heard of. I swipe the notification open. "HELLO ERIN, SAY DN-YAY! WE'VE JUST FOUND YOUR FIRST SIGNIFICANT MATCH: A NEW HALF-SIBLING FOR YOU ON THE PATERNAL SIDE! CONGRATS!"

I read the message several times.

This must be a mistake.

Blaide swoops back in. "Sorry about that, babe."

"It's cool." I push my hair back and clear my throat. "Don't worry about it."

"So…" Blaide grits his teeth in subdued excitement as he turns his mug. The nose is pointing towards the door again. "You're ready for tonight then?"

"Yep." I put my shaking hands in my lap instead of reaching for his mug to set it right. "I'm ready."

Evan & The Unacknowledged Eggplant
<u>Chapter Two</u>

The first part is always easy. The room darkens. An unexpected rap or pop song from several years ago plays over the PA. For us, it's meant to represent a song we loved as preteens, a time in our lives where we were more open and innocent. For the audience, it's meant to just be funny. We're nerdy theater kids and here's a cool, fairly hardcore, explicitly boastful rap song with booming bass. It works for both of us in the same way, it loosens us up, prepares us for the unexpected.

A strobe light pattern flickers over the room. The audience starts clapping and then we burst in from the left and right of the stage, Cam and Ashanti come through the door in the middle of the stage. Guinevere follows close behind. Tony tumbles through the window opening. As always, Ro is right with me. Sierra and Mose crowd in closer. We start clapping too. Adrenaline tingles from the back of my neck all the way down to my feet.

On cue, the music fades, lights steady. This is it. The moment I've been counting down to since our last show. The moment I thought of as I swung the tassel to the left side of my cap earlier this week. The moment I've thought of since I saw the look on my parents' faces when I gave that impromptu speech at my birthday/congratulations party. Here it is, the moment that's going to make everything okay.

We form a semi-circle and, as it was predetermined, I head to the center of the stage. I lean forward on my toes to enthusiastically proclaim, "Hiiiiiiii, we're Pizza4Sluts and we're so glad to have you all here. Does anyone have a suggestion for us?"

Look, I love the audience, okay? Even though we're up here and they're down there, we're creating this thing together. Their suggestions, laughs, and awkward pauses provide all we need to discover this story. But in some ways the audience can be super predictable. Like, there are almost always the usual attempts at humor from the audience when you're asking for a suggestion.

Tonight is, unfortunately, no different.

Some bro-dude shouts "Dildo!" Another says something vaguely sexual. "Eggplant!" I bypass those, don't even recognize them as possibilities, don't want to give them one iota of the attention they crave. A third guy across the room tries even less hard and just yells, "Penis!" I shrug that one off too. A single bead of sweat rolls down my temple. Never mind the two empty seats in the front where my parents are supposed to be sitting; the national scouts are out there somewhere. Mercifully, a polite girl in the front row says simply: "Owls."

"Yes! Thank you!" I clasp my hands and bow to her. "Owls," I repeat, turning to the rest of our group.

"Owls," they repeat as we reform in a cluster. "Owls."

"Whooooooo." Together we move as though we're soaring over a nocturnal forest floor. Tony mimics spectacles with his hands, because, ya know, owls are wise and all that. "Whooooo!" Ashanti calls. Swooping together as one, we establish the team dynamic and chemistry we hope to carry for the rest of the show, our hearts and minds are open, our bodies attuned to each other. Like a dance troupe, we're just conduits for the rhythm, everything else fades to the periphery.

"Whooooooo!" Ro echoes.

We glide as a collective, massive owl.

"Whooooo!" Sierra flaps one arm gracefully.

The crowd eager to laugh, chooses instead to be patient, many of them have been here enough times to trust the process. Still there are limits to how long they'll wait. You never want to go straight for the laugh, that's cheap, most of the time, the audience sees right through it anyways. Let the laugh come naturally on the way to something else. Allow the moment to create. Each second, the tension pulls tighter, I want it to stretch as far as it can until—

"Who! AM I?" I yell, an owl experiencing an existential crisis. The crowd erupts. This is going to be a good show.

Or at least it seemed like it was going to be.

Okay. So, this part is a little harder when we find ourselves here. The first two bits were sloppy and uneven: Tony and Guinevere did a slow moving two-person scene about an owl birdwatcher having a midlife crisis, which culminated with Tony down on his knees, shouting "WHO AM I?" Wonder where he got that idea? It elicited a few good-natured chuckles from Tony's stacked cheering section but little else.

The next scene was an ensemble with five of us performing as an owl family unit trying to encourage a young owling—if that's even the word—to take a chance and fly beyond our tree. It was lower-cased-g good, but not capital-g great. Sierra and Ashanti earned a few laughs, and Ro edited it well at the end. But still, we don't have much to go off of for our final scenes, no memorable characters, no real worthwhile lines to call back, so it's obvious we need to recalibrate some, need to go further to the left and do something truly weird or inspired or both. We really need to move off the whole owl thing anyways. A suggestion is just that, a starting point, a launch pad, not something the whole show should be based on. We're better than this.

I pull in a deep breath.

My team needs me.

Here we go.

Ashanti walks to center stage. I come from the other side, hands clasped at my waist, thoughtful furrow of my brows. Ro is close behind. Our best three performers versus twelve rows of shadowed faces, the scouts are somewhere among them. Then—we're looking out over the audience. Something only the three of us can see. Ashanti reaches up as though she's picking an item off a shelf. She looks at it. Ro and I at her shoulder also study the object. The tinkling of the piano offstage sets the tempo and accentuates the tone. Ro and I start shaking our heads a millisecond after Ashanti does. "No, this won't do," she says, returning the invisible item to the invisible shelf. We still don't know what it is, but that doesn't matter. In our collective mind it's beginning to take shape, something random only we know, the mystery makes it interesting, the arbitrary makes it hilarious. Ro goes next, reaches for something on a lower shelf, he shows it to us. "This is way overpriced compared to what I usually pay. Inflation is getting out of *control.*" A few tentative chuckles from the crowd. Ashanti and I nod. Now it's my turn. I reach for the shelf again and pull one back, screw off the top of the jar—yes, it's a jar now—and paw some of it into my mouth like Winnie the Pooh.

I'll be honest, I don't know what I'm doing just yet, but I'm getting there. "Oh, my God," Ashanti whispers.

The crowd pulses with anticipation.

"It's incredible," Ro chimes in. Scattered laughs from the audience. Ben, the pianist, plinks a few more notes, matching the oddball humor.

"Yes, we—" I start before I notice Tony crossing the stage from the other side. He breaks into a jog before sliding across the stage on his knees.

He flashes a fake badge. "Owl Task Force, you three dirty birds are going down for fowl play."

Are you serious? The crowd explodes in laughter and I'm left standing there with my mouth open. Tony sees me. "Oh, are you hungry, baby bird? Don't worry I got you."

I plead to him with my eyes. *Oh, no. No, no, no.*

Oh, yes, Tony proceeds to act like he's throwing up in my mouth to feed me. The crowd loses their minds. I have no choice but to go along with it.

Until, finally, the lights drop. Show's over.

I think there's a metaphor here somewhere.

Erin & The Exits

<u>Chapter Three</u>

A chorus of triumphant notes signals that the school band has completed their first number. Scattered applause follows. Ms. Bailey frantically waves to snap me out of my daze. It's time to take the stage. Okay. It's time. I got this. *You* got this, Erin.

In the stands, already exhausted people flap their programs in front of their faces. A massive fan rumbles in the corner of the old gymnasium while the band plays another pop song I recognize but can't name. I take my seat on stage with the other honor students. Madison slides next to me in her salutatorian gray and squeezes my thigh too tight with her well-manicured talons. "Erin, I'm so nervous," Madison whispers.

"You're going to be amazing. Everyone will love you," I whisper back.

Madison meets my eyes. "Are you sure?"

"Of course."

"Good." Madison swats my thigh where I'm confident the imprints of her claws will linger well past my first college semester. "You're going to do great too."

I nod.

"So glad you didn't break up with Blaide."

"Yeah."

"You got this, girlie." Madison whacks my leg again.

"I know," I whisper back. *Dad's Random Bits of Unsolicited Advice #34: If you can't summon confidence, project it. People will believe almost anything. They're not near as intuitive as you (or I) give them credit for.*

The rest of my classmates begin filing in. There's Steph Avery, the first boy to ever hold my hand on Luke Kaynor's hayride in sixth grade. There's Kayo Adams, she invited me to my first overnight slumber party when we were in third grade. We stayed up singing Forever Fifteen songs all night long. There's Zaire Howell, my secret crush all through junior high until Madison told him and all his friends in the cafeteria. There's Finn Jackson, the guitarist in Blaide's band, the one that helped set us up in the first place. Though we're all in the same class, have all survived the same awkward growing pains of the last twelve years together; I'm apart from them as much as I'm a part of them.

My speech will change that. It'll make everything better.

This is my moment.

I can do this.

I don't know if I can do this.

It's almost my turn. I shift my weight, crossing one leg over the other before reversing it. If only it were possible to hide both of my legs at once. Everyone's definitely looking at them. I should've let Mom take me to get new shoes, because these are way too tight. Images of a trash compactor swim to mind. Which then brings another thought to the surface—isn't there an island of trash double the size of Texas floating just off the coast of California? Then a different image…Once upon a time, two empty Sprite liter bottles were taped together, filled with water, blue food coloring added, a swirling whirlpool, Dad's wild beard and thick framed glasses, his eyes alight—What about that notification though? Did Dad have a secret that I don't know? A secret life? A secret family?

Nope. I shake the thought from my head and attempt to focus on the words of my speech instead. *My fellow graduates...exalted faculty...it's an honor...*The words keep dropping off from there. I try again. *My fellow graduates...*I clear my throat, but the dryness remains.

From the podium, all capped and gowned, Madison smiles back at me as she says, "Webster's—"

The gears of all space and time screech to a halt.

"Dictionary—"

Oh, no. No, Maddy. You're better than this.

"Defines—"

Dear God, this can't be happening. I'm going to throw up. I can't handle this. The exits mock me from the far side of the gym. I'd have to run to get there. Everyone would definitely see my legs.

"Excellence—"

A smile holds firm on my face. Please stop, I plead with Madison and my body. Both of them seem set on their respective paths though.

"As—"

Oh, I could always pull the fire alarm. To get there though, I'd have to navigate the stairs expertly in these shoes. That would be a disaster like...Oh, no.

*Aren't you...*Anxiety Brain begins before fully emerging triumphant again. "Aren't you supposed to be listening as your 'friend' stands up there lying to everyone about how great you are?"

Responding will only give it strength so I nod thoughtfully at Madison as I scan the crowd again. Back when I still went to counseling, Dr. Meera would tell me: "take in your surroundings whenever you feel the panic coming on. Ground yourself in the present moment. List the tangible."

So, I try that. Okay. Athletic banners hanging from the rafters: *Girls Basketball Sectionals 2019, Cross-Country Regional Qualifiers 2019, Wrestling Single-A Conference Champs 2018, 2019, 2022.* A man coughing too loud. There's Damon Severs, my first French kiss when I played spin the bottle at Zoe Hall's birthday party in seventh grade. The awful taste of his Dorito's and cool mint gum lingered in my mouth for days. Then I'm thinking of my legs and how I'll have to stand soon. Then I'm thinking—being here reminds me of sitting on the Homecoming Court this past fall. Even being voted on felt like a joke whose punchline still hasn't landed.

"Maybe they're waiting to dump a bucket of pig's blood on you during your speech tonight instead," Anxiety Brain starts in again.

Oh, please shut up. I squeeze my eyes tight and thankfully the voice disappears. Still, I check the rafters overhead again, trying to find solace when they're empty. Meanwhile, at the podium, Madison continues, "So while I would like to thank Webster's for their excellent, pun intended, definition." Madison pauses for the audience's gracious laughter.

I look at my knees so no one can see me wince.

Madison picks back up, "I would like to define excellence a little differently. I have known Erin Drexel since we were both little girls.

While I wanted to be a star, she was more of an astronaut, and in that way, she always…"

It'll be my turn to speak any second. Motivational words scroll through my mind in masse, all mismatched and mashed together. The countless hours of commencement speeches I watched for research, all the phrases I used to get myself out of bed every single day since October, the many clever anecdotes about Dad I want to share, the words I prepared to put an end cap on all the pain we've been through, they've all joined forces against me in the moment I need them the most.

Heat washes over me. My chest tightens. This has only happened once before. That time, the fear leapt up and took over before I even saw it coming. I didn't know what it was then, but now I have a name for it: a panic attack. I'm having (or am going to have) a panic attack. Despite what Dr. Meera says, *giving a wolf a name does nothing to dull its fangs*.

I glance out to the crowd again. Red exit lights and soda machines shine from the darkened corners of the gym. Each face in between blends into the next except for—

Blaide locks eyes with me and elbows Mom to get her attention. They both beam brilliant smiles that radiate their pride for me. Seeing them calms me some. I fake a smile in their direction, knowing well that even my best fake smile isn't fooling anyone. For exactly half-a-second hope flickers in my chest that I will be okay.

Then *it* comes into view like an out of focus ghost in one of those b-minus horror movies Dad always liked. For months, I've been avoiding *it*. Instinctively sidestepping the recliner in the living room each morning and then again, every evening on my way upstairs. Taking dinner in my bedroom so as to avoid the dining room table entirely. Eschewing the office at the end of the hall regardless of what I may need from there, even asking Mom to retrieve the stapler or "Hey, can you grab that off the printer for me?" Knowing that everyone would grant me a little more leeway with my being so close to locking down valedictorian. Now though? Now that I've arrived at this day that I hoped would silence the hallway whispers and the *I've-been-praying-for-you-and-your-family*'s once and for all. Now that I've tunneled through the grief, heartbreak, humiliation, and despair, I've reached the light at the end only to realize what it has been all along.

A trap.

"So, without further ado…" Madison turns from the podium beaming a fluorescent death ray smile, whitening all teeth in its path.

Okay. Okay. You can do this.

"No, you can't." Anxiety Brain smirks. A bowl of popcorn rests in its lap.

"Langford Miners welcome your Class Valedictorian, Erin Drexel!"

Applause echoes through the auditorium. A few whoops are thrown in there for good measure. Everything sounds like it's happening in a tunnel while my heart thumps the score of a shark attack movie. I stand and start the long walk to the podium, avoiding the stare of *IT* with every step. The stage hums beneath my feet. Sweat trails down from beneath my cap. I receive Madison's hug. "I'm so proud of you, Erin," she whispers.

"You're going to let them all down," Anxiety Brain cackles giddily between chomps of popcorn.

All I can see is the vacant chair to mom's left. A cone of light shoots from the ceiling highlighting the chair's existence. I step to the microphone. "It's an honor…" My voice is a cresting wave about to break. "It's an honor," I try again, but the words I started writing on that night in October, the same words I rewrote over and over each night in between, have been backspaced out of my mind. Shuffling my notes doesn't help. The perfectly transcribed words that fill each line blur together.

"It's an honor…" I sputter again. I'm a plane with a failing engine, hanging in the air for a brief hopeful moment before it falls from the sky.

Somewhere in the gym a man coughs. A young toddler whines. A few underclassmen break into a fit of laughter before a woman shushes them quiet. I look out amongst the faces. I can't stop thinking the same thing.

My mouth opens then closes.

Say something.

Say anything!

"We're all going to die…" I start.

My voice echoes, hovers high above everyone, everything, all of it, all of us, desperately alone. I raise a trembling hand to my mouth as if I can retrieve the words that have already spilled out. "I—I'm sorry," I say, before retreating from the microphone a few steps. Then I turn and walk quickly off stage to stunned silence.

Evan & The First Rule

<u>Chapter Four</u>

The first rule of Improv is: YOU DO <u>NOT</u> TALK ABOUT IMPROV. Just kidding, the first rule of Improv is quite simple, it's to never say No in a scene, or more specifically to say "Yes, and…" You are to agree with your scene partner's contribution and then build on it in such a way that the scene goes to better, more interesting places. It's a simple attitude I try to carry with me into other parts of my life ever since I did my first improv scene years before as a gangly, closeted seventh grader. *Oh, sweet naïve little Evan. How I wish I could protect you.*

After the show, I wait outside the theater as the crowd lets out. I make small talk with everyone that comes up to say how much they enjoyed it. Each pair of hands I shake, I make eye contact and wonder, *"Are you the scouts? Do you love me?"* I hold a smile, assume the identity of gracious humility, attempting to soak up whatever compliments that come my way, because inside I know the truth: that was not my best show.

Not by a long shot.

"We crushed it!" Tony yells, smacking a five with Mose as they come through. Tony, the answer to the question: *What if we re-created Jimmy Fallon but without the charisma or talent?*

I give a big, obnoxious, fake laugh when Tony slaps me on the shoulder. My smile fades into a scowl once he and Mose are out the door with a whole crew of Tony's friends and family trailing behind them. Say what you will about Tony, but the guy is no slouch at self-promotion.

Then I'm alone again. Instinctively, I check my phone. Nothing except another spam notification from DN-YAY. I swipe it clear. I can't believe I ever let Ro talk me into taking that stupid test. Right on cue, Ro comes through the stage door next. "You coming to the party?"

It almost hurts to make eye contact with him. This was our last show. Most of us have been in this group for four glorious, highlight-packed years. To go out with this for our last show is an absolute travesty on par with the unholy invention of Peeps or the time they tried to make a live-action movie based on *CATS*.

Ro lightly shoves my shoulder. "C'mon, man, that was a *fine* show. Both of us have tomorrow off anyway. It's your actual birthday. You'll feel better if you come out." Ro allows a half-smile. "I mean you've already done that once this week, right?"

"Exactly, and after that, I've earned a lifetime of staying in."

"I bet Christian from The Bean will even be there."

"Oh, really?" I arch an eyebrow. "Even though he has no idea I exist, and I know for fact—not because I stalk his work schedule or anything—he actually has a shift tonight, he's going to drive an hour out of his way to come to a high school improv group's finale party?"

"Yep. As soon as you came out, all bets were off. An amber alert went out that the hottest, funniest, most talented young man in the distant-outer-suburbs was on the market."

I shake my head to hide my smile from Ro. Thing is, I'm always the life of those parties. I just don't have it in me tonight. Bad shows have a way of just draining the life force straight out of your soul. "I just need to hang out here a minute."

The glimmer in Ro's brown eyes says he knows I'm not coming. "Drive home safe, okay?"

"No, *you* drive safe or better yet, don't drive at all."

"You got it. See you at work on Sunday."

"See you." Ugh. The only thing worse than thinking about the show I just had, is thinking about working even one more grease-soaked shift at Charlie's Burgers. The National Team's going to be my escape plan from that, from my parents, from everything.

I scroll aimlessly through my phone until Aidy, our fearless mentor/team-leader, bounds through the door, all bright twenty-something, greeting me with a grin made more powerful by her short brown hair, stylish maroon pants, dark gray hoodie, and footwear that appears as though a local dad just donated his lawn mowing shoes to Goodwill. "Good show, Ev."

"Was it though?" I ask. No compliment can be trusted until it has been thoroughly interrogated. I have to deconstruct it. Tear it to pieces. Lay it out there on the table for all to see. If there was a brief moment of hesitation, or misdirection, that I missed in the show that could've led to a bigger, weirder, more humorous scene, then I must know so I can wallow in it, roll around in it, breathe it in, wrap it around myself, fully submerge myself in it like a cocoon of depression until I emerge days later that much stronger and devoted to the craft I love and want to dedicate my whole life to. Oh, sure, some people can just welcome the healthy little spike of serotonin that accompanies a compliment, but haha not me. Affirmation rules, no question, but I can't just like...accept it.

Aidy digs her shoulder into mine. "You all were magnificent. I'm a proud mama watching her pretty owlets fly." Aidy chuckles as she briefly mimics soaring through the air.

Ah, so that's the word. *Owlets.*

"But no…what about me, specifically."

Aidy furrows her thick eyebrows. "Evan, you know you're the strongest performer of your group. They all look for your lead. Even Tony knows it."

Something about the way she said my name there makes me feel guilty for being so needy, but still I can't come off it. "That can't be all. There has to be something I could be doing better."

"Well…" Aidy sets her tote bag down. "Sometimes you get caught watching."

I force a swallow. Though I wanted it, the medicine always tastes so bitter.

Aidy shrugs. "It's not always a bad thing. I've seen a lot of truly gifted performers do this. You're very trusting of the process, always believing that the scene will just work itself out, but sometimes, I just want you to get in there and take control when something's obviously not working."

I can't believe I ever thought this night could've went any other way.

"Yeah, yeah, you're right." I muster my best million-dollar smile. "Thanks for telling me. I'll do better."

"You do plenty. It's just something I've noticed and like I said, we all do it sometimes so don't beat yourself up over it or anything."

"I won't."

Extreme narrator voice: *Oh, he definitely will.*

"Anyways, I heard something about an after-party. You all put in a great four years of work. You should go celebrate that with your team."

"Yeah, I'm definitely going."

Narrator: *He's definitely not.*

Growing up, the only non-obvious-Christian artist my mom would play around the house was Patsy Cline. Mom would wash dishes and I'd dry them while she sang "Crazy" into the scrubber. Her eyes sparkled with each line. Mom told me once how Patsy died in a plane crash in 1963 after she performed a charity concert in Texas. I don't know why this memory comes back to me now, but I pull up Patsy's Greatest Hits on my phone and let it play on my drive to the party.

I park my mighty Toyota Yaris in front of Guinevere's parents' house. My friends' cars line the street. Just the sight of their vehicles, the pseudo-anarchist stickers decorating their back windshields, is almost enough to make me cry, or at the very least, maybe I *could* just go up for a bit. Booming music echoes from the backyard. It's a song we used to warm up with. It's a song that's awesome and over-the-top silly yet also sentimental to us in the same way. What's it called when you're nostalgic for the moment you're currently missing?

Aidy's pointed criticism completes its seventh round through my head, devouring all other thoughts, growing into something bigger and more monstrous than it was ever intended to be. I shift back into drive and ease onto the street to start my hour drive home. Patsy's singing "I Fall to Pieces." I turn it up and sing along to every word.

By the time Aidy's heartbreaking remark that I'm simply not cut out for this makes its thirtieth trip through my head—I know that wasn't what she said, but also, it pretty much is—I'm ready to lay down in the middle of the street.

Mercifully, my house comes into view.

I slam my car door, not worried if I wake my parents. Maybe it's better they missed my show. It's not like they need another reason to be disappointed in me. Even getting my bag out of the backseat seems like too much. I leave it there and start for the backdoor. There's an envelope taped to the glass with my name on it. This is weird. My parents are a lot of things, but they aren't the surprise-birthday-card type. But what's even weirder is that my key doesn't fit into the lock. It takes me a few seconds to notice the lone duffle bag under the carport. I glance from the unread letter to the backdoor to the duffle. I tear open the envelope. I think about the dark clouds that must have filled the sky when Ms. Cline boarded that plane in 1963. The view from her window as the turbulence hit; the crackle of the pilot's voice over the intercom; her reaching out for a hand to hold.

I'm alone in the glow of the porch light.

The paper shakes in my quivering hands.

A single tear falls, blotting out the ink where it lands on the word, "love." Much like Tony running a joke into the ground, life took this shitty night and made it shittier.

Yes *and*, indeed.

The Letter from Evan's Parents

Dear Evan,

The last few days have held a lot of heartache and sorrow for your father and I. The decision to lock you out wasn't one we reached lightly. I hope you know that. Your father and I love you very much. But the life you have picked to live is your life, not ours, and it cannot be accepted nor allowed in our house. This absolutely breaks our hearts, but we cannot stand idly by while you play with fire!

I have packed a few essential items in your duffle bag. The rest of your things will be kept in your bedroom until you're ready to move them into a place of your own.

In time you'll see that we made this decision out of love. It's what's best for you. By law, you're old enough to live your life how you want to, you'll just have to do so on your own. All we can do is pray that eventually you'll learn the error of your ways and step back onto the path of righteousness. We love you so much.

May God be with you & guide you in the right direction,

Mom

Erin & Plea From A Cat Named Chevy

<u>**Chapter Five**</u>

I can see it in my mind, the embarrassing "Congratulations, Miss Valedictorian!" banner drooping over the arched entrance to the dining room; the balloons creating low-level static electricity as they dance on the carpet in the air conditioning; a lone, half-eaten piece of Ice-Cream Cake (Fudgy the Whale, always) melting in the kitchen sink, chocolatey syrup spiraling down the drain. The party guests, of course, never arrived, they more or less understood following the ceremony that the Drexel family wouldn't feel much like celebrating tonight, or ever again. My mom sits on the couch in front of the TV playing the third-consecutive episode of Gilmore Girls. A near-empty glass of white wine warms on the coaster just beyond her reach. Then, through the living room, up the stairs, past the smiling family photos arranged in ascending ages, my door sits, shut to the world.

Graduation clothes scatter around my bed in little pools. Dad's Post-It notes ripple on my wall from the air conditioner. Blue light fills the corner of my room. Each flick of my thumb only pulls the knot in my stomach tighter. For months, I've been trying to avoid social media since it's hard enough to deal with my own anxiety brain, let alone everyone else's.

But this time it's worse, much worse.

It finally happened.

I've been…memed? Mememied? Memified? Whatever it is called, I don't like it one bit. Still, I scroll on. There's me on the verge of tears behind the podium. TFW YOU REALIZE CRUSHING STUDENT LOAN DEBT IS IN YOUR FUTURE.

"Dang, that's a pretty sick burn," Anxiety Brain cracks. "You know, because you bypassed those full ride junior college scholarships since you just *had* to go to a university."

I doubt they know all that. I think it's more in general terms.

"I don't know. You've been pretty outspoken with your college plans. I think this is about you specifically."

Maybe.

"Definitely. Do you think that whole thing puts more pressure on your mom since, you know, she lost her job and now you're making her pay for college? Your dad left a stack of medical bills higher than his pile of failed manuscripts."

...whatever.

Texts keep coming in from Madison and Blaide, among others. I know they mean well, but I just don't have the energy to reassure anyone else right now that I'm okay. I'm not losing my mind. It was just...allergies?

Then, there's another meme of me storming off stage. I SHOULD NOT HAVE ATE THAT MCHUGH'S DOUBLE CHILI DOG BEFORE GRADUATION.

Ah, at least that one kinda sucks.

"Are you kidding me?" Anxiety Brain guffaws. "It's brilliant. What's worse—people thinking you stormed off the stage because you're a baby or because you're about to crap your pants?"

I squeeze the power button off as though I'm choking the life out of my phone. It's scary how satisfying it is when the screen goes blank. Then I stare at the ceiling and try to take in the silence. Even that is interrupted though by the occasional tap-tap-tap of Chevy the Cat pawing for me to open the door.

I close my eyes and try to think of Dad.

Much like the mess of charger cables in my nightstand drawer, my memories tangle together, forming one giant indecipherable bundle. Dad's trapped in my mind somewhere, or at least my memory of him is (really what's the difference anymore though?). Conversations that truly happened in the glow of Christmas lights mash up with a passing anecdote shared beneath the never-ending summer sun. One clear, definitive image of him—arms in the air, face lit up like the sky above Disney—cheering me on could've came from anywhere (seriously, a bowling alley after my first strike, tee-ball as a six-year-old or my—not so humble brag—three debate championships, constant honor roll, etc.). Now that I truly need my memories, they're as intangible as whatever new digital currency Blaide's obsessed with this week.

Well, except for the bad memories. Those? Those are as clear and ever-present in my mind as every awkward moment I've experienced since the third grade. The times I disappointed Dad by getting caught in a lie, calling the neighbor kid the dreaded F-word (look, I was eight, okay? I didn't know what it meant), the time I quit softball after less than half a season. "We always finish what we start, Air-Bear. Are you sure you want to just give up?" And then right before he passed…the one thing he asked of me…

I can't.

So, I try to untangle the massive ball of good memories, picking a simple strand at a time. A warm kiss on my forehead after a bedtime story, always waiting to turn out the hallway light until he thought I was asleep. The smell of salt and grass clippings that clung to his clothes on Saturday afternoons during the summer. I remember the pleasant smile hiding beneath his untamable beard, the wildness of it offset by his kind brown eyes. I remember the way he got rude whenever I bothered him when he was reading or how much worse it would be when he got interrupted from writing. The way he would be so bummed whenever he got another rejection for one of his stories. The way he always left those damn Post-It's around the house. How annoying that used to be until I found out he was dying. Then I couldn't collect enough of them.

None of it is enough.

Remembering the notification on my phone negates each happy memory snippet I replay. A half-brother? How could that even be possible? As far as I've always heard, Mom and Dad were each other's first and only's. They never shut up about it. There's not a single Post-It he ever left around the house saying: *Random Bits of Unsolicited Advice #Whatever: Start a second family, it's good to have options!*

Half an hour later, there's a soft knock at my door. Not Chevy the Cat. Human. Would anyone believe I'm not home? I slide off my bed, not bothering to stand straight. I flip the lock open, barely twisting the knob so the door will drift open on its own before I walk back to my bed and fall into it. Never one to miss his opportunity, the black and white blur known as Chevy the Cat bursts through the open door and under my bed. Cautiously, Mom steps into the doorway before leaning against the frame with her left shoulder. "Hey Air-Bear."

I wince at my old nickname. Mom's been doing that more often lately. Doesn't she know it causes me pain? "Hey," I manage.

"There's still ice-cream cake downstairs. I'm watching Gilmore Girls." Mom offers a small consolation smile. "Again."

"No thanks."

"You sure? I think it would help you feel a little better."

"Mom, please."

Mom pulls away from the doorframe as though she's considering coming in and sitting next to me. She thinks better of it, leaning against the frame again with her right shoulder. Watching her be so grim makes me long for the days when her laughter would come so easily. Nowadays, the last time I saw her laugh was two weeks ago when she found out she was being laid off from her job at the Autism Center (budget cuts). She joked that the coming months could be the Summer of Laurie and Erin. "Isn't that just what you want?" She asked. "To spend your last summer home hanging out with your mom?" I laughed, but like most things, the futile attempt at spinning bad into good, just made me sadder.

Dad's Random Bits of Unsolicited Advice #13: When faced with one of life's many problems, laughter is often a damn good alternative to crying (But there's nothing wrong with crying either btw).

"Erin…I…" Mom starts. "I—I wish you had just talked to me if you were still…we could've set up an appointment with Dr. Meera again. You were making such great progress."

She's right, of course, but I couldn't keep going after I found out how much it would cost Mom after losing Dad's insurance. Not to mention the fact that Dr. Meera mentioned that I should maybe start taking medicine, which freaked me out on at least two levels. Plus, I hoped (stupidly) that I was okay now since I had the commencement speech to look forward to.

Mom shakes her head. "Just—you seemed fine this morning, honey. What was it that upset you so much?"

Five seconds pass and then another five. *The notification. The chair. The notification and the effing empty chair,* I want to say, but fear that I'll sound like a total lunatic. There's also the added wrinkle of my lying to Mom about even taking the DN-YAY test in the first place.

So, I say nothing.

Mom sighs again. "Erin, I—I know you worked so hard to get there. You're always so hard, way too hard on yourself. You just— anyone would crack under all that pressure."

Yep. Mom thinks I'm losing my mind too.

"Mom, I'm sorry," I say, mainly for myself, because I know it'll help me feel better. Apologizing always feels so good. I'll never understand why some people have such a hard time with it. If I had my way, I would just apologize to everyone everywhere all the time. Really though, who says I can't? Maybe I could drive around town with a giant megaphone strapped to the roof of Fiona blaring I'M SO SORRY FOR EVERYTHING. Or one day when I die maybe my headstone could just play a constant apology on a perpetual loop. That technology will have to exist by then.

"It's okay, honey." Mom's voice brings me back. "Do you want to read me your speech? I know you've been working on it since…for a long time. I'd really love to hear it."

I shake my head.

"Well, could I *read* it then?"

"Mom, no." I cover my face with the pillow.

The floorboards creak as Mom takes a step backwards. "Erin, your dad is...he would be, he was..." Even though it's been seven months, Mom always struggles with what tense to use. "Always so proud of you. We both were—are."

I look at Mom standing in my doorway. She's right here, right now. The months haven't been so easy on her either. For a split second, I consider running to her, crying in her bathrobe, feeling it brush against my cheek.

"Thanks," I say, staying put. "Please shut the door back, okay?"

"Okay. Love you." Mom eases the door shut.

"You too," I say once the door's closed. My eyelids hang heavy. Regardless of how bad I want it; sleep will not come easily tonight. I'm desperate for a distraction so I turn my phone back on. That familiar blue glow that takes more than it gives. Another text from Blaide. Several from Madison. A few more have trickled in from members of the various clubs I'm in.

And then...the notification from DN-YAY remains there. All innocent like it's not a flag waving in the wind on an invading Viking ship, set to pillage and burn everything I love. Everything I think I know.

My finger hovers above the notification.

How much worse can things get?

I wait for Anxiety Brain to say something, anything, but when it doesn't—

I click the link.

Evan & The Cobwebs of Lost Youth

<u>Chapter Six</u>

The window air-conditioning unit coughs to life. Shadows line the walls and pile up in the corners. Ro pulls the cord in the middle of the room, bringing the shapes to life. Hockey sticks with scuffed blades drape over a battered goal. Dusty Power Wheels with popped hoods and missing batteries. A family of bikes leans against the wall, cobwebs in their spokes. An oil stain the shape of Australia covers the cold, concrete floor. "Sorry, it isn't much." Ro quickly sweeps rags off a dusty couch.

"Sucks you had to leave the party early," I say with my arms wrapped around the pastel comforter and Paw Patrol sleeping bag Ro gave me.

"Ehhhh, it was winding down anyway." Ro swats the question away. "I'm sorry you can't stay inside, but with my brother home for the summer already…he's sharing my room again and Dad gets up super early, so he didn't want to come through the living room and wake you in the morning, which is definitely for your benefit since Big Bill still rocks the tighty whities." Mint lingers on Ro's breath, not quite covering up the whiff of alcohol. "Both my folks said you can stay as long as you need."

Like my parents, Ro's parents are Christian too, but unlike mine, they actually accept and love people for who they are without any judgment. With any luck, I won't have to take advantage of their graciousness for too long.

"I can't thank you enough, Ro."

Ro sucks his teeth. "Well, I'd hold onto your 'thanks' if I were you. You're not afraid of spiders, are you?"

"Me?" I sweep back my deflated hair. "I'm very pro-spider. Sometimes I let them bite me just for fun. Heard it's good for their teeth."

"Good, good, because there are several hundred families of spiders that have paid rent through the end of the year so we can't kick them out."

I fight the urge to run over and hug Ro, because I know if I do, I'll surely break down. Ro didn't ask why I needed a place to stay and I didn't tell him. There's a version of this story where that shows how close we are, there's another where it shows the distance between us still. I don't know which version this is. "Thanks," I say with a sniff.

Ro shuffles his feet. He gives me a pat on the shoulder. "Sleep well, Ev. And if you hear a boy crying out in the middle of the night, don't sweat it, that's just Wyatt the Ghost that has lived here since the Great Depression."

"Oh, nice, he'll complement my personal demons well." I start making a pallet over the couch cushions, tucking the blankets in tight as though that will guard against spiders better. Like most of Ro's jokes, there's probably some truth to the spiders bit.

"He's pretty racist, which is unfortunate, but you're white so he should like that."

"Just wait until I lecture him on the statistical realities of white privilege."

Ro slumps his shoulders. "I tried that. He went on a rant about how *live* privilege was the true downfall of society. Also, I'm pretty sure he called me some 1920's slang for Mexican which was pretty offensive."

"I'd believe it." The couch squeaks as I recline back.

"Do you need anything else? Maybe some noise-cancelling headphones for the Cricket Orchestra that is due to start back up here in—" Ro checks his watchless wrist, continuing to dance around the question we both know he'll never ask. "Five minutes or so."

"Nah, that's the real reason I'm staying here." I kick my shoes off and pull the covers up. "I'm just a big fan. I can't wait until they play their hits like the Cherrrrrtttt-Cherrrrrtttt Concerto and The Ballad of Eee-Eeeee-Eeeeeeett. Maybe Wyatt will join them on the triangle with Big Daddy Long Legs on cello." We could riff like this into oblivion without either of us ever laughing. That's one of the problems with hanging out with performers. We always keep digging for a laugh that's never going to come, each of us too proud to give the other the win.

"Alright. Goodnight, man." Ro starts for the door before stopping. "Evan?"

"Yeah?"

Ro bites his lip. A look passes between us that says *I've known you from Veggie Tales Birthday parties to Drama Camp All Stars, from Charlie Burgers' screaming lunch rush to Lightning Thief Musical sing-alongs on the way home from work, from your failed hetero-dating attempts to your eventual coming out.* "Just be sure to really cheer when the Orchestra hits their crescendo during their finale number. They like that," Ro finally says before pulling the cord to the light.

"Sure thing. See you tomorrow." I watch him leave. Right on cue, the Cricket Orchestra stretches their strings and promptly launches into their first number. I stare at the ceiling. It's way too early for any word from the National Team, but still, I check our team group-chat. There's a round of messages congratulating everyone on a great final show, a couple of *missed-you-at-the-party-tonight-Ev*'s, but nothing about who may be picked for the team or when we'll know. It only makes me feel worse. Even if all of my teammates were singing my praises, saying how it's a sure thing I'll make the team, I still wouldn't buy it and I'd just feel anxious. Now that they weren't even doing that, I feel even more dejected and just as anxious. Another spam notification from DN-YAY pops up on my screen, I promptly swipe to delete it.

The corner of my parents' letter juts from my duffle bag. Tears sting my eyes just thinking about it. The people that brought me into this world think my mere existence is an affront to God. It's not true. It's not true. I know that. Still…it hurts like the hell I don't think I really believe in anyway. My cheeks are warm and wet. I stare at the cobwebbed wooden rafters overhead, feeling sorry for myself. My life story is being written in disappearing ink. It's fading to a blank page before it can even be finished. A sob almost escapes my chest before a laugh slips by to take its place.

Hopefully, Ro was just kidding about that ghost kid.

Erin & The Promotional Materials

Chapter Seven

Filtered with faux-grainy 1970's Panavision, the video opens on a classic game show host named…wait for it…Dean Enay. Gripping a long old-school microphone, Dean declares, "Welcome to Punnett Squares, the game show where you ask the questions, and your genes provide the answers!" The camera pans around to the colorful boxes outlining the room in packs of four. Each box has its own smiling, waving couple and matching theme. For the bright blue box, the man and woman wear bright blue doctor's scrubs. For the light-yellow box, the man and woman wear giant straw hats and sunglasses as though they're on a beach vacation, and so on.

"Playing today, we have Lisa from San Diego, California!" Dean gestures to a young woman dressed in the exaggerated pastels and bell-bottoms of the seventies. "Tell us about yourself, Lisa!"

"Well, my name is Lisa. I'm adopted. I love surfing, my Golden Retriever Ace, and my two boys, Kevin and Jimmy!" Lisa blows a kiss off-screen toward her nonexistent children.

"Oh, that's just wonderful. Please tell the audience what you're playing for today, Lisa."

"I'm playing for the continued health and well-being of my children because I want to know if there is a history of heart disease in my family!"

"Terrific! For health history, we go to Square 17!"

The camera zooms in on the orange square where two folks enthusiastically wave. Glasses filled to the brim with Florida Orange

Juice sit in front of them. "Thanks for playing, Lisa. We're happy to tell you…" the man turns to his female counterpart. They inhale deeply, preparing to time their statement together. "You have NO! HISTORY! OF! CONGENITAL! HEART DISEASE!"

The audience erupts into applause as Lisa collapses sobbing with joy into Dean's arms. As the scene fades out, information for DN-YAY scrolls across the screen. A deep movie-trailer voice narrates: "For an easy one-time payment of $49.97, you too can unlock the mysteries of your own family health history. Simply lick the popsicle stick when it arrives in your DN-YAY family pack. Then stick it back into its protective sleeve. Drop it in the mail and wait four to six weeks for your results to come back! Lick, stick, and sit! Then say DN-YAY! It's that simple!"

Blaide spins from my desk, thumbing over his shoulder. "That's it?"

"Yep." I can't even lift my head from my pillow. "That's it, except they left out the whole 'discover your dead dad has a secret love child' thing. Probably had a hard time coming up with a cute color-coordinated theme for that one."

"And you did this for…" Blaide squints at me. "What exactly?"

"Extra credit in Ancient Civilizations." God, I'm so glad Mom isn't home right now.

Blaide rolls his eyes, because yeah, the idea that I'd need extra credit in anything is laughable to most people. But don't they realize that the fact that I take these extra precautions is why I'm so effing good?

"It was just distant cousins at first," I say to the ceiling. "For a while it was super exciting whenever there'd be a random match on my dad's side. I never ever wanted to meet them, no way. It was just nice to know that there were all these possible new connections to him roaming the earth, unaware that he or I even existed. This? This I wasn't planning for. The worst thing is—" I throw my hands towards the computer screen. "That's not even how Punnett squares work."

I wait for Blaide to acknowledge my joke, but he just looks at his phone.

Normally, I'd make another (usually worse, much worse) joke or throw something at him, but I just don't have the energy today.

"You've been giving yourself that excuse a lot lately," Anxiety Brain says. "When was your last shower?"

I raise my t-shirt to sneak a sniff. Oof, not exactly fresh. If anything, maybe it will keep this afternoon platonic.

Blaide looks up from his phone just in time to catch me smelling myself. "What'd the link say when you clicked it?"

"Just the guy's name: Evan Prucasyk and his email," I say with my nose still in my shirt. What I don't mention is how, for the last five days, that name has droned on in my thoughts like a doomsday clock striking midnight.

Dum. Evan Prucasyk.

Dum. Evan Prucasyk.

Dum. Evan Prucasyk.

Blaide rubs his jaw where he's started growing a faint beard. It looks…dang …great, actually. On second thought, I could always throw on some deodorant. Just to, you know, keep my options open this afternoon.

"You're doing a great job with this whole breakup thing."

Anxiety Brain does the chef's kiss. "Just spectacular. Step One: Have a freak out at graduation. Step Two: Stinky desperation make out session. Master Class work here, Erin."

Whoa, is Anxiety Brain really trying to slut-shame me right now?

"Eh, shaming you comes easy."

Whatever. I'll do what I want.

"Sure. Hey, what was that name again? Evan, what?"

EEP! Evan Prucasyk.

"Sorry." Blaide puts his phone down finally. "So, what are you going to do?"

"I'm not sure yet."

Blaide does his impression of the squeamish emoji by just showing his teeth. "Just don't reach out to him, okay? That could be kind of dangerous. Who knows, he could be a three-hundred-pound creep hoping to lure you to his basement."

Ugh, why does his creepiness have to be attached to his weight? I don't challenge Blaide on this though, which I guess says as much about me as it does him. "What else can I do?"

"Well…" Blaide stretches with a big yawn. "You could just wait for him to reach out to you. He probably got the same notification too, right? So why hasn't he contacted you yet?"

I really hate when Blaide makes sense.

"I mean," Blaide continues. "If he is in fact real, how can you be sure he even wants to hear from you?"

"Why would someone take the test if they didn't want to know where they came from?" I counter his question with a question of my own, reminding myself of this game Dad used to play on long car rides where we could only communicate in questions. He called it 'Be the Askhole,' which always made me laugh.

"You did that. You said yourself that you didn't intend to learn of all these family members coming out of nowhere," Blaide answers plainly. "Maybe he doesn't realize your dad is also his dad. That's the only way it could work right?"

"Yeah..."

I know it didn't, but I swear the temperature just dropped in here.

I see it then. A dark thought creeping in, crouching low like an apex predator ready to pounce.

Maybe if I stay really still it won't sink its teeth in.

"Or else..." Blaide starts.

No. Don't acknowledge it, Blaide. Don't even look in its direction. Don't do it. Just, for once in your life, shut up.

Blaide laughs and just says it, "Who knows? Maybe you both come from the same anonymous sperm donor or something."

I grip my bedspread to anchor me.

"You know, I saw this documentary once where this fertility doctor got like a hundred different women pregnant with his own, um, fresh specimen and they didn't know it came from him, and..." Blaide trails off possibly noticing that all the blood has drained from my face. "Are you alright, babe?"

I manage a nod. "Just fine."

"Okay, good." Blaide leans forward. "Anyways, so in this doc..."

And he keeps talking and talking and talking, but I really can't hear him. The more he talks, the smaller his voice gets, the further my own mind floats away from my body like a lost balloon caught in the wind. I'm a little kid watching it disappear, calling: *Come back, mind. Come back.*

Until...

One of Dad's Post-It's comes unstuck from my wall.

It glides to the floor like the first leaf of autumn.

Blaide's still in the room with me, still talking.

I find myself moving to retrieve the fallen orange scrap.

Dad's Random Bits of Unsolicited Advice #23: "The truth isn't always easy to face. But face it we must."

A sound leaves my throat that's somewhere between a laugh and a sob.

Evan & The Play Tunnels of the Damned
<u>Chapter Eight</u>

After the play-place tunnels are navigated and wiped down. After every discarded straw wrapper and forgotten fry are expertly swept from the nooks and crannies of the floor. After the trashcans are emptied, bags tied up, carried dripping across the parking lot pavement before being hoisted into the dumpster out back. After we play rock, paper, scissors, to see who gets bathroom duty, before deciding we'll both just do it together like always. After Cheryl sends our fellow cook Weird Allan home early since it's a slow night. After the lobby doors are locked and Cheryl leaves too, saying, "Just one more hour for the drive-thru, boys, enjoy!" We're finally left to do our favorite thing for the final stretch of the 11-12pm of a Charlie Burgers' Sunday night shift: riff aimlessly, mocking the void of existence until we disassociate from our lives and all our problems.

If only that were possible tonight.

The screeching wheels of the mop bucket announce Ro's presence coming around the corner. "Have you heard anything about A-TIT?"

"Nope." I exhale sharply. A-TIT's the funny acronym we came up with to take the power away from the thing looming over us. In our minds, A-TIT stands for America's Teen Improv Team. Please just ignore the fact that the team is actually called the National Young Adult Improv Team. NYAIT just didn't have a funny enough ring to it. Though we did try it out like it would be pronounced NYET, the Russian word for "no," but with the current political climate and all that, we just decided that wasn't the kind of funny we're going for. So, it became A-TIT. "It's Sunday night. Aidy said we'd know by the end of the weekend. I'm over here refreshing my email every thirty-five seconds."

"You're handling it well then."

"Aren't you anxious to find out?"

"Nah, not really." Ro squeezes the mop out. "I don't put much faith in those kinds of things. Don't get me wrong, I would love to be on the team or eventually have a career in comedy, but it's all so dependent on luck that I try not to think of it as a possibility. I prefer it that way, keeps improv pure."

"True," I say even though that's definitely not true for me. My obsessive competitive nature renders Ro's kind of approach impossible. Just last week, I nearly flipped over the table during Settlers of Catan with Ro, Sierra, and Ashanti. Instead of doing that though, I just laughed nervously and faked a phone call to exit the room. "It just sucks to have my fate in someone else's hands, to just be left waiting."

Sometimes you just get caught watching, Aidy's words echo in my head again.

"Man, you're *going* to get it. Though, if all else fails you can join me at Illinois State in the fall. You can help me make the extremely bad, cringey student film I've always dreamed of. Even if you do make the team, that's just going to get you through the summer anyways. You need to have something planned after that."

I don't say anything as I help Ro ease the mop bucket over the lip in the floor separating the lobby from the back of the house. We can't allow a repeat of last winter when—after an exhaustive double shift, which saw not one, not two, but three different buses of basketball teams come through—I tripped the bucket over the cursed tile spilling dirty mop water everywhere. Ro, really putting the Best in BFF, didn't even cuss or say a single word. He just grabbed a fresh mop bucket and helped clean up the mess. It was two in the morning before we finally closed up that night.

Headlights turn into the parking lot. Ro and I lock eyes like a couple in a slow-motion car crash. We're both holding our breath as the Jeep pulls around the building. I brace for the inevitable beeping in my headset for a new order that will require at least seven minutes cooking, assembly, cash exchange, and delivery via the drive-thru window. Seconds pass, each one holds more hope than the one that came before. Until, finally, the Jeep leaves the parking lot entirely. "OH, praise Charlie." Ro drops to his knees, his folded hands held to the sky to honor the Patron Saint of Subpar Regional Fast Food.

"So…" Ro hops up on the counter to sit facing me. He pops a cheese curd in his mouth. "When you made out with Missy Hamilton after Sophomore Sock-Hop? You knew then."

"Oh, yeah."

"And again, with Sarah Debowski after Junior Homecoming?"

"Yep. Same with Niya Green after Spring Fling. Every time felt off, but I faked my way through, hoping it would eventually feel alright, but it never did." I shake my head. "Especially not with Sarah Debowski though, she was getting *particularly* handsy, so I had to get out of there."

"I remember that!" Ro claps. "Everyone saw you leaving the party and Sarah, not so subtly might I add, inferred that you, uh, maybe got a little too excited."

"And I went along with it, because I didn't want to let anyone down."

Ro looks me dead in the eyes. "Honestly, I've never been prouder of you."

I look away and clear my throat. "What about the time I spent a whole shift taking the drive-thru orders as my Australian alter-ego, Mick Wallabie?"

"I've actually been trying to forget that. That voice haunts me. You—" Ro stops as both our phones buzz simultaneously.

I nearly drop mine as I pull it from my pocket. It's a message from Tony in our group chat: "I got it! They picked me!" I steady myself on the counter. This has to be a joke.

"It might be a joke," Ro says in the tone he normally uses to calm upset customers.

I nod, unable to look up. It's definitely the kind of "joke" Tony would make. Last summer, he told us all a convoluted tale about being deported to Canada following an elaborate maple syrup sting.

Man. If only.

The group chat keeps vibrating every few seconds. Each buzz brings a new bout of "Congratulations!" a new explosion of confetti. Each buzz diminishes my hope that this is just a cruel joke. I can't stop from swiping through though to scroll for an extra message that doesn't exist.

"Congratulations, bro!" Mose chimes in.

"You sooooo deserve this!" Sierra comes in next.

"You're gonna have the time of your life this summer. I know

I did," Aidy adds. That one may hurt the most.

"Good job, dude," even Ro texts in. Okay, actually that one hurts the most.

I glare over and Ro just shrugs. "He's our teammate, man. I'm going to congratulate him." It stings like betrayal, but he's right.

It's my turn to text in my well wishes. Several times I start tapping out a text before backspacing it out entirely like the modern-day Sisyphus.

My phone vibrates in my hand again. It's Tony. "Thanks, y'all."

Okay, I'm all for saying 'y'all.' It's gender inclusive and a positive message of acceptance, but when Tony says it, I don't know, it seems so phony. Tony texts in again: "I couldn't have done it without you folks." Ugh. The false humility. Like Tony, it's all just too much. I can't do it.

"So that's pretty fucked up, huh?" Ro has such an eloquent way of putting things. He puts his phone down again. "It's like we joked about that happening, because it would be the worst-case scenario, and then it did. Really, it's our fault for putting the idea out there."

"Yeah."

"Looking back, we should've known it was likely. All the worst people win all the time. I don't even have to state the obvious examples but look back throughout history. The Lannisters won Game of Thrones."

"Um, that's not really history. And I wouldn't say they won."

"Batman," Ro continues.

"Again, not reality and Batman is a good guy," I cut in. "And don't give me your whole 'Batman is a billionaire kicking poor people's asses, ergo he's a villain' take."

Ro tsks, continuing with his list, "Chris Pratt in all those Jurassic World movies. Tom Brady won like ten Super Bowls. *Green Book* won best picture once. I mean...consider literally any Silicon Valley tech bro selling our online souls for ad buys. Compared to those dudes, Tony is actually an alright guy."

"Yeah."

"Look at it this way, at least you get to spend the summer living and working with your best friend." Ro flashes a cheesy smile in my peripheral. "That has to be worth something."

"Yeah."

Ro slides down and puts his hand on my shoulder. "Just wait until you hear the Cricket Orchestra's summer concert series. Word is that they're going to take on *Pachelbel's Canon*. They last did that three summers ago after my dear sweet Nana passed and I swear to you, it reduced me to an absolute puddle of tears every single night."

Reflexes kick in again. The circuits of my brain explore the different puns and places Ro's joke could go. If I allowed it, I know it would make for a nice distraction, but I shut it down. Maybe I'm just not funny or talented. Maybe the reason I haven't found an audience for my humor is because one doesn't exist beyond Ro.

"Look, Ev." Ro digs his shoulder into mine. "You know this is all subjective right? None of this has any bearing on your abilities as a performer or worth as a person. You're super-talented. Do I need to recite examples of now-famous people who thought they missed their one shot and then went on to great success? Do I? Cause I will, if you make me." Ro pauses for not even half a second. "Okay, here we go,

Jordan Peele, Stephen Colbert, Michael Jordan, Megan Rapinoe, the Joker."

"Ro, it's cool. Thank you for trying to cheer me up."

Our phones buzz again. Another message from Tony: "Also, the coach, Jabari, said they're picking one more from our team too."

Ro slaps me a stinging high-five. "You're sure to be in now!"

"I don't know. It could be any of us really," I say without looking up from my phone. Suddenly, I've found the resolve to text Tony congratulations. My fingers go to work: "Wow, just now seeing this, this is all such great news. You totally deserve this. Congrats, Ton!"

"Ton?" Ro hits me with his patented arched eyebrow. "You got a nickname for him now?"

"You know, the moment overtook me and I kinda went for it."

Ro places his phone screen down and faces me. "Ev, you haven't mentioned what's going on with your parents, but I'm smart enough to figure out how they'd handle you coming out so what's your plan?"

"What's the problem?" I ask gently, putting my phone screen down by Ro's. "I thought it was okay for me to stay with you all for a while."

"Oh, it is…it totally is." Ro holds up his hands. "Most importantly though, are you okay?"

"I'm…" I stop short. One of our phones is buzzing on the counter. "It's them!" I snatch my phone up before slumping in defeat. My screen is dark.

"It's them," Ro says as he picks up his phone in disbelief, the screen alight with the Greater Chicago Area number.

Erin & That (Not So) Funny Feeling

<u>Chapter Nine</u>

Light leaks from Mom's room even though it's almost midnight. The quirky fast-paced dialogue of Gilmore Girls is barely audible, as though Mom would even need to hear it. She knows all the episodes by heart. I pad across the carpet and knock lightly on Mom's open door (it's sad that I don't remember when the door exclusively became Mom's and not "Theirs"). "Hey, come in," Mom calls.

Her nightstand light is on. Her laptop and an assortment of job applications cover dad's side of the bed. The down comforter is pulled halfway up making Mom seem like some beautiful, exhausted mermaid that has washed ashore. The calming scent of her lotion lingers in the air. Mom probably got in bed two hours ago. It will likely be another two before she finally falls asleep.

Mom takes her reading glasses off. "What's up, Air-Bear?"

"I…" Dang. I spent so much time since Blaide left trying to talk myself out of talking myself out of actually talking to Mom that I didn't come up with what exactly I wanted to say. I guess I figured I would end up wimping out anyway.

"Your track record does speak for itself," Anxiety Brain says as it applies its own night lotion.

Gross. Why do you even need a skincare routine? You're already covered in wrinkles.

"That's the point." Anxiety Brain continues lathering.

Concern flashes in Mom's eyes. "Erin?"

"Mom…" My throat cinches up. "Do I have a half-brother?"

Mom chuckles. "Sure, you do. His name is Chevy." At this, Chevy the Cat looks up from where he's nestled in by mom's feet. The little black patch of fur over his eye makes him look like history's cutest pirate.

"Mom. No. I took a DNA test." It sucks to admit a lie that I've been holding in for months, but one of us is holding back an even bigger lie and it sure isn't me.

Mom's smile abruptly vanishes. She sits up straighter in bed. "What are you talking about?"

"For extra credit in Ancient Civilizations Class," I give the half-truth again. The full truth is that after Dad died, I leapt at the chance to learn there were more small connections to him out there. This is *not* what I signed up for though.

"I thought we talked about that." Mom's not necessarily trying to turn the tables on me, but she's definitely trying to buy time until she figures out what to say. "I thought we agreed you didn't need the extra points." Mom runs a hand over her face and shakes her head. "I can't believe you'd do that."

"Well, Mom, I apologize for keeping such a massive life-altering secret from you. I know my taking a DNA test means you could get caught for all the bodies you buried in your serial killer past."

"Well, they hardly ever expect the frail, widowed, white woman to be the killer as you well know…"

"Mom."

"Erin…I don't know what to say." Mom's eyes dart back and forth between her hands as though they hold the words she's searching for. "Your father…he…I don't know what you expect me to say."

"I expect you to tell me why—" I stop myself because I want to drop a big ole f-bomb so badly, but I still can't bring myself to do it. "I want you to tell me why it says I have a half-brother from Chicago." I slap my hands down at my sides.

"I think…" Mom draws in a breath and exhales. "Erin…are you sure you don't want to wait until another time?"

I nod that I'm sure, even though I'm not. Mom gets out from under the covers. She's wearing an oversized t-shirt from a 5k that Dad barely finished and purple plaid pajama pants. Mom sits on the edge of the bed, facing me. Her hands rest just inches away from mine as though she wants to reach up to take them, but she's hesitant. "Erin. Your dad…"

Just hearing the two words lodges a sob in my throat that feels like trying to swallow an ice cube. Still, I nod for Mom to go on.

"Your dad…before you were born…we had a couple of…close-calls…miscarriages…three. We never made it past eight or nine weeks. I blamed myself while your dad blamed himself for continuing to put me through it." Mom's voice breaks, but she keeps going. "After the last time, he asked if he should get a vasectomy and I told him he should. He did. A year or so passed. We learned of a new fertility clinic up near Chicago. Your father wanted you so badly. I wanted you so badly. He was willing to try anything…for one last chance." Mom looks up, trying to meet my eyes.

I look past her to the carpet underneath her feet. The same carpet Dad and I used to wrestle around on when I was six-seven-eight years old.

"And your dad, he tried, they tried to get the procedure reversed but it didn't take. The fertility doctor said we had other options. They said our best bet was an anonymous donor. The donors were all vetted, some in medical school, no history of genetic diseases. I—I was scared, but your dad encouraged me like he always did."

I clinch my fists tight. Release them. Then clinch again. "But why didn't you guys just tell me?"

"Your dad was afraid you'd look at him differently, but then…" Mom sniffs. "Then as years went on, and we both saw how much you loved him, and you were—are like him in so many ways, ways that go beyond genetics ever could, we decided that something like that wouldn't matter as much. He was—*is* your dad still. So, we decided we were going to tell you when you were older, but then after he got sick…after everything…you just took it so hard, and I didn't know how I could tell you without him here." Mom's bottom lip quivers. "Everything is harder without him here."

Dad's Random Bits of Unsolicited Advice #53: "No one (and I mean no one) will ever have your back like your mom."

The inner workings of my head must be present in my eyes, because Mom's searching them, waiting for my response. "I don't even know who I am anymore," I say finally. Sometimes saying harsh truths aloud sets you free, other times it causes you to recede further into yourself. Unfortunately, this feels like the latter.

"I don't want you to feel that." Mom shakes her head with tears streaming down her face. "You are who you've always been. None of this changes that."

I don't agree, but I'm too tired to voice it. There are just too many things to say, too many feelings to put into words, too much pain to make sense of. In my mind, I see pages of my life's history book being rewritten. I see myself fading like the protagonist in a time-traveling story that can't convince her parents to kiss for the first time. I see my family tree reshaping itself into a gallows. I see my double helix getting pulled apart like a wishbone.

I see my dad dying all over again.

Like everything ever, I know what I *should* do…I should fall into Mom's arms, crying into her t-shirt, allowing the release to wash over and calm me, allowing her to let go of whatever grief she's still holding onto, whatever guilt that has weighed on her shoulders for keeping this from me for so long…but like everything…I don't do those things. Instead, I look down at Mom coldly. "Thanks for finally telling me," I say and then I leave her room, heading straight for mine. I close the door behind me before crumpling into a heap on the floor.

Dad is not my dad.

Nothing will ever be the same.

JUNE

I'm a can on a string.

The Origin of Bio-Man (Part One)

His face never appears. She sees everything from his viewpoint, from behind the same set of eyes that possibly account for her brown when her mother has blue. His clothes are neat, cool, but not too stylish. His footsteps are quick and deliberate. If he is experiencing any doubts about whether or not he wants to go through with this, it isn't apparent.

A clipboard is given to him with the paperwork. He fills it in, checking the appropriate boxes, and supplying the requested information. Sometimes his signature appears, the looping consonants and messy vowels of a doctor to-be. But his name is never legible, not that she even wants to know. It's his face that she strains to see: are his earlobes attached or detached? Does he have the same dimple when he smiles? Is his chin defined or rounded? Is his nose small like hers? Or does he appear like a complete stranger? After all, that's what he is and what he will always be. Regardless of how many times she has this dream.

The nurses keep smiling at him so he must be handsome. Or, perhaps, they recognize his anxiousness and want to put him at ease. His voice is all Charlie Brown Christmas wah-wah-wahs in her head as he responds to their questions. They smile again, pointing to a door down the hallway. No child wants to imagine how they were conceived, whether it's a romantic getaway to Costa Rica or a drunken hookup in a dingy dive bar bathroom. But for Erin, she can't stop seeing the door. This is where she begins. And, thankfully, it's where her dream ends every time.

Evan & The Too Lates
<u>Chapter Ten</u>

The Bean is exactly the sort of faux-risky-corporate coffee shop one would expect my try-hard hometown to have, but I still like it. The décor straddles the uninspired equator between back-to-school Target ad of a dorm room and record store that still thinks Pink Floyd is cool. It always smells of incense mixed with caramel. There's a large coffee bean above the oval entryway. The paint worn where everyone taps it on their way in. The few times we've met here after improv, Tony wouldn't stop giggling about the sexual innuendo. Makes sense that he would like a joke so hacky and lazy.

Today, there's some 70's rock song playing overhead as I swing open the door. *Yes, I still tap the bean as I enter. I'm not a monster.* I order a small hot chocolate from Christian, the cute barista. Dyed blonde hair hangs down as he works. One of his eyes is always half-shut, something must've happened when he was a kid. He's lean but I still notice the hint of his biceps underneath his black t-shirt. An apron smeared with powders and syrups is tied around his trim waist. Do I make eye contact as I order? Hahahaha. No. I do not. Keeping my head down, I grab my middle school drink, mumble something that resembles "thanks" and take a table in the middle of the room while I wait for Ashanti.

I wonder what Ro's doing right now. For the first couple days he was gone, I thought it was okay that he hadn't texted me at all. I figured, sure, he was probably busy with practices and meeting all his new teammates from across the country. But now, it's getting downright scary that I haven't heard from him. Has Ro been kidnapped? Was the whole National Improv team thing just some kind of subversive human trafficking thing? Stranger things have definitely happened.

The last text he sent to me said: "We're staying in Louisville tonight before we head over to Cincinnati in the morning for a show there." This came after I asked where he was and how he was feeling A-TIT so far. That's it. That's all he said. No joke—or even an acknowledgement of my joke. No big run-on sentence telling me about the rehearsals. No person-by-person breakdown of his new group, telling me who is a for-real team player and who is out for themselves. No paragraph-upon-paragraph descriptions telling me about the dorms they're staying in with little insights like how his roommate moans in their sleep. No personal details like who he thinks is cute and who he's vibing with. No downtime texts telling me about the so-bad-they're-good movies and shows he's binging so I could watch them too. Nothing. I know he's busy, but it would be nice to get a bit more detail on the life & times of my best friend. Maybe he's just being considerate and doesn't want to rub it in. Maybe he's replacing me. Maybe…

I quickly type out: "Worked with Weird Allan today in the hole for seven hours. 9-4 shift. He told me about seeing a snake outside and then he of course did an impression of said snake. So, I asked him to join my new improv group and he happily obliged. We're going to take over Whiting now. Alas, I'm not sure Weird Allan isn't a lowkey member of the alt-right, which makes it all a little less endearing." I start to send it before immediately stopping myself and deleting it.

Why did I do that? I stare at my phone screen. The empty message field doesn't have an answer for me.

This is a new feeling. I don't like it.

"Hey, Ev!" Ashanti sets her bag down beside the chair opposite from me and immediately leans over to give me a hug. She's wearing a white pocket tee, tight tucked into a pair of light blue flared jeans. A cream-colored cardigan covers up the tattoos that go down each of her arms. Both her moms are artists and have always encouraged her eccentric side. Must be nice. Her necklaces hang down to my lap as she hugs me. I'm probably the envy of every straight dude in this place right now.

"How're you?" Ashanti asks once she sits down. Her brown eyes shine behind her windowpane-sized glasses.

"I'm good." I place both my hands on my cup of hot chocolate. Warmth radiates through my palms. "How's the gallery doing?"

Ashanti's face falls, taking her posture along with it. "Oh, Evan, it's terrible. Just terrible."

"What do you mean? The preview was barely a week ago. Seemed like people were really into it."

"Well, that's part of the problem." Ashanti pushes a spiral-curl of her hair back. "Word has definitely gotten out. And since we nabbed everyone's phones when they came in, that meant only descriptions of my artwork made it onto social media. For the most part, the reviews were positive. But by the time word hit Acquaintances several days after the fact, it seems a local church congregation heard about some of my more *adventurous* paintings."

"Ah," I say with a nod. I don't need more than one guess to pinpoint which group that could be. "I had no idea. I've been staying offline the best I can."

A few more tight, dark curls come loose from behind her ear as she shakes her head. "It's happened so fast. I got to enjoy the warm reviews for maybe two days. Now, there are people picketing outside. Sophia worries we may not be able to do the grand opening if it keeps up like this. She already pushed it back to the end of the month."

Christian brings Ashanti's Chai Tea. I glance in his direction before quickly looking away like he's an eclipse that I'm scared to look at directly. Ashanti brings the cup to her mouth with both hands and takes a sip before setting it back down. "We're just hoping the storm will die down, but it doesn't seem to be letting up."

"But...the church congregation, they haven't seen the actual paintings, right?" I ask this knowing that it doesn't matter if they've seen them or not. It's never about the actual art. It's always about the power to harass others into submission. Once when I was in fifth grade, my parents' church protested the local library for what the church called a 'flagrant advancement of the homosexual agenda' when, really, they just had a story hour by two dads who had written and illustrated a picture book for their young daughter.

"Turns out, they don't have to see a piece called *Judas In Heat* in order to know they hate it."

"I can imagine." Boring platitudes like 'it's better to be hated than ignored' or 'controversy builds careers' run through my head and are rightfully ignored. "That sucks," I say instead. "I know how hard you worked. It isn't fair."

"Thanks, Ev." Ashanti locks eyes with me. "I did want to ask...and if it's too much with you staying at Ro's or too awkward or anything, then please don't feel any pressure…"

My palms begin sweating. I know where this is going. "Yep, I'll talk to my parents about calling it off."

Ashanti's face lights up. "You will? Oh, my God, Evan. You're a lifesaver."

"It's no big deal." I attempt to wave her off, because no, it's not merely a big deal. It's an effing monster truck of a deal. In fact, it's one of those monster trucks with a name like *Evan's Dilemma* written on the side of it in energy-drink font and then lying all around it are the flattened car carcasses of all my actual problems. Here's a totaled Buick Skylark that's my lost childhood. Here's a smashed Pontiac Grand Prix that's my parents' love for me. There's a destroyed Dodge Dart that's me ever going home again. There's a crushed Kia that's my dreams of ever leaving this town. "Totally not a big deal," I say again.

"You're the literal best." Ashanti shrugs out of her cardigan, draping it over the back of her chair. "A few of us are talking about doing a show later in July. There's a small theater that will rent us the space. Aidy has said she would coach us again. What do you think?"

I feel myself smiling; a placeholder while my brain catches up to what's happening. The thought of talking to my parents again sends my mind reeling into crisis mode, but I can't let them take this thing away from my friend. At some point this summer, I'm going to have to face them anyways, right? "That sounds awesome," I finally answer, maintaining a smile that weighs a ton.

A searing sensation rises in my chest as I get to my feet. My knees threaten to buckle beneath me. "Hey, Ashanti, sorry, I gotta go. I just remembered somewhere I need to be, but let me know when you want to get together for practice and I'll work on my parents, cool?"

"Sure." She furrows her brows, studying me, then tilts her head. "You alright?"

"Oh, yeah." I wave her off again, trying to keep cool even as sweat dampens my forehead. Getting out of here will be the only thing to save me. My legs are sparkles and pins. I loop my arm through my bag. "Thanks for meeting me. I'll get back to you with an update soon."

"That would be awesome. I'm foolishly hoping the whole thing will just blow over anyways." Ashanti narrows her eyes. "Just call me if you need something, anything, alright?"

"For sure." I swallow, but I'm already walking towards the exit, watching my feet as they go over the smooth, cold concrete, trying not to imagine how flat and cool it would be against my skin if I just laid down right now, right here.

I burst through the door and the relentless June humidity slugs me in the face. I walk quickly to my car in tight steps. Once the door's open, I collapse into the front seat. My breaths come rapidly. The more I try to steady and slow them down, the more they speed up.

One spring, a few years ago, our family's trashcans got blown over in a windstorm. They started rolling downhill, picking up momentum as they went. Knowing that it was my responsibility to take out the trash, and that my dad was going to be so pissed, I jogged after them. Only they were going too fast, each in a different direction, and as they bounced, their lids opened up and trash flew into our neighbors' yards. Fast food paper bags, paper towels smeared with BBQ sauce, the contents of Bridgette's litter box, overdue bills, all the things we were embarrassed of, just laid bare for all to see.

That's how I feel as I lose my shit in my car. I know I'm in a public place. I know my windows aren't tinted. I know anyone walking by can see me. But I can't help it. Everything is moving too fast downhill for me to contain it.

The only thing that can stop my rapid breathing is screaming into my undershirt. Spit and snot soak the now stretched-out collar. Still, I grip my eyes tight and continue letting loose, picturing the lid popping open, everything spilling out, not caring where it ends up, just knowing it needs to go.

Until I hear someone tapping on my window.

Double take.

It's Christian.

Erin & The Social Media Bump

Chapter Eleven

Dad's Random Bits of Unsolicited Advice #22: No better time than now to do something that scares the absolute shit out of you.

It's taken over a week, but I finally type his name into the search bar. Evan Prucasyk. My finger hovers over the key. It's probably just a fake name or perhaps it's a phishing scam to steal my online soul (haha, if so, joke's on you, fuckers!). Maybe there won't even be any relevant results anyway. Chevy the Cat hops up into my lap. I tousle his black and white fur. I hit enter.

My first hit is a LookAtMe photo that Evan Prucasyk is tagged in. In the pic, he's with eight other teenagers, their arms all around each other. The rest of them mug various degrees of goofy faces and gestures, but he stands in the back, taller than the rest, giving the biggest, cheesiest smile that still seems genuine. I study the picture. Though I know it's unlikely (re: impossible) at this point, I can't stop myself from looking for some faint resemblance to Dad that doesn't exist. Where Dad has— *had*–round jowls and scraggly, curly hair, Evan's blessed with the jawline of a lost Hemsworth brother and straight, swooped hair that could rival any late-night host. It makes sense that he doesn't look anything like Dad, but he also doesn't look anything like me.

His eyes = bright blue.

Mine = brown (like…Dad's).

He's tall and I'm so short that I've not once, not twice, but thrice, been mistaken for a middle-schooler when I've gone to the Junior

High to tutor kids in math. Also, he's incredibly good-looking and seems to know it. While I…well, occasionally I've heard guys say that I'm cute or, once, "surprisingly attractive," which didn't boost my self-esteem near as much as one would think.

Anxiety Brain puts it more aptly: "He's definitely too hot to be your brother."

"No crap." I bite my lip and keep scrolling.

The location for the photo tags a comedy theater in Chicago. There are even a few more photos under "High School Performances" that show his group acting out some scenes. There's one with Evan holding a chair over his head, yelling in mock anger. Another where he's lying on the stage with his hands clasped over his heart. In both, the audience is lit up with laughter.

Next, I find his Acquaintances profile, but it's locked, and he uses the same profile pic found on LookAtMe of his improv group. His full LookAtMe account is also locked with one having to make a request to follow him. For what it's worth, my LAM(E) account is locked too, but there's no way I'm bold enough to request a follow just yet.

Evan's BLRTR account, however, is unlocked and mainly showcases his numerous RifRaf videos, which include a series about some extreme archconservative fake politician that I hope is satirical named Cliff Shackleboot and an awful Australian personality called Mick Wallabie (maybe the badness is the point?). Then there are a number of film reviews for movies that seem made up and clips from a silly (yet surprisingly great) musical he and a friend filmed in the back of a fast-food restaurant. Naturally, there are also memes.

Lots and lots of memes.

I doom-scroll into oblivion. I even move onto searching about his hometown. It seems a lot like Langford, just further north and closer to Chicago so it has to be way cooler than being from southern Illinois. At the very least, it's gotta be less backwards and ultra-conservative than here. In nearly every category, even with the social media boost taken into consideration, Evan seems too good to be my brother. He's too cool, too popular, too talented.

"You said it," Anxiety Brain adds. "You'd just scare him off if he saw you pop up in his mentions looking like you just crawled out from under a bridge. Oh, I know, just go ahead and send him the graduation video right away so you can inspire yet another meme."

This is too much. I mean, I licked a freaking popsicle stick and put it in the mail just so I could get some extra credit. I never asked to learn that everything about me is a lie. I'm a lab experiment, a mistake. I shouldn't even be here.

"Now seems like a good time for a good ole fashioned panic attack. What do you say?" Anxiety Brain says while chomping on a cigar.

"Where'd you get a cigar?"

I shake my head. The fact that I even have a moment to consider that a panic attack may be coming is all the warning I need. There has to be a way to get this weight off my chest. Otherwise, I'm going to freak the eff out.

Dad's Random Bits of Unsolicited Advice #31: Never be afraid to tell someone that you're afraid.

Confide in someone, the message blares through my mind like a red alert in the hull of a sinking submarine. Confide in someone! Confide!! Confide!!

Blaide? Not after last time. He'd just make it worse. Mom? Um, that's an all-caps HELL NO.

"It's getting closer," Anxiety Brain whispers.

I consider screaming. I consider crying. I consider shaving my head just to have something to control. I consider running away. Bursting through the front door to gasp fresh air, but then I'd have to go past the Callery pear tree in our front yard. The one that Blaide always says smells like sperm in the springtime.

Awesome.

I'm afraid of trees now. Just fantastic.

"Time's running out." Anxiety Brain wiggles its bushy eyebrows.

Without wasting another second, I grab my phone and rapid fire off a series of texts to Madison.

"I need to talk to someone"

"Like face to face."

"Are you free?"

Madison promptly texts back, "Sure thing. Meet you at Dr. Koolz in fifteen."

Evan & The Crush

Chapter Twelve

Christian gives a little 'just-wanted-to-make-sure-you're-okay' wave. I pull in a deep breath and crank my window down. In improv, it's fun to steer scenes into uncharted, uncomfortable territory. Places where you're not entirely sure what's going to happen next. That's when the real magic happens. In life? Not so much.

"Sup?" I ask once the window's down. This is something I've never said before in my entire life.

"I just…it seemed like you could use some help." Christian gives a half-smile. He's so much cuter up close. A curl of blonde hair still hangs in his eyes. It's probably an accident, but it's so perfectly messy it's hard to tell.

"Oh, yeah." I fake a laugh. "I'm fine. Just rehearsing a scene for an upcoming play I'm in."

A little glimmer appears in Christian's eye. "Is the play called, 'Panic Attack'?"

"Close. It's called *This Is Our Youth* and in it I play a teenager that's experiencing an existential crisis at eighteen. Kicked out of his overly conservative parents' house, no plans for the future, abandoned by his more successful best friend, gay and out but still pretty much closeted," I slip in the last line. "But the panic attacks are pretty much a new development."

Christian cocks his head. "*This Is Our Youth*…isn't that a play by Kenneth Lonergan?"

"Holy shit, yes." I resist the urge to leap through the car window and shake his shoulders. No one around here ever knows this stuff. Well, except Ro.

"That's not how it goes though, right? Isn't it about a couple of teenagers in the eighties?" Christian asks. A pack of cigarettes stick out of the front pocket of his jean jacket. Smoking is so gross. Yet, damn it, with Christian, still sexy.

"Wait, how do you know this?"

"I know a lot of stuff, man, you don't know me," Christian says with a light laugh.

"Oh, yeah, right."

"I'm kidding." Christian starts to offer his hand and then stops. "I'm Christian."

I know who you are. "Evan." I shrug.

"I'm just on a break. Do you…" Christian thumbs over his shoulder. "Want or need to talk?"

"Um." I rest my hands on the steering wheel. Ahead of me stretches a scene where I lie and tell him, "thanks, but I'm okay," I put the car in drive, blast Patsy Cline and sing until my voice is shot or until I end up back in Ro's hot garage, fending off spiders on the couch. The other option is I say, "Sure," and then…then I'm not sure what happens. That seems like the bolder choice. "Sure."

Christian steps aside as I open my car door. I point to the alley behind The Bean. "I have a friend that's still inside and I don't want them to see me like this…could we?"

"Yeah, for sure." Christian jams his hands into his pockets and starts in front of me. He even walks with confidence. His jeans are tight, yet not too tight. He fills them perfectly.

"So how long do you got?" I ask with an uneasy smile. My cheeks feel warm. *Are you seriously blushing right now?* Performing, keeping my head under pressure, being able to think on my feet, that's supposed to be my thing, but in Christian's presence it's nearly impossible.

Instead of checking his phone, Christian shoots out his right wrist and checks his watch. "I got about…seven minutes left." He shrugs. "I know I'm just a stranger. I just couldn't let you drive off when I saw you were so upset. You don't have to say anything if you don't want."

I nod, wondering just how much I should say if anything. My lips part, but that's as far as I get. The aroma of freshly ground coffee beans leaks from under the side door, mingling with the acidic smell of the dumpster. It's not as unpleasant as you might think.

Christian catches eyes with me. "I've felt like that before." He tilts his chin in the direction of my magnificent Toyota Yaris. "I used to feel like that all the time."

I wait for him to go on, maybe into a spiel about how he found God or some new age religion that helped him get his life together. He doesn't though. It would be wrong to be intrusive, but there's something about him that seems so open. Rather than asking what caused his panic attacks, I ask, "What made it better?"

Christian lets out a short laugh. Dimples appear under the stubble on his cheeks. "I started self-medicating with pain pills."

"Oh." I resist taking a step backwards. He definitely catches my recoil though.

Christian meets eyes with me again. I never noticed how blue they are, like this lake at the bottom of a cliff I went swimming in with the other boys in my cabin at church camp so many years ago. "It's okay," he says. "My senior year of high school, I did the whole cycle of R's. Rock bottom, Rehab, Relapse, Rehab again, and now Remission." He raises his left wrist. A single white piece of string is tied around it. "I'll always be an addict, but I'm doing better right now."

"So, I just need to acquire a debilitating drug addiction so I can wrestle with that instead and eventually, if I make it, I'll feel alright again?" My face does the grit-teeth emoji. It's always hard to know if my humor will go over with new humans. Something about Christian seems like I've known him before or he's a part of my soul-family. Bad jokes are often a litmus test.

Christian laughs. It's goofier than any sound I would expect to come out of his body. "I wouldn't recommend that, no." He locks eyes with me. "Talking with people though." He motions from me to him. "In rehab I learned it helps. I'm still learning through counseling. You have to talk about stuff with honesty instead of just trying to solve your shit on your own. Otherwise, you may end up leaving a path of destruction behind you full of people you've hurt and bridges you've burned."

This kind of earnestness is so refreshing and intimidating at the same time. I look at my shoes. I don't even feel like making a joke right now. Instead, I want to tell him everything, but compared to what he's gone through…I open my mouth. "I'm—"

"Christian," the other, considerably less cute, barista, Owen sticks his oversized head out the side-door. "C'mon, break's over man. We need you."

"Sorry," Christian says once the door slams shut. "I gotta head in. It was nice talking with you though, Evan, however briefly." He reties his apron around his waist and starts to head in. This is where our scene ends. Unless…

"Wait…" I reach for his shoulder. It's harder than I expected. I withdraw my hand like a little kid caught reaching for their parent's phone.

"Yeah?" Christian stops. After initiating this whole thing, he's really not making this any easier on me.

"Um." I cross my arms then uncross them. "Could I text or call…you know if I wanted…to talk more?"

"I am kind of between phones right now—" Christian starts.

"Oh, yeah, right. Don't worry about it." I back off. The sense returns that this scene is going to end the way it was always meant to: me alone, feeling the full magnitude of the word.

"No, it's not like that. It's just with my recovery…I got rid of my phone. Too many old threads, both to and from, you know?" Christian pulls an order pad from the front of his apron. He scrawls then tears off the sheet. "Here's my email. Hit me up on there or just come by here if you want to talk."

I take it from him like it's a hundred-dollar bill. "Cool."

Without another word, he disappears inside. I don't know what comes next, but for the first time this summer, I'm excited to see where this leads.

Erin & The Questionable Degrees

<u>Chapter Thirteen</u>

Dad's Random Bits of Unsolicited Advice #9: Empty calories are a temporary (yet delicious) cure for most problems. Hey, there are worse things.

"Welcome to Dr. Koolz! Home of a million and one toppings!" A blonde freshman girl that I recognize from school tells me as I enter. "Do you know how it works?" She asks with a forced smile.

I grab an empty green cup, the biggest one. "Yep. Been here a lot thanks."

"Great. 4.7oz is the Surgeon Selection Size of the Day so if you get that weight then it's on us. Otherwise, enjoy!"

"Thanks."

I proceed straight for the Frozen Chocolate Banana Blast and nearly fill my cup (it's been a long couple of weeks, alright?). The Oreo crumb toppings are always a little stale for my taste, so I just add a shot of Nutella, a few M&Ms, and a spattering of sprinkles. Minus the Oreos, this was dad's go to creation. He called it My Calorical Romance, which was some lame old emo band joke that only he and mom understood.

Shoot. I overshot the Surgeon's Size of the Day by a good three ounces. I pay and take a table near the back. It's pretty empty in here since the little league games haven't let out yet. Madison will have no problem finding me whenever she gets here.

I glance over at Dad's old table, the place where he and mom told me about his diagnosis, thus forever changing the happiness that was once contained within the molecular fabric of that lone red table and four solo chairs.

"I mean it's likely the chairs are switched around pretty regularly," Anxiety Brain says matter of fact over its own large bowl of syrupy frozen yogurt. "You could be sitting in one of those chairs now."

No one asked you.

"Just saying…right now, you could be sitting in the exact same chair where your dad told you he was going to die. If I were you, I'd switch," Anxiety Brain says between mouthfuls. "It's bad luck."

I switch seats.

"You know, this seat could be it too. Any of them could be THE seat…also look at the other empty seats…remember the empty chair…remember how that was a thing?" Anxiety Brain gleefully adds.

I switch seats again and try to return to my previous plan of ignoring Anxiety Brain. I take a bite of yogurt, letting it melt on my tongue. Madison should be here any minute. She's hardly ever late. Something must be going on. Maybe—

The shutter-click of a phone disrupts my thought. I look up in time to catch the blonde girl behind the counter taking a picture of me before triumphantly typing in her phone. Did she—did she just snap a pic of me to send to her friends? I can just imagine her text now: *Hey, remember that girl that freaked out at graduation a few weeks ago? Well guess what? She's in the shop eating a massive bowl of yogurt all by herself. LOL.*

"Welcome to Dr. Koolz!" The blonde girl calls without looking up from her phone as Madison comes through the door. Despite it *just* being a Tuesday, Madison is dressed as though she stepped straight from the screen of her best LookAtMe pics. She's wearing a pair of tight black jeans, factory-ripped (modestly) at the knees, and a loose, flowing purple blouse that accentuates her skinny frame perfectly. She bypasses all flavors of yogurt to come straight to my table.

"Erin. How. Are. You?" Madison sits across from me and quickly places her bag underneath the table. Unlike Madison, I didn't feel the need to dress up for an impromptu yogurt meet-up. Dr. Koolz doesn't discriminate. I once saw a dude wearing dripping wet swim-trunks in here and nothing else. Still, I wish I had dressed up beyond the same stretchy pants I've been wearing for three days and a t-shirt from my favorite murder podcast, *2 Dead Broads*.

"I'm okay." I take another bite. "Just pondering the authenticity of Dr. Koolz' doctorate—like did he go to medical school? Or is he one of those people that just took a ton of extra classes in college, racking up insane debt, just so they can go around telling—nay, *making*—everyone call them 'doctor' for the rest of their lives?"

Madison blinks long eyelashes at me. She doesn't like it when I try to banter, even when I've given her plenty of fuel to fire something back. Like, *why do you presume Dr. Koolz is a man?* Or *what kind of classes would Dr. Koolz major in? Creamology?* And then we could laugh about how gross of a word creamology is (like maybe it's a disease?), but Madison's not that kind of friend.

Madison reaches into her purse to retrieve some lip-gloss, which she promptly applies without breaking eye contact. "Sorry I'm late, love. I was just over at Kennedy's house helping her prep for her Pals Party on Friday night. You should come."

"No, that's alright." I haven't been to one of Kennedy's overnights since sophomore year when they set up a fake HookUps profile for me (with my actual phone number!) after I fell asleep. When

I woke up, it seemed like every creep within an eight-mile radius had messaged me. Hilarious.

Madison puts her lip-gloss away. "What was so urgent, girlie?"

"Well—" I start before Madison interrupts me with a sharp inhale.

"Oh, no." Madison puts her hands on top of mine. "Blaide broke up with you, didn't he?"

I wish. "No, it's a bit more complicated than that...do you remember the DNA test that Mrs. Phelps offered for extra credit in Ancient Civilizations?"

Madison clutches her pearls like a scandalized Southern Belle who was just told that *The Help* is problematic. "No. Erin, you didn't."

When I nod that in fact I did, Madison whisper-hisses, "You should never give the government your DNA, who knows what they'll do with it!" She then shoots a quick look to the door like the Men in Black will bust in any second. Which, I mean, honestly, Chris Hemsworth can come wipe my mind any time he wants. Tessa Thompson too for that matter.

"I got matched with a half-brother...on my dad's side."

Madison gasps. "Oh, no, Erin."

"I got the notification on graduation day."

"After all you've been through..." Madison's huge eyes well up with tears like she legit might cry and I'm reminded of why we've stayed friends for so many years. "What does your mom say?"

I shake my head. "Do you want to see him?"

"Oh, God, yes!" Madison yelps. A few guys that have sat down in the corner look our way and laugh.

I hand her my phone to show her my favorite of Evan's RifRaf videos, the one where he's singing the ballad of the perpetually broken milk shake machine ("the real brokenness is in *myyyyy* heart").

"Wow, he's so tall."

"Yep."

"And so cute."

"Yep."

"Actually, I'd call him downright hot." Madison shakes her head with a tsk. "I don't necessarily see the resemblance though."

"Yep." I reach for my phone back. *ANNNNNDDDD* just like that I'm reminded why I don't enjoy hanging out with Madison all that much anymore.

"Also, he seems kind of…" Madison flicks her wrist with a smirk.

I know what she's implying, but I don't push back on it. I hate myself for this more than anything. I take my phone and put it away as quickly as I can, lest it records this painful conversation.

Actually, you know what?

I jab at Madison with my spoon. "What did you mean by that?"

Madison's smile lingers. "What did I mean by what?"

"The wrist thing. What was that supposed to mean?"

Madison tilts her head with a pout. "Erin, honey, are you okay? You look so tired."

"Oh, I'm fine. I just want to know what you meant by that, with the little smirk."

Madison shoots a look to the boys in the corner to check if they're paying attention to us. They're not. "It was just a joke. I didn't mean anything by it."

"But where's the joke?" I point again with my spoon. "I don't get it."

Madison grabs her bag and starts to stand. "I should really get going. Kennedy is expecting me back. I just wanted to check on you." Madison taps on the table before leaving. "Text me if you need me and please get some sleep, okay, dear?"

I watch Madison leave and continue eating my yogurt.

I know what I need to do now.

But I don't know if I can.

Erin & Is This Thing On?

Chapter Fourteen

There's this lame (actually I think they're cool, but it was more fun to give him crap) super-old emo band that Dad used to like called The Promise Ring. They have this album called *Nothing Feels Good* that is full of all these short, reflective songs about being young and sad. Once, when Dad was driving me home from one of my volunteer shifts at the shelter, he turned up the title track from that album and told me how the title holds a double meaning for him, "like how sometimes in life, nothing feels good, but if you lean into it then that feeling, that nothing-feels-good feeling, *feels* good, ya know?"

A marijuana dispensary had just opened in Langford, so I politely asked, "Dad, are you high?" Then he laughed that deep booming giddy sound that he was known for. The kind of sound that I could always hear no matter where I was in our house, the kind of sound that I used to imagine seeping into our walls, flowing down to our floorboards, down into the foundation of our home.

It's memories like that, the ones that seemed pointless and inconsequential, that I'm most thankful for when they come trickling back in. I'm hanging onto this memory right now like a piece of driftwood. Perilous water surrounds me on all sides, but I'm ignoring it. I'm not going to think about what Mom told me. I'm not going to think about Dad not being my dad. I'm just going to keep hold of this memory like my survival depends on it. Because I've been in bed since I got home from Dr. Koolz last night and this is the first time I've felt myself smiling.

Nothing *feels* good, ya know?

It's strange how a small crack in depression can send you into action, because before I know it, I'm drafting an email to Evan. *Must take action before the despair takes hold again.*

"Hi Evan! So, I guess you're my long-lost half-brother! Haha!" I type and then promptly backspace out. Too many exclamation points, what am I, a serial killer?

Okay. Try again. This time with a bit more chill. "Hi Evan, so I guess you're my long lost (half) brother. Haha." Shoot. That's way worse. The only voice I can read it in is Eeyore's. Backspace. Let's just nail the beginning.

"Greetings, Evan." Backspace out. I'm not an alien trying to colonize his hometown. Nor am I an Internet bot that has just gained sentience.

"Good morn—" Delete. It may not be morning when he reads it.

"Good eveni—" Same. Also, I'm not reporting from the local news here.

"Hello." Ugh. GTFOH. Delete.

"Dear Evan…" What's with the ellipsis there? Am I my Noonie writing an email from California? Delete.

"Evan." Nope. I'm not sitting him down to tell him that it's not his fault, but his dad and I are getting a divorce. Highlight. Delete.

Fine. No intro then. Let's get down to it. "My name is Erin Drexel. About eight months ago, my dad died." I pause, reading those last three words. I've thought them a lot. They're the way-too-hot water

I splash on my face each morning. They're the cold brass doorknobs in my palm when I pad around the house in the middle of the night double (then triple, then quadruple etc.) checking that the doors are all locked. They're consistent and everywhere. Still, I've never said them so plainly before. It's almost refreshing. I keep going.

"It was really hard, and I didn't know what to do with myself," I type out. I reread that sentence several times. Highlight. Delete.

I try again. "Eight months ago, my dad died. Then just a few weeks ago, I got this notification that you may be my brother." I stop and read that sentence again. You know what? It's fine. I'll leave it (for now).

"Then my mom recently explained that my dad wasn't my BIO-dad and that I came—" Um, that's going to be a big fat NOPE. Delete.

"My mom recently explained that her and my dad went to a fertility clinic called Michael Reese Hospital and that they used an anonymous donor to help my conception." Pretty cold there, but it gets to the point. Let's roll with it.

Actually, wait…am I really doing this right now? Spilling my guts to a complete stranger? A stranger that—might I add—is super cool and funny and interesting and isn't from a hick small town whose only redeeming quality is having not one but two Casey's gas stations? No way. This is all so embarrassing. I'll stick with my brutal true-crime marathons while wallowing alone in my bed, thanks. Select all, delete.

My mortal nemesis the blinking cursor returns.

Breathe.

Okay.

Try again.

Nothing feels good.

Erin's Introductory Email to Evan
(That She Actually Sent)

Hi Evan,

So, we (significantly) matched on DN-YAY. You know I don't really like the gratuitous all capped out name (like it always feels like I'm in trouble and they're yelling at me), but I have to admit, I was pretty stoked (stunned? Flabbergasted?) to finally match with someone that was more than a fifth aunt or a twelfth cousin thrice removed.

Anyways, I know this may all be a bit much, so I just wanted to send along a quick Email to say: 'hey' (insert waving emoji) in case you have any questions for me. I'd be happy to chat some more. Just let me know.

Thanks,
Erin

Erin & The Regrettable Double Downs

<u>Chapter Fifteen</u>

Centuries from now, at the height of knowledge, when all that is knowable will be known, long after all diseases have been cured by microscopic nanobots, when the arbitrary divisive borders around our countries cease to exist and human beings have finally learned the pointlessness of hating/killing each other, one lone mystery will remain to puzzle scholars until the sun explodes: *How is Erin's email to Evan the single worst message ever sent in all of recorded human history?*

Just keep it simple, I told myself. Keep it light. Make a joke if you can. In what world would that thing about the unnecessary capitalization ever be mistaken for a joke? And the mother-effing waving emoji? I don't know if I'm more embarrassed that I forgot to actually insert it or if it's better that I didn't. Let's not even start on the sign off: *Thanks.*

Actually, now that it's been mentioned…*Thanks?!* Thanks for what? Thanks for sharing 24.7% of my DNA? Thanks for putting up with the email equivalent of a cat hacking puke on the carpet?

It's no surprise that Evan hasn't written me back yet (it's been a whole twelve hours after all). He's taken one look at the obvious desperate mess that is his (probable) half-sister and decided to never speak to me. Why would he want to?

I pull my blankets up to my chin and click play on another *2 Dead Broads* live podcast video. The hosts, Kay and V, continue riffing about the little-man inferiority complex of the Cry Baby Bridge Killer. They have a way of talking about the crimes so that it makes the women (who are almost always the victims) seem more human and less like objects, while not fawning over or idolizing the men (who are almost always the killers). Also, they're funny as hell. Their show is better than almost anything at getting me out of my head for a bit.

"You want to know what else may help?" Anxiety Brain peeks up from its Ted Bundy biography.

Oh, no. Please.

"You should…"

No.

"Check."

Come on.

"Your."

No. Please. I'm sorry. No.

"Phone."

I just did and there was nothing there.

"Well, what if your email app just hasn't updated?"

Hmmmm. That's actually a great point. Let's take a look. Tap. Swipe up. Little circle regenerates and fades. "No new emails." That's what you think, little circle. Swipe down. Little circle regenerates and fades. Nothing. Again. Nothing. Again. Nothing. Again. Nothing. Again. Nothing. Ag—

Okay, stop. I gave it a go, Anxiety Brain, but it seems Evan just hasn't seen my email yet.

"But wait…"

No. I did what you wanted. Please. No.

"What if…"

No. Not again. C'mon. Seriously, we've been through this.

"Just hold on. Hear me out now...what if..."

Nooooo-oooooooooo-oooooooo-oooooooooo-oooooooo-oooo.

"What if you recheck your email to see if it's as bad as you remember it? Maybe it wasn't so bad. It wasn't so bad. I promise if you check it this time, you'll see it wasn't so bad and you'll feel better."

Argh! You win, Anxiety Brain. You always do.

"I know, bitch."

I click on my Sent folder and open up the message I sent Evan. I read it again. The spiral continues.

Deeper and deeper down I go.

Now, it's 1AM and my room is pitch dark other than the light from my open laptop screen. No sound comes from Mom's room, but I feel like she's awake. Crickets thrum beyond my window. Even they have more of a life than me.

With a sigh, I roll back towards my computer screen again. "You're seriously going to do this, aren't you?" I ask myself, already knowing the answer. And then—

Oh, no.

"How can you be sure he's seen the email?" Anxiety Brain asks over its midnight snack of olives and mayonnaise.

You're so gross. But to answer your question, well, who would sign up for DN-YAY take the test and then not check their email for results?

"He's definitely seen it then. You're sure?"

Yes.

"What if he hasn't though?"

Do you have to do this?

"You're avoiding my question." Anxiety Brain sits cross-legged in a chair tapping its mayo-covered spoon to its lips like any respectful therapist.

Fine. Maybe he hasn't.

"Oooooh. Now I have a fun thought…"

I hate you so much.

"But what if he has?"

Then the only possibility is that he's read it, deemed that I'm an emotional mess, thus unworthy of his time and moved on.

"Checks out."

So that leaves me with only two options:

A.) Okay, sure, not email Evan again, but then go on feeling the way I do now until Anxiety Brain takes over Logic Brain and then the rest of my body, like one of those ants in the rainforest that get taken over by zombie fungus.

Or

B.) Write another email to Evan. But this time—oh ho baby, THIS TIME—I'm going to be so mind-blowingly charismatic and charming that he won't be able to help himself from wanting to be my friend. I'll even be a bit more thorough (and a little less desperate) thus hopefully proving to Evan that I'm not a lunatic seeking a kidney transplant or money or even love, necessarily.

With my fingertips on the keyboard, I already feel calmer. There's potential here and it's up to me to unlock it. Maybe that's all this is, without schoolwork or graduation to distract me, my anxieties have just gotten out of control, an existential crisis running amok like a drunk dude wearing a sumo-suit in an antiques shop.

This will help.

I'll just write. I've missed this.

I don't even have to send it if I don't want.

Before long, it's 4am and I've written a three-page rant covering (almost) everything from before Dad got sick to my commencement speech meltdown to the past month of separating myself from everyone, even leaving in the part where I learned that Dad isn't my bio-dad. I scroll back through. Ugh there's no way I can send this one. If he didn't think I was a mess before then he definitely will now.

Select all—except before I hit delete, I double-tap the Enter button and whoosh, it's off.

Without me signing off.

Or putting goodbye.

Or apologizing for my rant or anything.

He may be my half-brother and now he's going to already know all my crazy before I ever meet him. AND he's going to see that he got it at...4:13AM.

I let my head fall to my desk. I want to laugh at how ridiculous this is, but after the last ten months...

I just can't do it.

Evan & The Farmer Tans

<u>Chapter Sixteen</u>

Outside Ro's house, I sit in the car for a few minutes to let "Maybe This Time" from the Cabaret soundtrack finish before I head into the garage. The sun sets over the Holloway's house next door to Ro's. Poor, eternally sunburned-shouldered Mr. Holloway is out mowing their yard in shorts and a Bulls jersey. I wave and he waves back. Maybe I won't even stay inside too long tonight. I could text Ashanti and apologize for leaving early the other day, see if she wants to meet up. We could head into the city and see a show. Afterwards, I could tell her why I can't actually ask my parents to call off the protest. About how just that thought alone sends me into a full-blown freak out. Never before has talking about any of this seemed even remotely possible, but right now, I don't know, I could just open my mouth and let it all out. *Maybe this time, I'll be lucky.*

That feeling vanishes once I enter the garage and find Ro's parents, Big Bill and Carmen, waiting for me. "Hey, Evan," Carmen says, patting the couch for me to sit beside her.

"Hey." I cross the floor and sit on the edge of the couch. Carmen is wearing yoga pants and a zip-up jacket. Big Bill's still wearing his suit from work, albeit with his tie loosened and the sleeves of his white dress shirt rolled back to reveal the tattoos from his more rebellious days.

"Evan." Big Bill clasps his hands and leans forward on his backwards folding chair. "We need to talk."

I nod for him to go on. There exists a handful of ways for this to go and none of them are good.

"We love having you stay with us, honey," Carmen says. "You've been such a good friend to Ro since you both were little. We've gotten to watch you grow up into a wonderful young man. In a lot of ways, we feel like you're a son to us."

And much like watching Magic Mike here comes the...

"But..." Big Bill nods. "You need to have a plan."

"We told Ro before he left that you can stay with us as long as you need to." Carmen puts her hand on my shoulder. "Which is true. We're not going to have you out on the streets. You'll always have a place here. You just need a plan for what's next."

"For sure. I've been thinking the exact same thing," I say, meeting Carmen's kind eyes.

Narrator voice: *He has not.*

"I've been saving money to get a place of my own." I turn to Big Bill, also making eye contact, connecting like a true performer

Narrator voice: *His bank account is currently at twenty-two dollars.*

"I've started looking at apartments even," I go on.

Narrator voice: *Where is this coming from?*

"Good. That's great, Evan." Big Bill nods at me.

"We're just so proud of Ro for getting on the improv team this summer." Carmen smiles and shakes her head. "He's been checking in everyday about how much fun he's having. Though I don't have to tell you that. I'm sure the two of you have been texting all day every day."

My heart sinks. "Yep. All day."

Big Bill stands, offering his hand. Even though I'm over six feet tall, he still has a solid four inches on me. His hand swallows mine as he shakes it. "You can stay with us as long as you *need* to, but not as long as you *want* to. Got it?"

"For sure," I say, holding his eye contact like it weighs four hundred pounds. "I feel the exact same way. I appreciate you both so much. You'll never know."

"Aw, we appreciate you too, honey. Remember that God loves you and we do too." Carmen holds her arms out. I bend over so she can wrap me in a tight hug. "We just want to see you grow beyond..." Carmen glances around the garage and tsks. "This."

I offer a small laugh. "Me too."

As they leave, Carmen's phone begins ringing a piano riff. "Oh, there's Ro right now." Beaming, Carmen raises the phone and answers it on speakerphone. "Hi honey, we were just out talking to Evan."

"Oh. Cool," Ro says flatly on speaker.

"Do you want to talk to him?" Carmen's eyes sparkle at me.

"No...uh..." Ro clears his throat. "I just wanted to talk to you and Dad real quick. I need to get backstage soon."

"Oh, okay, honey." Carmen and Big Bill wave at me as they exit the garage.

Once they're gone, I'm left alone with the opening salvo of the cricket orchestra and my thoughts. Just hearing Ro's voice felt like being dropkicked in the gut. Added guilt comes from the fact that Big Bill and Carmen even had to come out here for that talk in the first place. For a distraction, I log into their WiFi with the new rickety phone I had to get since my parents cut me off. It's been a bit since I've been on LookAtMe and I can't say I miss it. Old habits though, I start scrolling through.

Here's a pic of Ro in front of a comedy venue in Dayton, Ohio. Here's his team at a small diner. Here's him and Tony laughing about something I'll never know. It hurts. I double-tap-heart them all anyways as quickly as an assassin, a small reminder to him that I exist.

I flip over to Acquaintances. It offers nothing in the form of a dopamine spike. Sure enough, my parent's church has launched an attack on Ashanti's art installation. Since I've long since unfriended my parents and their church friends, I only see the backlash to the backlash. I scroll until I've found a backlash to the backlash to the backlash. And then I close it out. Yep. That just made my anxieties much worse.

I start to tap over to BLRTR before stopping myself. Nope. Absolutely not. There's no way there's anything there to make me feel any better. Dang it. I was feeling so good just a bit ago. Maybe I could finally email Christian. It's been two days. The thought alone would surely pass a few hours.

My inbox overflows with invites to Improv shows that I will never go to and musicals I would like to but can't afford. There are a slew of notifications from DN-YAY and then an email from someone named Erin Drexel, two emails actually. I open one up and...oh...oh, my.

Evan's Email to Erin

Hi Erin,

Thank you so much for reaching out and sharing your story. I haven't checked my DN-YAY site since I submitted it, so I hope you haven't been waiting long. Personally, I don't know how my dad could've ever had another kid that wasn't me. At the risk of TMI, he and my mom have made a HUGE deal about only ever having one partner, each other. Which, yeah, I know, is super-gross and something no child should have to envision of their parents, but still, they've preached that...and God, so many other things...since I was young. Still, I was born at that same hospital so who knows? Maybe a switch up or something happened there. Otherwise, I have my doubts about the accuracy of DN-YAY's science too. I mean, as a rule I try not to trust any corporation, especially those with such a devotion to overcapitalization. Still, of course I'd be happy to text if you'd like, my number and contact info is attached. I'll help you on your path any way that I can.

-Evan

Erin & The Four Custodians of the Apocalypse
<u>Chapter Seventeen</u>

When I first see the email in my inbox, I scream and throw my phone behind the couch. Then I approach it cautiously like it's one of those spricket (spider + cricket, trust me, they exist) bugs we used to have in our basement. I peer over the couch. My phone sits there all innocent like it didn't just have a life-altering, reality-shifting email on it.

I swipe through the photo of Dad and I at the local Comic-Con. There it is. It takes me maybe five seconds to read it the first time. Then I take a full five minutes to read it the second time. Then I read it a third, a fourth, a fifth, a sixth…a twenty-eighth time. *Don't read too much into certain phrases,* I preemptively tell myself.

"Like what?" Anxiety Brain baits me.

Nope. Not falling for it.

"No seriously, what's there that I would even read into?"

Oh-ho-ho-ho, eff you, that's not going to work, pal.

"It seems like a perfectly good email to me. What is there to even be upset about?"

Nothing. Just move on.

"Oh, I was moving on. I was totally moving on, just minding my own business, but you said for me to not read too much into it, which leads me to believe there is something to read into. So, what is there?"

Well…

"Yes?"

There's the way he said, "thank you so much for sharing your story."

"Oh, yes, that is troubling."

I mean shouldn't it be our story?

"It should be."

And doesn't that phrasing make it seem like—dang it—both my emails were a bit insufferable for him? Like I just went on and on and on and shared my whole life story?

"That's precisely what I was thinking."

I fall back on the couch to read the email for a thirty-seventh time. Another *2 Dead Broads* live show plays on mute.

Thirty-eighth time.

Actually, you know what?

Thirty-ninth time.

I think…

Fortieth time.

I think…

Forty-first time.

Yep. I'm going to text him. I am. Let's do this.

"You can't be serious," Anxiety Brain says. "He was just being nice. He doesn't actually want you to do that."

Screw you. I don't care. I'm going to do it. I'm going to text him.

In a flurry, I tap in his contact info and write my opening: "Hi Evan, this is Erin Drexel (the weird-yet-hopefully-endearing girl from the emails). Just wanted to say hey. Feel free to write back whenever you'd like. Thanks!"

Hit send, I tell my thumbs.

"You wouldn't dare," Anxiety Brain halts me.

HIT. SEND.

Whoosh. It's off.

It's out there. I can't believe I just did that.

"I can't believe you just did that."

What? Shut up. That was fine. There's nothing wrong with that message.

"I'm just surprised is all."

What was wrong with it?

"Well, since you asked. Don't we normally have a protocol for this sort of thing? You didn't work through multiple drafts. You didn't even edit it!"

I didn't need to. It was just a simple message, you know? Nonchalant. Off-the-cuff. Flowing from the top of my dome.

"You sure about that?"

Yep.

"Let's reread it just to see."

Fine. Whatever. This message is good.

"Okay. I believe you."

It's just fine.

"Sure."

Just fine.

"Yep."

I'll read it just to prove it to you... Oh. Oh, God. What have I done? First, I say "Hi" then in the very next sentence I say, "I just wanted to say 'hey'." There's even a long parenthetical phrase with a super-extra hyphenated word! Why does anyone even trust me with a phone? How did I ever think I could do this? How am I a person?

"I tried warning you. This is why you should always listen to me."

I bury my head in the couch cushions. Why do I—my phone buzzes on my lap interrupting the spiral. My impromptu pillow-fort lights up blue.

It's him. I swipe through again.

"Hey Erin, I was hoping it was you."

Wowowowowowowowow.

The little ellipsis bubble pops up.

Dot.

"Hey, you know he could be—" Anxiety Brain tries.

Nope. Shut up.

Dot.

The sun explodes, the earth dies and is reborn again while I watch those three dots pass from left to right and regenerate before disappearing again.

Dot.

Finally: "So I'm sure you have a lot to ask/tell me, but for now, tell me this…what do you think about the Purge extended universe?"

That's it?

I waited an eternity for…that?

It's such a short message. Either he's the slowest texter ever (which is doubtful) or he had a whole other, much longer message all typed out and he backspaced it out for this. The possibility that it's the latter fills me with hope. If he really is my brother (which I of course have never been anything other than a True Believer of the brilliant science behind DN-YAY) then maybe he's just as neurotic as I am.

I type out, "The Purge, the awful b-rated, gory, horror movie? The WHAT IF ONE NIGHT ALL CRIME WAS LEGAL IN THE UNITED STATES tagline automatic green light premise? The uniquely American irony of 'hey, let's make murder legal rather than just making therapy more affordable or guns just slightly more difficult to purchase.' Please let's talk about the extended universe."

"Whoa, you really just fucking went for it, huh?" Anxiety Brain chimes in.

"Uh, shut up, go to sleep," I say, but then I reread the message and dang, I did just fucking go for it. This is the moment where my long-lost brother (okay, *half*-brother, but who's counting?) decides I'm a lost cause, deletes my contact, changes his number, gets an order of protection, files for a name change, moves to a different sta—

Whoops! My phone buzzes in my hand.

Evan: "That's the one."

Evan: "It's just they've made like six installments of that movie, but they never show the part of that world I care most about, the part that would actually be interesting."

Me: "Which is?"

Evan: "Well, since you asked."

Evan: "I want to know who's responsible for cleaning up after everything."

Me: "So...The Purge: Custodians of the Apocalypse?"

Evan: "Yes! Exactly! Those are the stories I want to see. Those are the lives I'm interested in. Like in my mind, they wait out The Purge in their homes with their families, trying to get a good night's sleep despite all the screams and chainsaws and, for some reason, tricked out death-mobiles, because they know the next day they have to go and clean all the crap up. I mean someone has to, right?"

Me: "For sure."

Evan: "And I just can't help but imagine what they're conversations must be."

Me: "It's definitely a buddy comedy."

Evan: "Totally!"

Me: "Screenplay: open on a post-apocalyptic hellscape then a slow zoom out reveals a Krispy Kreme parking lot with a Jimmy John's next door. Enter Toby, dressed head to toe in an orange HAZMAT suit, pushing a large trash bin. His friend Geoff (who has a bad British accent—came here for thus far unknown reasons) walks close behind him, just throwing in random body parts and bloody-secret-society masks into the bin."

Evan: "Toby to Geoff: Oh, sweet!

Geoff casually picking up a foot: What's that?

Toby: This guy had a coupon for a free dozen glazed in
      his pocket.

Geoff: No blood?

Toby: No blood!

Geoff: You gotta take it.

Toby: I can't take it.

Geoff: Why not?!

Toby: I need to locate his next of kin.

Geoff looks at Toby they both erupt into laughter"

Me: "That kind of took a dark turn."

Evan: "It's a *dark* buddy comedy. Did I not mention that?"

Me: "Ah, I see. It's not supposed to be funny. Got it."

Evan: "No. That's the brilliance of it. No one will like this installment of the Purge universe at first. It will be panned by critics and audiences alike. Its Smelly Eggs aggregated score will be a nausea-inducing 8%. Then slowly, over time, The Purge: Custodians of the Apocalypse will find its fans. Highly intelligent, snobby weirdos who will find its complete lack of humor hilarious in a so-bad-it's-brilliant move."

Erin: "Ten years later there will be midnight showings at prestigious theaters in big cities across the country."

Evan: "Fifteen years after its release there will be a special Criterion Blu-Ray edition released with exclusive bonus features like the deleted scene where…"

I wait for Evan to finish his thought, but he doesn't. It's like he's setting me up for the punchline.

Me: "Toby and Geoff dance beneath the mostly-broken lights in the soccer stadium (they're secretly in love with one another)."

The little bubbles pop up and then disappear without a message. Oh, no, maybe I messed up. A meteor strikes the earth and New Orleans is erased by the rising sea level as seconds pile up on one another.

Huzzah! My phone buzzes in my palm.

Evan: "I love it!"

Me: "Can I make a confession?"

Evan: "Please."

Me: "I've only ever seen like half a Purge movie."

Me: "I kind of hate horror movies because they're scary and awful and though I know that's a creature-comfort kind of entertainment experience for some, it's not one I enjoy at all."

Ellipsis bubble. Ellipsis bubble. I'm holding my breath. Then finally—

Evan: "Oh, me neither! I've only seen the previews. Those movies look terrible. My best friend Ro loves movies of all types, especially awful ones, but even he can't get me to watch them."

I fall into the couch cushions.

A blowtorch couldn't remove the smile off my face right now.

Evan & The Most Sacred, Hallowed Chain Restaurant

<u>Chapter Eighteen</u>

For the next week or so, Erin and I stay in almost continuous conversation. Showers are halted so I can text a funny thought. Drive times to and from work have doubled, as I often have to pull over to read what she's written before replying back. Once at work, the little vibrations of my phone in my pocket let me know that I'm not alone and it will just be a matter of time until my next break so I can talk with her again.

Despite the fact that we've talked about everything from our hopes for the future—Erin: college, career in whatever. Me: HAHAHA IDK—to how we'd potentially react to an alien abduction—Me: probably go along with it. Erin: no way in Hell and actually got a bit heated at the mere mention of aliens—we still haven't discussed the real issue at hand: how exactly are we related? The subtext of that question is there though. It lurks behind every one of Erin's messages. Almost like she wants to bring it up but...won't for whatever reason.

There's a lot more than just Ashanti's art show that I need to talk about with my parents.

Naturally, Mom picked Applebee's as a "neutral meeting ground." Though Applebee's is without a doubt my parent's turf. A true neutral meeting spot would be the Target parking lot at dusk or the so-sparsely-populated-it-resembles-a-postapocalyptic-hellscape Outlet Mall food court, but I wasn't about to argue over something so petty.

Waiting for my parents to get here just makes me nervous though so I text Erin.

Me: "Meeting my parents for lunch."

Erin immediately texts back: "Oooohhh, lunch is my favorite. Where are you eating?"

Me: "Applebee's."

Erin: "Ugh."

Me: "Yeah, for sure. It's like they should change their tagline, Applebee's: We Have As Little Personality As Those Who Eat Here."

Erin: "Applebee's: Hope You Like Microplastics!"

Me: "Applebee's: Half-Priced Apps Because Who Gives An Eff, Really?"

Erin: "Applebee's: Because Your Marriage Is A Sham."

Me: "Applebee's: It's Divorced Dad Weekend Somewhere!"

Erin: "Applebee's: Depression You Can Taste!"

Me: "Applebee's: Proof That You Will Never Truly Leave Your Hometown."

Erin: "Applebee's: The World Is Lukewarm Artichoke Dip & I'm No Longer Afraid to Die."

Whoa. Not even Ro can beat me in this kind of back and forth. Man. Ro. Maybe, I should text him.

Across the lot, my parents pull up in their white Chevy Traverse. Also not discussed between Erin and I, my estrangement from my parents and/or the reason why. Everything about her makes me believe she would be totally cool with who I am, but I've definitely been wrong before.

I slide my phone into my pocket and step out of my car. The heat is so intense that I already feel drained and ready for a nap and lunch hasn't even started yet. My parents appear mid-argument as they come around their vehicle. Dad hush-snaps a few dagger words to my mom as I approach. His face contorts in the same confused anger he usually carries with him, like he's always just mistakenly eaten a ghost pepper and he doesn't understand who is to blame.

"Evan!" My mom acts surprised when she sees me like this whole thing wasn't prearranged. "You made it."

"Yep, I'm here," I say with my hands in my pockets.

Dad cuts in front of Mom, offering his hand. "Evan."

"Dad." I shake his hand, holding his eye contact. *I didn't want to hug you anyway.*

My mom looks from my dad to me and then back again. A quiet dance between wanting to hug me but not wanting to just offer a handshake like we're strangers. The initial impulse triggers in me to just hug her, I could even lock eyes with my dad while I do it. Maybe his germaphobia will combine with his homophobia and send him into apoplectic shock. But no that's not what I want. Not here in the parking lot of the holiest of all chain-restaurants.

Once we get to our table, we sit in silence, menus used as a flimsy defense against the awkwardness, until the waitress arrives to take our drink orders. "Diet for me, hon." My mom makes eye contact and smiles at the waitress.

"Just water's fine," I say.

"Coke, please." My dad folds his menu. "And actually, we'll go ahead and order now to save you time. I'm sure you've had a very busy shift," he says without checking to see if I'm ready.

Rather than rushing to order when it comes my turn, I say, "I'll just stick with the water for now, thanks."

The waitress starts to walk off before coming back. "I'm sorry. I just realized who you were…you're with the Sunny Days church?"

"Sunny Days Church of Christ. Indeed, we are." My dad clasps his hands together and beams a smile up at her.

"I just wanted to say, you all built my sister a beautiful new home after hers burned down and it was such a huge blessing. She and my nieces would be out on the streets if it wasn't for you guys."

"Oh, that's incredibly kind of you." My dad holds his smile. "But He is the one deserving of your thanks."

The waitress ducks away, raising a hand to her cheek as though to brush away a tear, and Dad raises an eyebrow at me like *see?*

"Your mother said you wanted to meet with us?" He then asks. Gray has claimed the entirety of his mustache other than the hints of brown right above his lips from the occasional cigarette sneak. He would rather eat an entire pack of Marlboros than let anyone know he smokes.

I glance from him to my mom. My heart begins to pound. My palms itch. Another freak out could be in today's forecast. Then, my phone vibrates in my pocket, followed by a second and third burst. Knowing Erin's with me gives me what little strength I need. "I want you to ask the church to stop protesting my friend's art show."

"What?"

This is a power-move of his that I'm not unfamiliar with at all, but still, it takes me off guard every time. He wants me to repeat the question because he knows that the repetition of it will make it seem more ridiculous. Kind of like repeating the word "pencil" over and over, if you say something enough times, eventually it stops meaning anything. My parents have successfully done the same thing with the word "love."

"Why is the church protesting Ashanti's art show if it hasn't even officially opened yet" I ask a question of my own.

"This…this is what you asked us to meet for?" He fires back a question to answer a question. Ah, yet another tactic they have used since I was a kid, ask questions in response to my questions so that I'm the one on the defensive. *How do we know the Bible's one hundred percent real if people wrote it?* I used to ask. *How can you doubt the word of God?* was the answer I got.

I look to mom for help, but she isn't any. "Yes," I answer. My knee bounces beneath the table. "What did you think I wanted to meet you for?"

"We…" He gestures from my mom back to himself. "Presumed you were ready to come home now."

"Come home? You wrote me a letter saying that as long as I 'practice my lifestyle,' I couldn't return home. So, what're you really asking?"

Both of them look away from me, casting careful watch over the dining room of this fine Applebee's. Made-to-appear-vintage pennants decorate the walls exclaiming "Go Wildcats!" Decade-old photos of sports teams from my high school date the existence of this hallowed site. Truly oblivious, my parents are just looking around to make sure they don't know anyone here. I watch them watching out for everyone else. These are my parents. These are the people I came from, yet they may as well be strangers.

"Evan." My mom turns her eyes back to me, reaching both her

hands across the table for mine. I don't move. "We want you home." She puts a hand on my dad's shoulder. "We *both* want you home."

I narrow my focus on them. "How would that work?"

"Evan…" Her sentence trails off as she cranes her neck to check again that no one is eavesdropping on us. "Your father and I…we love you so much."

So much that you missed my last show?

So much that you kicked me out of your house?

So much that you've disowned me?

So much that you want me to hide who I really am?

Instead, I say nothing.

"We want you home and we just want what's best for you," Mom tries.

My dad works his jaw before snapping, "You need to just end this silliness and come home."

"What silliness?" I clap back.

"Joseph," my mom says, attempting to calm my dad before he can react.

"This…" He tosses his hands up at me as though I'm the walking embodiment of the demonic gay agenda that cable news and his misunderstanding of the book he's supposed to love have taught him to fear. "Are you done with *this* now so you can just come home?"

"Are you really trying to ask if I'm done being gay now?" My voice rises like I'm in a low budget theater production.

They both hold out their hands to shush me. "We just thought that if you got it out of your system, maybe by staying at Ro's for so long, that you'd be done by now," my mom says.

I can't hold back a smile. "That's what you thought I was doing there?"

"No judgment," my mom says in a soft tone.

I can't take this. Unfortunately, it's super awkward to get out of a booth when you're pissed off. I bang my knee on the table as I slide out.

"No judgment?" I ask now that I'm standing. Okay, people are definitely staring now, but I've always liked an audience. "Judging others is the sole thing the two of you can do to ignore the fact that our lives are temporary, one day we're all going to die, we're ultimately alone, and nothing that we do means anything in the grand scheme of the universe!" I start to storm off before stopping. "And to answer your question. No, I'm not done yet. I haven't even gotten started."

A table of college-aged guys starts clapping as I make my exit.

When I get to my car, I fumble to unlock the door and then fall in. My breaths are all trying to rush out at the same time. I put a hand to my chest and try to space them. My phone buzzes in my pocket and I pull it out.

One message from Ashanti: "So how did it go with the parents?"

The mere thought of letting her down again just makes me want to freak out even more. Luckily, there are several more messages from Erin, each one just another dumb rejected Applebee's slogan. Just seeing them steadies my breathing.

I text her: "I like you."

Then: "We should meet up soon."

Erin & The Pronouncing G in GIFs
<u>Chapter Nineteen</u>

There's this feeling between elation and absolute dread that I've always had a hard time nailing down. It's like when a band you love puts out a new album, but you're not sure it's any good. Or the nervous butterflies you get on the first day of a new school year when you know all the good days and bad days are still out there ahead of you. This...this text I just got from Evan, it's something even further beyond any of that.

It's like the thing I've wanted most in this world these last couple of weeks AND the thing that scares me more than anything.

Anxiety Brain coughs itself awake then says, "Would you say it's like being picked to give the valedictorian speech at your school's graduation when that's all you've worked towards for years, and then freaking out when it actually comes time to speak?"

Shut up.

Anxiety Brain then says, "Or is it finally getting the cute boy you've been lusting after for two years and then deciding he's boooorrrriing?"

Ugh. Go. Suck. A. Butt.

"Very mature," Anxiety Brain pouts, but then, rather mercifully, stays quiet.

Actually, it's neither of those things. It's something better. I mean, I'm sure we'll set our meeting date for some distant, safe point in the future. Like September or even March next year. Of course, I want to meet Evan. I just need some time to mentally prepare myself for it.

By like meditating in a space swamp, doing some lunges while putting myself through emotional immersion therapy by watching forty straight hours of Hallmark movies, getting all the cries out and then watching forty straight hours of the cheesiest sitcoms to get all the good feels in.

I'm pulled over on the side of the road, just two blocks from Blaide's. My phone is cradled in my hands like it's this sweet, innocent baby bird whose mother may come any second to peck my eyes out. A post-it is taped to my dash. *Dad's Random Bits of Unsolicited Advice #3: Texting & driving is almost as bad as drinking & driving, or perhaps it's worse. I'm not sure, but don't do either, please. Love, Dad.*

"Let's do it," I text to Evan.

Me: "Any time."

Me: "Any place."

The little ellipsis bubble appears but it doesn't make me as nervous as it used to. Anxiety Brain raises an eyebrow. "You sure about that?"

"Positive," I puff. "He said he likes me. I think we're good." What's probably not good is the fact that I've been consistently talking out loud to my own brain. The added fact that it seems to be gaining more physical attributes in my mind isn't that promising either.

Evan: "Awesome. What're your plans…"

Evan: "Next Wednesday."

What? Next Wednesday? That's next Wednesday! That's barely a week away. He can't mean that soon. Come on. No way. I read the text again. It's confirmed; he does indeed mean that soon. Oh, wow. What *am* I doing next week? Ummmm, potentially meeting my long-lost (half) brother. No big deal. No big deal at all. This room isn't on fire, it's just warm and I'm a cute dog with a hat. This is fine.

I text back: "No plans at all."

Evan: "Where do you live again?"

Me: "Langford, Illinois, Home of the Unemployed Miners."

Evan: "Right. Do you want to meet for lunch at the…"

Evan: "Raindrop Café?"

Evan: "It's in Hoakie, Illinois, pretty much midway between us. Looks like it should be about a 2.5 hour drive for you and a 2.5 hour drive for me."

"Sounds incredible," I text back. "Count me in fo sho."

What are you doing? I ask myself in the rearview. You just said 'fo sho,' Who even are you, Erin Drexel?

Evan: "LOL."

Evan: "It's a date."

Evan: (GIF of Gaston gyrating)

I've never met someone who likes GIFs as much as my mom does. I think about calling Evan on it, pointing out that he's technologically old fashioned, basically from a previous (like our…um, Bio-Man's?) generation, but instead I just reply with a GIF of my own (Snoopy dancing).

I watch Snoopy bouncing around to see if Evan will respond. He doesn't. My stomach does a toddler somersault. It's the halfway point between exhilaration and an all-out panic attack. A two and a half hour drive each way.

Erin & The Sunset Tree

<u>Chapter Twenty</u>

I park in the overgrown grass in Blaide's front yard like Kevin, his dad, has requested I do so as to not block anyone in. Crashing cymbals and heavy guitar riffs ring out from the open windows of the living room. Kevin's 90's cover band is practicing. I don't blame them for having the windows down. It actually feels pretty great right now. The sun melts like orange sherbet on the horizon.

You know what? I may actually miss coming here.

No. No-no-no-no-no. You're not talking yourself out of this. We're going into our first meeting with Evan with as little baggage as possible so that means we're breaking up with Blaide now. Tonight. We've put this off far too long.

"You know—" Anxiety Brain claps its book on Didacticism in Modern Philosophy shut. "One could argue that not breaking up with Blaide will actually give you *less* baggage since you'll have that added emotional support. Plus, it wouldn't hurt to have another, hhmmmmm, let's just say roll around on his couch—"

"You shut up too," I say as I crunch over the dried-out grass to the basement steps.

Unlike his dad's rock out session in the main house, Blaide's basement lair is eerily quiet. Each creaky step down, as the spores of mildew get stronger, I imagine walking into a surprise party or a murder scene, a pool of blood growing beneath Blaide's body, or maybe he forgot I was coming and he's having some, um, personal time. None of these scenarios are what I find when I reach the bottom of the stairs though. Instead of lying face down in a pool of his own blood, Blaide is sitting on his couch with his head in his hands.

I sit on the edge of the couch, unsure of what to say next. Blaide doesn't even acknowledge my existence. In a way, this is way stranger than catching him in the act of something embarrassing. Blaide's always so upbeat and free of self-doubt or self-awareness that I've never really seen him exhibiting much sincere emotion unless he's playing music or listening to it.

Ugh. You know, that's actually pretty sweet.

I run my fingertips over the felt of the couch, so soft yet rough at the same time. Glancing around Blaide's room, I wrestle the urge to be nostalgic. I won't miss the vinyl albums tacked to the walls or the old handmade show flyers for crappy punk bands with as little regard for equal rights as they have for learning to properly play their instruments. I won't miss the mismatched patches of carpet that cover the floor in inconsistent squares and rectangles, united only in the equal disbursement of stains spread out over them. I won't miss his crooked bookshelf overflowing with "philosophy" books written solely by dumb white dudes *for* dumb white dudes. Nor will I miss the drunken Polaroids of his friends taped on the wall. Ugh and I definitely won't miss the can't-stay-in-tune acoustic guitar leaning in the corner like a crotchety drunk. The one that he'll pick up sometimes when I'm in the middle of a story and just start playing like I'm not even there, making that pinched-together face like he's sucking on a lemon drop while pondering the inanity of trying at anything when life is so mercilessly short.

I take a last look around the room.

Nope. I won't miss any of this.

My eyes fall back on Blaide. He still hasn't said anything. Maybe he knows that I'm going to break up with him? Which, how would he even know that? I did mention it to Madison...but she and Blaide hardly hang out with the same people. She wouldn't dare go to the VFW halls, crusty punk houses, or dive-ass dive bars where Blaide and his friends play shows. Hell, I hardly go to those places anymore. Then, a comfortable warmth spreads over me like I just got a text cancelling plans.

What if....

What if...

What if he's actually going to break up with me?!

Oh, my, I've never been that lucky in my life.

"Blaide..." I start.

"I—I just can't believe it," he says while looking at his hands.

"Blaide?" I slide down from the arm of the couch.

"I thought we'd always be together," Blaide says in a weak voice.

My mouth hangs open.

"It's like my life has no purpose now."

"Whoa...that's uh, a little too...wow." Madison definitely said something to him. She always goes on about how hot he is. "I don't..."

"You're totally crushing this right now," Anxiety Brain says.

Shut up and go eff yourself.

"You realize I am you, right?" Anxiety Brain pushes back.

Just...please stop. Not now.

Blaide meets my eyes. "I feel so...so betrayed."

Locking eyes with his steely blues eradicates my shallow resolve. Is this how breakups are supposed to go? Am I the aloof partner that emotionally detaches themselves so much that the other person finally catches on and just ends it? It feels like a whole onion is lodged in my throat. I swallow. "How—how so?"

"We broke up."

I nod, maybe if I play along with this it will all just be over soon. Years from now, scholars will look back at the fading embers of our relationship with awe. *Here it is, folks, the first break-up to ever occur through shared general apathetic telepathy.* Move over heated toilet seats—here's a new miraculous occurrence! It's one of those inventions that makes so much sense that you can't imagine there ever being a time it didn't exist like plastic tips at the end of shoelaces, GPS, or the skip 15sec option on podcasts so you can blow through ad reads. Welcome to your new life, Erin. Everything will be different now.

"What am I supposed to do?" Blaide asks. "I'm all alone."

I am the human embodiment of the shrug emoji, still too scared to speak for fear that it will ruin whatever this…this is. What do I do here? Should I offer advice? *Ah, don't be so hard on yourself, there are plenty of pretty faces to swipe through out there, kiddo,* I could say to him with a slug on the shoulder. Maybe that would push all of the tension to the edge of the room and then I could tell him it was a good run and I appreciate him being there for me after my dad and all that. Then I can leave here and go get the milkshake I desperately crave. Or maybe that would make him laugh, then I'd laugh, and we'd lock eyes, and I'd just naturally lean in for a kiss since my body would definitely want to feel the flatness of his chest and stomach, his weight on mine again. Then, before I know it, we'd be a tangled mess and the break-up would be an afterthought.

Anxiety Brain does the chef kiss. "Again. Totally killing it."

Blaide shakes his head. "I thought we'd never break up."

"Well, never is a long time…" I start but trail off. How many more words do I need to say before I can just leave here? That milkshake is so close I can taste it. Then I can clear the remaining few hours of this evening to just obsess about meeting Evan next week. Gulp.

"We had such potential." Blaide rubs his jaw.

I narrow my eyes at him, *did we though?*

"It's just not fair," Blaide says with a sniff.

He's taking this way too hard. Sure, he's told me he loves me (and okay, I've said it back) but we've only been together for like ten months, which is long in high school time, but not in real life.

This doesn't add up.

Oh.

OH. HOLY SHIT.

HE'S TALKING ABOUT—

"Your band broke up?" I blurt out.

Blaide looks at me dumbfounded. You'd think I just asked if he'd like to see a movie with a female director AND a female lead. "Yeah, what'd you think I was talking about?"

Just do it now, you coward. You've already done the emotional labor of it. Just do it.

"Us?" I ask, my intonation betraying me yet again.

"What? Us?" Blaide laughs. The blissful tone reverberates through his eyes, giving them their carefree light once again. "You're pretty much the only person I can trust any more. Without you, I'd be really bummed out."

I reflect back a weak smile. What am I supposed to do? Break-up with him on the worst day of his life?

Blaide hooks his muscular left arm around me and pulls me into him. As much as I hate to admit it, it doesn't feel too bad. His lips find mine and then he's leaning into me and, okay, I'm leaning back into him.

There are worse places I could be with worse people. A little stress relief never hurt anything either. But then, as he's kissing my neck, I catch sight of his calendar hanging crooked on the wall. More than half the days of June are marked out with a hastily sharpied star. Something Blaide has always done because he said he wants to mark off each day that gets him closer to where he's going. Blaide's sad attempt at motivation isn't what bothers me though.

If only, but no.

It's the plummeting realization that this coming Sunday is...

Father's Day.

A Tale of Two Father's Days (Part One)

It takes the Sunday Church Lunch Rush lasting longer than normal for it to hit me.

"It's *fucking* Father's Day?" I ask to no one in particular as beef patties pop on the flat top grill in front of me.

"Father's Day is a scam," Weird Allan answers from his own flat top grill beside mine. "I saw this video on ViewMe. Father's Day was invented by the liberal elite to delegate men to just having one day a year, you know?"

"Wait." I stare at the crackling beef, perplexed, before turning to him. "What?"

"They want to marginalize men by giving us just one day out of the whole 365."

"That doesn't make any sense. What about Mother's Day then?"

"They just did that to appease the women."

I turn from the grill, balancing three greasy burgers on my spatula. The screen overhead beeps in with a new incoming order while I assemble three Charlie Specials. "I thought you hated your dad?"

"Oh, I do. But I'm also a dad, and it's bullshit I just get one day."

The news that Weird Allan has offspring turns my stomach more than the smell of beef. I really shouldn't ask any further questions, but I can't help myself. "How many kids do you have, Allan?"

"Three with one more on the way."

Huh. All this time, I thought Weird Allan was the stereotypical lonely misogynist who hated women as much as he feared them. Turns out Weird Allan's just a straight up normal misogynist.

Work's so busy that I'm not able to check my phone. Fortunately, I forgot it in the break room, which helps remove the temptation. The thought of all the messages Erin may be sending me is the only thing getting me through my eight-hour shift. When I finally clock out, I rush to the break room and swipe through my lock screen. My shoulders slump. Only one new text and it's from Ashanti: "Sophia cancelled my show opening because of the protest. Thanks for trying though, Ev."

I start to type a response, but there aren't enough emojis or words to express my regret to Ashanti. I don't send anything. The guilt is too much. I know Erin would make me feel better, so I start to draft out a text to her before deleting the whole thing. Maybe she just needs to be left alone today. Our meeting can't come soon enough.

A Tale of Two Father's Days (Part Two)

For most of the day, I'm able to avoid social media like an invite to Blaide's new band practice. However, doing this gives my mind nowhere else to go other than focusing on how my dad isn't *technically* my dad, and *am I really going to meet Evan in three days?*

So, after about eight hours of fighting it, here I am doom-scrolling through picture after picture as my friends, acquaintances, and random follows, wish their dads Happy Father's Day. As I scroll on, I'm surprisingly not able to muster a single drop of pettiness when every post declares their dad as "THE BEST DAD EVER!" Nor am I able to muster any when I try wondering who these posts are for, since it's doubtful any of their dads are on LookAtMe. A part of me honestly feels happy for them that they still have their dads. But mostly…mostly all the posts just make me sad.

Really, really fucking sad.

But then—and please believe me, I know this is messed up—I start drafting out a post for Happy Father's Day to the Best Dead Dad Ever!!!! I'm half-smiling through the tears, through the pain, as I find the right photos of us and begin typing away, because I'd know he'd think it was hilarious. "After all, most dads in the history of human existence are dead," he'd probably say. "So, when you think about it, being the Best Dead Dad in heaven or in the never-ending void of nonexistence is wayyyy more impressive."

I sob out a laugh and keep typing on LookAtMe, knowing I'll never post it, but saying everything I would want to say to him if he were in the room with me and/or watching me from above and/or had ghost WiFi wherever he is now.

Creaking floorboards announce that I'm not alone. The momentary escape I felt quickly vanishes. I delete the post and tuck my phone away as my mom steps into my room. "I was going to go see Dad and get some dinner, want to come?" Mom asks while leaning against the doorframe.

I feel the contempt burning in my eyes as I look at her. If Mom knew anything, she'd know that I hate casually mentioning a stop by the cemetery as "going to see Dad." She would know I haven't been there since the funeral. She would know that Dad's warmth isn't found anywhere in that cold, hollow place. God, if it really were possible to go by and see Dad anywhere…if it really *were* that simple…I would walk. I would run. I would swim. I would (preferably) drive that distance, no matter how far (even if my Check Engine light blinked at me the whole way). Mom is still looking at me for an answer though, so I just shake my head.

"You sure?" Mom tries to remain upbeat. "We can go get milkshakes afterwards."

That actually sounds pretty good, but it seems like too much effort just to feel okay. Again, I shake my head.

"Okay." Mom clicks her tongue and nods, waiting a half-second to see if I'll change my mind.

That's not happening though. Once she's gone, I return to scrolling through my phone. Dim blue light fills up my room. I imagine my life source draining in direct proportion to my phone's battery. It's so messed up that my first Father's Day without Dad is also my first

Father's Day with the knowledge that he never was my birth dad in the first place (good luck making a greeting card for that one, fuckers!).

I'm so tired.

The garage door whirrs open beneath my bedroom floor. Mom's car backs out and leaves. Knowing that mom is gone, wishing that I would have gone with her, I feel more alone than ever.

I wish I could just miss him the same way I used to.

Erin & The Ice Tub

<u>Chapter Twenty-One</u>

Then, just like that, in a blur of anxiety and depression, it's *Next Wednesday*. My phone GPS leads me to the Raindrop Café with little difficulty. Hoakie is even smaller than Langford and as it turns out, it's pretty easy to find anything in a small town (*except for a good time, amiright?*). After stalking out the parking lot, I determine that I'm here early enough that I don't have to worry about Evan showing up any time soon. I've shared my location with him, but he hasn't returned the favor. "ETA?" I text him but when the little bubbles don't pop up, I figure that he's being a smart driver and not looking at his phone.

"Maybe he won't come at all," Anxiety Brain starts in.

Jokes on you, shitbird, that actually sounds like a dream scenario. I'd be pumped to just drive home now.

I should've known better to mouth back, because then Anxiety Brain cracks its knuckles and decides to really let loose. "It's probably some Catfish scheme to get thousands of dollars from you."

Eh, I don't have a thousand dollars, let alone thousands of dollars.

"You have kidneys though, right?"

Um, yeah?

"How much do you think each of those bad boys are worth?"

I grip the bridge of my nose. *Are we really doing this again?*

"Honestly, it's a little concerning you haven't truly considered that yet." Anxiety Brain dons a pair of thick joke glasses with a bushy mustache for whatever reason. "The least you can do is scope the place out, so you have an escape plan if he turns out to be a creepo."

"I hate you," I say out loud. As much as I hate to admit it, Anxiety Brain has a point though; I should go inside and check this place out. After a quick glance at my hair in the rearview, I leave the safe confines of Fiona for the Raindrop Café.

"Table for one? Or meeting someone?" The hostess asks as a little bell announces my entry. The way she asks these two questions, one after the other, is more matter of fact than condescending. I immediately like her but refrain from asking her to fill my new best friend vacancy.

"I'm meeting someone, but he probably won't be here for another—"

"Erin?" A tall glass of impeccably shaped hair, hipster glasses, and perfect teeth waves at me from a table in the back.

I glance from the exit to the hostess to Evan. A bathroom beckons to me from beside the kitchen entrance. There are options, but really, there's no turning back now. I start toward him. He's getting to his feet like he's going to offer me a hug.

This is really happening.

Evan & A Vin Diesel Impersonation Saying, "Family"
Chapter Twenty-Two

I beam at her as she crosses the restaurant. My heart thumps so hard in my ears that I'm convinced it's further amplifying the impenetrable smile on my face. I'm smiling so freaking hard it hurts. When she finally gets to me, I go straight for the hug. Let's just get that awkward hug-handshake-I-don't-know-what-to-do shuffle out of the way. I hug her tight, but not too tight; long, but not too long.

"So…?" Erin runs her hand over the front of her blouse as she sits.

"So," I say with a smile. Uh-oh, this is exactly what I was afraid of. It's that thing where we clicked so well over text but then have no chemistry in real life.

She must be feeling that too, because she covers her mouth, trying to hold in a laugh, thus spurring me on even more. Then, we're both laughing without having said anything at all.

"So, I was thinking," Erin says and just stops. Her hands are folded calmly in her lap. She's way cooler and prettier than she even begins to give herself credit for.

"You were thinking that the Fast & the Furious franchise has brought numerous installments and a few blockbuster spinoffs, but they still haven't gotten to the good stuff yet?" I nod like I'm finishing her thought.

Erin gasps and touches her chest. "How did you know?"

"I just sensed it all around you." I wave my hand like Erin has an invisible aura of Fast & the Furious thirst. "As soon as you walked in, I was like 'ah, there's a girl who needs more Vin Diesel in her life.'"

"Don't we all? Even though it's the Rock that I'd really like more of."

"You said it." I watch Erin for a response. This is my oh-so-subtle testing of the water. So many people *seem* nice at first, but then they do the whole backwards defensive move of *"Well, I'm not saying it's wrong, but ..."*

Erin just smiles, and not in a "oh, that's silly because you're a boy" way or not in a way that she doesn't take me seriously. Just in the least pandering way possible.

"You know what I really want?" Erin's eyes light up with the question. She doesn't even wait for me to respond before she says, "A movie about the fast-food place where all the Fast & the Furious people go for lunch."

"I love it!" *I love her.*

"I'd call it..." She trails off to either build suspense or to find the right punch line. "The Fast & the Furious: Drive Thru or Die In!"

I teeter my hand. "The tagline could use some work, a little too wordy, but I'd see that movie."

She laughs, this time I think more out of nervousness. "So..." she starts again.

"So..."

Erin exhales with a question. "So, are you always this early?"

"Sometimes. You?"

"Almost always."

"Why?" It's nice to be the one to ask questions for a change.

Erin's brown eyes sparkle as she shrugs. "General fretfulness, I guess."

"How so?"

"I don't want to keep anyone waiting. Like if I'm not running *at least* thirty minutes early then the whole time I'm driving somewhere, I'll feel that low-level hum of uneasiness vibrating through my body that something is going to happen to make me late. Then I start playing out the scenarios of how whoever is waiting for me is already mad and resenting me for being late."

"Did you even feel that way with me?"

"Oh, God, of course!" Erin scoffs. "Especially you."

I nod. That makes sense. The way she says that last sentence lets me know that she feels it too, that connection through our text conversations.

"I brought you something." Erin reaches into her bag and pulls out a DVD-sized wrapped present.

"You didn't," I say with exaggerated surprise as I reach for it. I begin ripping the Grumpy Cat wrapping paper away. Horror font peaks through. "This is so thoughtful." I clutch the original Purge trilogy to my chest like it's a beloved childhood toy that I believed lost forever.

"I thought maybe we could watch them together." Erin's eyes dart away from mine. "You know, since we're going to write an award-winning expanded universe screenplay together for millions of dollars."

The thought flickers in my mind to give her a hard time by playing coy. It's so easy to mess with someone when they put their entire selves out there. It's also incredibly rewarding, but I can't do that to her.

"I would love that."

With that, her tense posture eases a little. The waiter comes by to get our drink orders, both waters, no lemon.

"Hey, I want to show you something." I get out my phone. "I wanted to show you some pics of my family. If we're related, then they're your family too. Who knows, maybe you'll see some resemblance?"

"Oh, cool," Erin says, but her eyes say the opposite.

Erin & The Fishbowl of Oblivion
<u>Chapter Twenty-Three</u>

A few years before we found Chevy the Cat, when I was just a little precocious five-year-old, I used to beg my parents for a sibling. Blissfully unaware of the complex mechanics of conceiving a child, I used to whine all the time about how I was so lonely (I was quite dramatic—good thing I aged out of that, huh). Until, finally, for my sixth birthday, they got me a goldfish. I named him Digby. He came in a plastic bag that we sat in his bowl to acclimate him to the water temperature of his new home. That's how I feel sitting across from Evan, like I'm in stasis, just getting used to the climate of my new reality. I can't stop staring at him thinking, *this guy is my (slightly) older brother.* He's the missing link to a whole half of my genetic makeup that I thought was lost forever. He's the sibling I used to throw tantrums so hard for that I got carpet burns on my elbows.

Then he swipes through to old family photos on his phone and it's like, *oh, no, he thinks his dad is my dad instead of us both coming from the same anonymous donor or even my dad being his dad* (which I know is impossible but dang it, that doesn't keep me from hoping). Do I have to be the one to tell him? I hope not. I can't just shatter everything he thinks he knows about himself. Been there. Not fun. Zero stars. Nope. I'm just going to play along and hope he figures it out. He seems like a smart guy (I mean, if he's my brother he's got to be). He'll figure it out.

Maybe he just needs to get used to the water too.

"And this...this would be your great uncle," Evan says,

pointing to a man wearing a light blue suit standing between two people that Evan doesn't specify despite their appearance in so many of these photos. "His name was Valentine. He used to always make baked potatoes dance like a little silly vaudevillian show at our family dinners. I don't know why he did that, but I'm glad he did."

"He seems really nice," is all I can say, because he does, but I don't feel any kinship to this man in the picture. It's obvious this is important to Evan though, so I sit and look through the photos hoping our food arrives soon.

"I just figured if I was you, I'd want to know who I came from. I'd *have* to know who my father was…even if he's a complete asshole."

I shrug, because, honestly, after finding Evan, I couldn't care less about finding anyone else on Bio-Man's side of the family. The thought alone spikes my fight or flight.

The waiter places my plate of chicken fingers in front of me. Yeah, that's right—chicken fingers. What? Chicken fingers rule. They're not just for little kids so don't believe what the joyless overlords behind Big Salad want you to believe. Yes, there was a part of me that wanted to order something more hip like, I don't know, kale with chopped cucumber, but I figured that if this relationship is going to be a thing, he might as well see the real me. And the real me effing loves chicken fingers.

"So how do you think we're related?" I ask between bites like this is not the most loaded question in our new little world.

"I was thinking *if* we are related then it maybe worked like this…" Evan pauses to finish chewing his chickpea salad sandwich. You know, it hurts that he uses the qualifier of "if"…but also, I get it.

Evan swallows then continues, "I was born at the same hospital as you were, just a couple months before. My parents had trouble conceiving. My mother used to call me her little miracle baby, so they must've ran some tests on my dad's—"

"SPERM!" I interject and then try my best to suppress the giggles. I've never shouted any word in public before, let alone the word "sperm." The thought of that just makes me want to laugh even harder. There's something about Evan and this whole stupid awkward mess that makes me so perfectly comfortable with being my real self. Hey, we're talking about my dad not being my dad here.

I've got nothing left to lose, motherfuckers!

"I was going to say jism, which is far more tasteful if you ask me," Evan adds before joining me in the giggles. "Wait, wait, that doesn't sound right." He holds out his hand, nearly spitting out his food.

There's something even grosser that I'm struggling to say, but I can't because we're both laughing too hard. The seriousness of my question, the stakes of it all, the fact that we're even here, all of it just adds to the absurdity of the situation, propelling us further into laughter. Yes, other people are looking at us. Yes, some of them seem pissed. Yet somehow being with Evan makes it all seem okay.

We keep laughing for longer than I thought possible. It helps dispel the lingering awkwardness in the air after he used the word, "if," which, IF I'm being honest is still there too.

"Okay, okay." Evan dabs his napkin at the tears in his eyes. "I was going to say…" He fights off further giggles. "That his c—nope, I can't even say it—his stuff must've been outside his body at some point so maybe…it got mixed with your dad's or maybe he made a donation?"

I wait a few more seconds to see if he recognizes the inherent flaw in this hypothesis. IE: *If your parents had trouble conceiving, it's not like your dad had Super Sperm™ so why would the hospital then allow him to donate it?*

"What did your parents say when you asked them?"

Evan looks away. "I haven't asked them…it's kind of a long story."

"No, it's okay. I under—"

Evan looks back at me. "They kicked me out."

"Oh."

"Because I'm…I told them, I'm gay." Evan narrows his eyes at me as he says this almost like he expects me to yelp, flip over the table, and sprint out of the restaurant.

"That's…fucking stupid," I say, not caring that the table next to us may overhear. Though yeah, okay, there's a cute little kid coloring a bear on the back of a menu that looks right at me after I dropped the eff bomb. *Sorry, little guy. I don't normally say those words…out loud.*

Evan wipes his mouth, raising his eyebrows without making eye contact. "You said it."

Well, look what you've done now, Erin. If I say too much more to over-comfort him, I could come off like some self-congratulatory person who takes selfies of themselves working in a soup kitchen on Thanksgiving or if I don't say anything it may seem like I don't care.

Uh-oh, I know where this is leading.

Anxiety Brain polishes its monocle on its white linen shirt and says, "You have royally sabotaged this whole situation, my dear. Just like we all knew you would."

"I'm sorry," I say to Evan. He looks up at me. Then I surprise myself by reaching over and putting my hand on his. "That sucks they would do that."

His eyes glisten behind his glasses. "Thanks."

We return to our food and soon the conversation flows freely like we hadn't just toed up to the edge of oblivion in our conversation multiple times. We talk about spin-offs for the Conjuring movie universe. Even though neither of us have seen a single one of those terrifying movies, we make up humorous installments for movies about the neighbors living next door to these haunted houses, the teachers at the schools for the kids who own haunted dolls, the home repair people who get assigned to fix the washing machines that keep spewing blood in these haunted homes.

We laugh and feel alright.

At least I do.

This water feels just fine to me, thanks.

I think I'll stay here for a while.

<u>Chapter Twenty-Four</u>

After the waiter clears our empty plates and refills our water glasses for the fifth time, after I realize that the tables around us are now filled with different people, after I see them paying their checks and their tables are bussed and wiped down for a new crowd coming in, after the shades are pulled over the huge window since the sun is seeping in from the west, after we take our third selfie together—my idea—with Raindrop Café menus held up by our overly excited faces, after Erin and I devote way too much time to coming up with indie band names despite the fact that neither of us play an instrument (Erin: "You just put your name with 'and' plus any noun and voila, you have a good indie band name."), after our waiter came over and asked again if he could get us anything else before politely mentioning that his shift's over, Erin and I know that we don't have to go home, but we sure as hell can't stay here.

When the waiter sets down the check, there's no awkward dance for who is going to pay. "Split check?" I ask with a conciliatory grin.

Erin sighs as though she too felt the pressure of should-I-pay-even-though-I'm-dead-broke? "That would be perfect."

Then, standing on the balls of our feet in front of the Raindrop Café, we rock back and forth, torn between the uneasiness of saying goodbye or pushing this further. I don't want it to end and I can tell that she doesn't either.

"Sooooooo…" Erin leans forward on her toes.

"So?" My eyebrows do that thing where they go halfway up my

too-tall forehead. The first time I noticed that in photographs I cringed. Eventually though I learned to wield my eyebrows as my secret weapon on stage.

"So?" Erin's smile widens.

"So?" I can do this all day.

"So, what do you want to do now?" Erin's smile lilts. "Or if you've got somewhere else to be, I could just go back. It's a decent drive for both of us."

"Erin, there is nothing I'd rather do than spend the rest of the day exploring the limitless sprawl of culture that is Hoakie, Illinois."

With a small fist pump, Erin says she'll drive, and I try to hide my relief that she won't have to see my Yaris. Her car is small and tidy with glimpses of her personality showing through at the edges, like a tiny Yoda that dangles from the rearview, an obscure indie band playing low on the stereo, post-it note reminders on her side of the dash, books elegantly laying over each other in the backseat like a spiral staircase, a random purple wig, and a stuffed Bulbasaur sitting in the back window. I've only known her for a few weeks, but in so many ways her car reminds me of her. I love it.

"Your car's really cool," I say.

"Thanks. The gas gauge is broke so it keeps life interesting." Erin continues tapping into her phone without looking up.

"I'm glad you're not one of those people who name their car like it has a personality."

"Uh-huh."

"What's the wig for?" I know Erin is trying to concentrate right now, which makes interrupting her all the more fun.

"Emergencies," Erin deadpans.

"Oh, like what?"

"It's a secret," Erin says with her head down, still scrolling through her phone. "There's a quilt museum."

"I'm in. Who doesn't love a cozy, handmade, patterned blanket?"

Erin shakes her head. "Apparently Hoakie also boasts of having the world's fourth largest Ketchup bottle."

"Excellent. I've already seen the top three."

"They have one of the country's last Chuck E Cheese's apparently."

"Also in. Out-dated animatronic animals being forced to play instruments against their will is my favorite genre of music."

"A bowling alley."

"Hmmmm. Hard pass. I swore I would never bowl again after the Great Alley Mishap of 2022."

Erin finally looks up with a grin. "What happened there?"

"Ooof, don't ask." I wipe the question away. "It was a whole thing involving a claw machine, an overloaded septic tank, and a not-so-subtly racist man named Yancy. If I go into further detail, you'll look at me differently."

"Understood. That's how I feel when people mention public swimming pools." Erin returns to scrolling through her phone. "There's a historical museum detailing the history of Hoakie."

"Sounds fascinating, judging from the appearance of Hoakie I'm sure it's a rich and layered whitewashed history."

"Ooooh." Erin turns to me. Her mouth forms a perfect O.

"There's a scenic hiking trail."

Whoa. Maybe she doesn't know me. Disgust must be evident on my face.

Erin holds up a finger. "Let me add, there's also a world-famous custard stand at the entrance of it."

"You just said the magic words."

And we're off.

<u>Chapter Twenty-Five</u>

"So, if you don't like him anymore, why don't you just break up with him?" Evan asks.

"I don't know…it's just hard." I peel back a limb so Evan can step around free of thorns. We both agreed to hike the two-mile trail before rewarding ourselves with custard, a decision that I continue to regret with each droplet of sweat that dampens my armpits.

"How so?"

"Well." I measure a breath.

How much should I share here?

"Be careful, Erin." Anxiety Brain waves around an oversized Stop sign. "Don't screw this up for us."

Oh, screw you.

"I'm scared," I say simply.

Evan just nods, equal measures "it's okay" and "I'm listening."

"I wanted Blaide for a long time. I literally pined after him, he was the hot musician guy, and I am—I was the overachieving smart girl. So, when he first asked me out, it was like a YA romcom come to life. I thought we were going to be together forever. I thought I loved him. That was almost a year ago. People still go on about how we're the 'best couple ever' and how we 'give them hope that love can work out.' When I still used LookAtMe or Acquaintances, any post of us easily got hundreds of ISeeYou's."

"But…?" Evan mimes playing tug-a-war like he's pulling the truth out of me.

"But I've kind of found that there's really not anything to Blaide, like nothing at all. At least not much that I like other than the fact that he's hot—"

Evan's eyebrows shoot up. "How hot?"

I pull out my phone and swipe through to a picture of Blaide.

"Oh, my! He is hot," Evan says, his bright blue eyes matching the sky. Evan hands my phone back to me. "But he's lame?"

I bite my lower lip. Maybe I should stop here. I've already probably said too much. Later tonight I'm going to lay awake thinking of all the stupid things I said, much like a hungover person regretting how much they drank the night before (sigh, not that I know what that's like). I've already gotten a good head start. *For example, didn't I say SPERM really loud earlier in a crowded restaurant? I also dropped a massive eff bomb out loud too. Oh, god.*

"But he's lame?" Evan asks again with a toothy grin. Darn him for having such flawless teeth.

I must have missed that gene.

"He's so uninteresting. It's like everything he says has been autogenerated by some BLRTR bot. It's just a random conglomeration of ideas that belong to someone else phrased in the least creative way possible with no actual insight."

"Wow," Evan says and just leaves it at that.

"I TOLD YOU," Anxiety Brain proudly boasts into a megaphone. "YOU RUINED EVERYTHING. HE THINKS YOU'RE A TOTAL JERK NOW."

I scan the trail for a cave to crawl into, a trashcan to climb in so I can roll off a cliff, a tree with a large crevice that leads to a mythical wonderland that I can dive into perhaps, anything that would allow a way out of the mess I've made.

"So, let me guess." Evan gives a smirk. "He's the kind of guy to space out whenever you're talking and totally miss an amazing joke?"

"Oh, my God. Yes!" My voice echoes off the cliff faces and my heart soars like the rare blue-footed wren, which, if the plaque we read earlier is to be trusted, is dangerously close to extinction. Dang.

"So again, why don't you just break up with him?"

"It's…it's complicated."

"I get that." Evan sucks his teeth. A few moments of quiet pass between us before Evan looks back at me with a smile. "You know, actually, just stay with him forever until you're in an unhappy, loveless marriage that imprints itself on your children."

I let out a single laugh. "Sounds like a wonderful plan." We start walking the trail again. "Evan, thanks for listening," I say to his back.

"Listening is easy," he calls back. "It's the sharing part that's tricky."

We keep on walking through the trail. Despite the extreme sweatiness, I feel lighter than I have in some time. There's a person I've always thought I had the potential to be, a person that I've always fallen short of regardless of how hard I worked. With Evan though, I become someone better, someone more self-assured, funnier, and more comfortable in her own skin.

Dad's Random Bits of Unsolicited Advice #14: Lean into the things that make you like yourself (same goes for people too).

Evan's my people.

Evan & Tom Cruise in Vanilla Sky
Chapter Twenty-Six

A small puddle of vanilla-orange swirl ice cream grows at our feet. We try to eat faster, but we can't stop talking. Each drop falling to the concrete is a sacrifice for our conversation.

"And you guys haven't actually met up yet?" Erin stoops to lick a streak of orange leaking from her cone. For what it's worth, she's holding her own. The Creamsters—Erin's word—made nearly foot tall towers of each of our cones before they handed them over to us.

"Not yet. He asked me to email him? And I just haven't had the nerve yet." I eye the line of Hoakians—also Erin's word—snaking across the concrete. A few of the guys look like the kind of red-hatted assholes that wouldn't take too kindly hearing about a same-sex crush.

"Is he hot? Do you have a picture? I showed you Blaide." Erin licks melted orange dream from her wrist. She's come a long way from hiding her mouth while she ate barbecue sauce-drenched chicken fingers at Raindrop.

"I don't. Christian doesn't have Acquaintances or any social media that I know of. He's super cute though," I say a bit too loudly and one mustached man in line cocks his head at me. I shake off his glare.

"Christian, huh?" Erin raises her eyebrows. "I thought you hated those."

My eyes drop to the concrete. "Ro's made the same joke. It's a...it's a good one."

Erin takes another bite. "I bet the two of you will make a cute couple though. He'd be a fool to not go for you."

"I don't really though."

"Don't what? Think you'll make a cute couple?"

"No. I don't hate Christians. At least I don't want to. They've…" I shake my head. "I don't know. It doesn't matter."

Erin's bottom lip quivers. "Sorry. I didn't mean…"

"Christian and I would definitely make a hot couple though." I drown the tension out with a brilliant smile, knocking my shoulder into hers. "What do you think our celebrity couple nickname would be?"

Erin watches me, obviously not yet used to the emotional whiplash of being my friend. "ChrisEv? Like Chris Evans. Captain America." I feign shock and wonder at Erin. "Captain GaMerica?!"

Erin's eyes search mine before she gives a little grin. "I personally like EvanTian, which calls to mind some New Age sex cult. Maybe you guys can start something there."

I fake a laugh with a mouthful of ice cream. "I wish."

A quiet descends over us. Before long, my cone becomes such a mushy, sticky mess in my hand that I want to throw it away. Erin finishes hers though, so I do the same. We take a selfie in front of the Cone. Mosquitos start picking their way through the warm bodies under the buzzing fluorescent lights. A baseball game must've just let out because suddenly we're surrounded by what seems like three hundred sweaty little leaguers with their tense parents. The sun has liquefied on the horizon not unlike the puddle of ice cream under our table. It's obvious that our day together is drawing to a close, but we're not willing to let it go yet.

Without another word, we each throw away our sopping wet

napkins, wash off our hands in the sink attached to the side of the Cone, and get back in her car to drive back to the Raindrop. The ride is soundtracked by the continued female-fronted indie rock pouring from her stereo with idle chitchat passing between us in sporadic bursts. As much as I don't want it, we're soon back in the strip mall parking lot. We each get out and lean against her car.

A few pops let off in the distance. Bright colored bursts light up the parking lot. We crane our necks back to look at the sky. There's no need for either of us to say anything. I've always kind of hated fireworks. They always start two weeks too early in the summer and stay two weeks too late. They're like the stupid-American-toxic-masculinity equivalent of some idiot revving up his truck engine. But standing here outside the Raindrop with Erin, after everything we've both been through this summer, this moment is kind of perfect.

"You know, all summer I've been waiting for it to feel like summer and finally now, here it is," Erin says, resting her head against the car.

"I know what you mean."

Erin leans her shoulder a bit into mine, so I lean back into her.

Twenty minutes later, after a flurry of pops, applause can be heard from the direction of the park. The smell of gunpowder wafts in with a gentle breeze. "Show's over, huh?" Erin leans away from her car and looks at me. "I usually get bored with fireworks, but I could've watched that for at least another two minutes."

"Yeah. You know, it's weird, but it kind of makes me miss doing shows with my group."

"Aren't improv shows another thing that no one usually likes?" Erin deadpans before offering a subtle smirk to let me know she's joking.

"You're not wrong. There's nothing fun about seeing a bad improv show, but when they're great, when the performers and audience are truly locked into the moment together, then it's a lot like that." I gesture up at the smoke outlines still filling the sky. "Something beautiful and magnificent, but once it's gone, it's gone."

Erin leans back against her car, working her jaw like there's something she's struggling to say.

"You can say what you want to," I say simply. "I promise a sinkhole won't open up beneath our feet and swallow us whole."

"You can't promise that." Erin points her keys at me. "Sinkholes know no God. They come whenever they want, wherever they want. Besides, I think we're on a fault line."

"You're avoiding the subject."

"I've had a really good day with you."

"I have too, is that a bad thing?"

Erin shakes her head. "It's just...is this it?"

"Is what it?"

"Do we just meet this one time and then never see each other again?"

I laugh. "God, I hope not."

"But you don't even believe that we're related."

"I—I just don't know for sure how it would even work." Like any true performer, I'm a people-pleaser, but I can't lie to her. "It doesn't make sense to me. But also, it doesn't make sense for DN-YAY to just randomly match people. That seems like a flawed business plan."

"It does, yes," Erin says. Again, it seems like there's more she's holding back. "And yet?"

"And yet, I'm sure it's not an exact science either. But we don't necessarily have to be related to be friends."

"There it is then," Erin concedes like a person well-accustomed to disappointment.

"Erin, I had a really great time with you today, and though I don't have all the answers right now, for me that is enough." I lower my head to catch her eyes. It doesn't seem to help much though. I wrack my brain for something that may make her feel alright. "What if we set up another meeting like this soon? That way you know that I won't just disappear from your life and I know you won't disappear from mine."

"I'd like that."

"And maybe I'll get some answers from my parents before then too."

"You sure about that?" Erin tilts her head. "You don't have to do that."

"Yeah, I do."

Erin & The Atlas Obscura

<u>Chapter Twenty-Seven</u>

For the two-hour-plus drive home, I actually feel pretty good. Windows down, summer wind ripping through, Boygenius at top volume, singing along as loud as I can to every song, it all keeps my brain away from inventing scenarios that I should regret from my meeting with Evan. Say like, I don't know, my total awkward joke attempt about Christians. Or…oh, no, damn it, I was way too tough on him at the end, kind of guilt tripping him into seeing me again. Also, I talked crap on improv, the one thing he really loves in this world. Dang it. Wowowowowow. Forget meeting up again. That won't be happening.

He must hate me now.

"What was that again about not inventing things to worry about?" Anxiety Brain asks as it files its nails.

When I park in my driveway, I look at my own eyes in the rearview, recognizing myself behind them for the first time in a while. Breathe steady. It's okay. You didn't do anything wrong. Evan said he had a great time with you, and it was his suggestion to meet up again.

Everything is all right, Erin. I promise.

There's a square of light on the asphalt when I get out of the car. Mom's light is on up in her room. A gentle breeze dings the wind chimes on our front porch. The air smells cool and sweet of grass clippings mingled with chlorine from the pool next door, and the Callery pear tree doesn't even bother me. Overhead, the stars shine through like pinpricks in a black canvas stretched over the bright soul of the universe. They stop me in my tracks. I stare up for several minutes, tracing imaginary lines between stars. If Evan and I are two stars of the same constellation, how many more sibling stars could there be out there? The possibilities are as vast and intimidating as the cosmos and make me feel just as small. A deep pit starts to take root in my stomach. I narrow my focus back to just two stars until the feeling disappears.

That's all I ever need to know.

Mom's door is partially cracked when I reach the top of the stairs. Her laptop is perched on her knees. Chevy the Cat is a puddle of fur beside her. The lamp on her nightstand casts the room in a butterscotch glow.

I step into her doorway. "Any luck with the job hunt?"

"Not so much. All the nonprofits around here are facing the same budget cuts." She closes her laptop and sets it aside. "How was Blaide's open mic?"

"I didn't go."

"Oh." Mom takes her reading glasses off. "Everything alright?"

"I went to Hoakie, Illinois."

Mom snorts out a laugh. "God, why would you ever want to go there?"

"You've been?" I pet Chevy the Cat as I sit down.

"Home of the world's third-largest ketchup bottle? Oh, yes, I've been. Your dad used to love pointless road trip minutia."

"Well, I regret to inform you…" I suck in a dramatic breath. "That Hoakie is no longer the home of the world's third-largest ketchup bottle."

Mom clutches at her chest. "Please say it isn't so."

"I'm sorry to be the one to tell you, but they are—" I wince as though I'm delivering life-altering news. "Now home of the world's *fourth* largest bottle of ketchup."

"I just...I just...my reality is shattered." Mom smiles before getting to the point. "So?"

"So, what was I doing in Hoakie, Illinois?"

"I assume it wasn't to visit the Home of the White Squirrels."

"I believe you're confusing your small-town Illinois ephemera. Hoakie is famous for Blue-Footed Wrens."

"Erin. Why did you go to Hoakie, Illinois?"

"I met someone."

"Oh." Mom raises her eyebrows, playfully scandalized. "I'm sure Blaide will understand."

"No. It's not like that. It's just...the DNA site I mentioned..."

Mom's face goes ashen. "You found the donor?"

"Oh, god, no, that sounds like a nightmare." I laugh. "Even if I lived a thousand lifetimes I would never, ever want to do that. I'd binge watch like the entire omnibus of Right-Wing Media before I'd ever do that. Like, I'm talking every single program from every single day for decades and decades."

Mom exhales. "Okay, so you met someone..."

"The previously mentioned half-brother. His name's Evan."

"Is he nice?"

"Yes, and funny."

"Sounds like he would be related to you."

"You aren't...mad?" My voice breaks as the question leaves my mouth.

"Oh, Erin." Mom sits up straighter in her bed and pulls me in for a hug. "How could I be mad at you? I've been upset for weeks wishing we'd told you the truth sooner."

"I was pissed about that for a while." I lean up so she can see my eyes. "But I understand."

"You do?"

"Yeah, you did it to honor Dad and you knew how hard it would be on me."

Mom's bottom lip quivers before she nods. She pulls me in for another hug. "Tell me about Evan," she says with her face buried in my hair.

"That probably smells like bug spray."

"Oh, it definitely does." Mom fakes a hacking cough. "Okay, so, Evan?"

I feel myself smiling. Then I tell her everything I can.

Evan & Big White Jesus

Chapter Twenty-Eight

I begin my drive home still floating high on my day with Erin. But as each mile marker brings me closer to Whiting, I feel myself getting more and more pissed off. Until, finally, here I am, sitting outside the home I grew up in, feeling like an alien looking at its toxic home planet, wondering how in the hell did I ever survive leaving this barren wasteland?

Ten minutes have passed since I parked on the curb. The light's still on in the living room even though it's well after eleven. There's a new Ten Commandments sign along with a pristine SUNNY DAYS CHURCH OF CHRIST sign posted in the garden bed. New landscapers have reshaped the planters around the porch. White stones allow bits of shrubbery to peek through like artwork. Though the grass is as neat and green as ever, it too seems different. Each blade is a sharpened point to protect against invaders. That's what I am to this place now. The inside of my car lights up with a blue glow, a text from Ro. I snatch up my phone hoping that things will be better this time. The air whooshes out of my lungs like the time Tony suspiciously mistimed a stage punch. The text just reads: "Show was good. Glad meeting Erin went okay."

That's all he has to say? I start to text him back before backspacing it all out. What is going on here? Ro doesn't get pissed. I mean, yeah, I could've definitely been a bit more supportive before he left, but he was the one saying all that self-deprecating stuff.

It's not like *I* said it.

The proximity light over the garage buzzes to life as I approach.

A small swarm of bugs plink against the glass, trying to get inside the light they desire so badly. I knock on the door hard, feeling the anger boil up inside of me with each strike. Inside, the recliner snaps into an upright position. The volume of the shrieking cable news show gets turned down. While my parents confer over who could be knocking at this hour, my eyes trace the flow of wood grain in the door. The same door I used to barrel through on summer afternoons, desperate for a drink straight from the faucet before I dashed back out to resume bike races with the neighborhood kids.

There used to be so many of us. Their homes still rest silently down the street like nothing has changed, but of course things have. Laura dropped out sophomore year. Jordan sells pills now. Todd is his number one client. Dez is doing alright, going somewhere for college, but we don't talk any more. Where I'm from, growing up often means growing apart. Is Ro the next to go?

"It's Evan." My mom's shadow peeks through the bottom of the door. More whispering follows.

Then, finally, a succession of locks click open and I'm face to face with my parents in their pajamas. They appear older and more vulnerable than they've ever been. "Evan," my dad says plainly.

"I need to talk to you." I look past him to my mother. "Both of you."

I'm invited in as a formality. A devotional lies open beside my mother's chair. A shouting red-faced man in an ill-fitting suit proceeds to yell from the TV despite my father muting it. Our cat Bridgette lifts her head from the back of the couch to acknowledge my presence, then finding me as boring as the man on the TV, returns to her nap.

"What do you have to tell us?" My dad asks.

"Well, I just wanted to come to you guys and tell you that I'm cured. I'm no longer gay," I say with my hands clasped at my waist. "All your prayers worked. Turns out you *can* pray the gay away. So, I was just coming to say—good job!" I give an overenthusiastic thumbs up, knowing that my eyes are wild behind my glasses.

"Evan?" My mom asks on the verge of tears.

My dad steps toward me. His frailty diminishes. "You just couldn't help yourself, could you? You just had to upset your mother."

"Who is my father?" I ask, fully aware of the edge in my voice, surprised by how unafraid I am of my dad right now.

"What do you mean?" My mom tries to misdirect. It would almost work if I didn't catch the worried expression she gives my dad.

My dad stares me down as he processes all this. His brain is a spent ashtray in an underground conspiracy bunker. "What're you talking about?"

"I was born at Michael Reese Hospital, a fertility clinic, why?"

"I've told you before," my mother says. "We had complications. You were our little miracle, an answered prayer."

"Can't you just tell me the truth?" I yell, my eyes burning. "For once in your goddamn lives, just tell me the truth. That's all I want."

I may as well have just sacrificed Bridgette on the rug. There's a five second recovery time for my parents to decide which route to take, whether they should douse me with holy water to expel whatever Beelzebub has taken hold of me or just simply answer my question. As always, they take the lazy path of self-righteousness.

"How DARE you?" My dad booms. "You come in OUR house

at THIS hour, using the Lord's name in vain. Are you on drugs too?"

It's the *too* that gets me. My fists clench at my sides. "I just want to know. I deserve that much."

"There are some things that aren't yours to know," my mom says.

"Leave now or your mother will call the police," my dad sums it up.

I start to walk out before thinking of Erin. I stop in my tracks. "No. Call them then," I say as calm as one of the porcelain angels that surround their Big White Jesus statue on the mantle.

"What?" My mom clutches the opening of her robe. "You can't be serious."

"I'm not leaving until I hear the truth. So you better call them."

"Evan…" My mom trails off.

My dad lunges another step toward me. His fists are clenched at his sides like mine. His whole frame trembles with fury. "LEAVE."

My eyes bounce between the two of them. They'd rather call the cops or let my dad hit me than just tell the truth. "Fine." My jaw quivers. "That's fine. You've both already told me more than I even need to know." I snatch one of the angels I always liked, a particularly pious one with big eyes and a golden harp. I go to throw it at the wall before restraining myself. "For what it's worth—" I point right at my dad with the angel. "I'm thrilled to not be your son."

Big White Jesus looks down at me with condemnation. Clutching the angel, I storm back through the kitchen and slam the door as hard as I can; an exclamation point to mark the end of my sentence here. I've been cast out of the place I once called home.

    Like

        lightning

            falling

                from

                    heaven.

Evan & The Yellow Lights
<u>Chapter Twenty-Nine</u>

I sit on the hood of my car on the side of the road watching the traffic light blink yellow in the empty four-way. Random fireworks pop somewhere beyond the darkened houses and the trees. Each car that turns on this road and drives past me is a reminder of how dumb I am for being hopeful that he'd actually show. My phone sits lifeless in my hand. Oh, sure, I could text Erin and she would immediately console me, but that isn't what I need right now.

I need a win. A big one.

Finally, a beat-up truck turns onto the road, slowing down to park in front of my Yaris. My chest thumps so hard and hollow it feels like it may cave in. Just play it cool. Just play it cool. The door shuts. I don't allow myself to turn back. Gravel crunches as he walks toward me. "Sorry if you've been waiting long," Christian says.

"No, it's alright." I clear my throat. "It's not a big deal or anything."

"Sorry you had a shitty night, but I'm glad you reached out."

"Me too."

A car drives through the four-way with blaring music. Neither Christian nor I say anything. Christian leans against my car. I watch the back of him, still surprised that he's actually here. It's dreamlike. Though I know I'm awake, because one thought keeps playing over and over in my head.

"I…" My quivering voice breaks the silence. "I found out

tonight that my dad's not my real, biological dad."

Christian doesn't even look back at me, so I continue.

"Which, I thought was going to make me feel better. But it didn't. Not at all."

"I understand that feeling." Christian faces me. The yellow lights carry on blinking on each side of his perfect face.

"Growing up, there were actually some happy times, ya know? Family vacations. The sound of my father's voice in the dark, comforting me when I had a nightmare, the feeling of his weight on my bed until I fell back asleep. My mother's hands making an action figure dance across the table. Either of them asking questions after they picked me up from play practice, they'd be like genuinely listening, actually caring how practice went. Then on opening night, they'd be right there in the front row, cheering me on." Now that I've started, the words start tumbling out like the tears rolling down my cheek. "But then, there were also bad times, a lot of them. Times when I'd be slouching in a pew while a thick-necked preacher yelled about the end times from the pulpit and my dad would snap at me to pay attention. Times when I would be like seven years old, standing on some sidewalk or another with them, holding a picket sign, feeling embarrassed as angry shouts surrounded me, not even knowing why they were so mad. Then when I was old enough to finally understand what was going on, I felt angry too, but not in the way they wanted. I've hated my parents for kicking me out, for filling my head with all this bullshit, all this guilt, for keeping all this from me in the first place. I guess I should be touched that my parents wanted me so badly that they went through all that to have me, but instead I...just feel...that anger still."

"Yeah?" Christian's hair hangs in his eyes. I want so badly to sweep it away from his forehead, but I don't.

"They went through all that…all that trouble…all that stress and worry…they should've done a better job of actually caring for me. They should've done a better job of loving me. I was apparently the miracle of their lives. How could they throw me away eighteen years later when I didn't turn out how they wanted?"

Christian softens his expression and shrugs. "I'm sorry. I wish I knew the right answer."

"You're okay." I shake my head. "It's just so crazy. My real dad could be anyone. He could actually want me. Just not knowing makes me restless. I know what I want to do, but it's scary."

Christian meets my eyes, so sheepish and cute in a black t-shirt and jeans. "I'm hesitant to tell someone what they need to do since it's your life, but again, don't let the fact that it's scary stop you if you want something."

A moment passes, and when I don't say anything, Christian apologizes again. "Sorry. I'm not really qualified to give anyone advice on anything."

"You have nothing to apologize for." I sniff and give an awkward fake laugh. "Do you give your email out to many people? Is this the kind of situation you regularly find yourself in?"

"No." Christian gives a half-smile. "Not just anyone."

"I was wondering." My heart picks up at the confirmation that I'm not just *anyone* to Christian. The number of ways this scene can play out narrows by the second. Only a handful of bold choices remain, I have to take one. "I know I hardly know you, but I think about you all the time," I say.

He holds my gaze. For a few seconds all I can hear is the rushing of blood in my ears. Christian's lips part and then close again. He puts his hand on the hood of my car, barely an inch from mine. I don't break his eye contact. The hunger in my eyes would be obvious from outer space. His fingers ease towards my hand and then his fingers intertwine with mine. The warmth of his palm radiates through my skin. My heart may hammer out of my chest.

If this were an improv show, I'd hop from the hood of my car, throwing him backwards and kissing him in an over-the-top gesture that would be sure to get a ton of laughs and applause, because you know, apparently nothing is funnier than guy-on-guy love. But this is real life, so I don't do any of that. Nor does he. We just sit here, holding hands, feeling the gentle breeze of the night, as my Yaris settles beneath our weight and the yellow lights blink in and out.

"Whatever it is you've been thinking about me," Christian says after a minute. "I promise I won't live up to the expectation in real life. I'm a person. I'm trying every day, like legit trying, but I'm still a mess."

"I know," I say. "Me too."

A big part of improv is picking up the internal cues of your partner, just listening and playing off what they're telling you they want, and what Christian is telling me he wants right now, is to just sit and talk with me for a while. So that's what we do. We talk about his disputes with his roommate Taylor, the highs and lows of being a Bean barista, as well as the drawbacks of working at Charlie's Burgers. I tell him about missing my best friend Ro. I tell him about my connection with Erin and how lonely this summer's been until I met her. He tells me a little about his past struggle with pills and how he burned every last bridge with every one of his friends. We talk about almost everything, with me conveniently leaving out how I live in my friend's garage and I have no prospects for the immediate future. Until, finally, we're both yawning, and it's been at least an hour since anyone passed through the four-way. This is his moment to leave, but he doesn't take it.

Christian faces me. Mere inches exist between his lips and mine. He places his hand on my jaw. Shivers run down my spine at his touch. I lean into him until my lips find his. When our lips meet, my whole body shakes like it's negative twenty.

Christian stops. "Is this okay? Are you okay?"

"Yeah." I gasp. "I'm just…I can't help it."

"That's okay." Christian leans his forehead against mine. "It's okay."

We lean into each other again. A series of short kisses lead to longer, more passionate ones. His tongue flicks in my mouth as an invitation. My tongue tangles with his. Soft stubble rubs against my top lip. The smoky-sweet taste of his kiss and the salty scent of his skin swirl together into one magnificent sensation. His stomach and chest press against mine, I can feel his breathing, I match his breathing. His shirt pulls up just a bit, I touch the small of his back, the skin so firm and smooth. My hands work up to the pitch of his shoulder blades. Adrenaline courses through my entire body. His fingertips trail the nape of my neck. Each move is a subtle signal, a brief improvisation, a gentle, natural progression. His hands move gently to my hips, pulling me ever so softly into him. The milliseconds between each kiss are electric. Each time our lips connect is a supreme affirmation that this *is* happening.

Kiss.

I'm seen.

I'm safe.

Kiss.

I'm alright.

I'm alive.

Kiss.

We're alive.

I can't get enough. Until Christian stops and says, "I should really go soon."

I sweep my hair back. "No, yeah, totally."

Christian touches my cheek again. "Not like that. I just need to work in—" He checks his watch. "Four hours."

"Oh, yeah. Me too," I say, knowing full well that I have no intention of actually showing up tomorrow morning. It's not like I *want* to let Cheryl and Weird Allan down, but there are bigger things going on than working the Charlie Burgers breakfast shift.

Christian pulls me in for a hug. His t-shirt smells like coffee beans, incense, fresh deodorant, a touch of smoke, and sweat. His forehead leans against mine. We kiss again, which, thankfully, leads to more kissing. It goes on for perhaps longer than Christian needs but still shorter than I'd prefer. There's a rightful joke about how Midwesterners have to say goodbye several times before they actually leave. I've always hated that, but right now, I don't mind it so much.

Then, we part. Christian gives me the number for his new phone. I long for another Midwestern Goodbye, but seeing as how "four hours from now" has turned into three, I don't push it. We say goodbyes. After he's gone, I get back in my car. Returning to Ro's garage doesn't feel like an option right now. I start my car and find myself heading towards the interstate. The angel from my parents' house rides in the passenger seat, down for whatever.

JULY

You're on the end.

Origins of Bio-Man (Part Two)

When Evan closes his eyes, he can see his face. Chiseled cheekbones, daggered blue eyes, stiff jawline, formerly thick dark blonde hair that's starting to thin in the front the way it is in the back. A face that looks just like his own, just perhaps more wary for what he's about to do. Should Bio-Man be wary though? Sure, it's considered a taboo, or at least it is to Evan's actual parents who are so ashamed they won't allow themselves to take ownership of it. Though the truth is it's not like Bio-Man is leaving an orphaned infant on a doorstep. The truth of it is, Bio-Man's just strolling into the nurse's station, maybe giving one of them a wink, to retrieve a clear plastic cup to leave his "deposit" in. That's what they call it—a "deposit." It allows grace for the moment. It provides Bio-Man a bit more dignity as he goes behind the blank white door to "do what he's got to do." They all know what he's doing in there though. Evan knows it too.

He doesn't want to see that part, but he can't unsee it.

This is his beginning after all.

After Bio-Man departs from the room, he returns to being who he was before he entered it. He returns to being a man with big, big plans for his future. A future-version of himself that doesn't involve being a father or having any greater responsibility to his "deposit" than screwing a little plastic lid on it, maybe checking a box on the label before leaving it on a shelf for one of the nurses to put in a cooler. There's no higher purpose to this for Bio-Man, he's not doing this for the couples that want so badly to conceive that they'll do whatever it takes. Oh, God, he's definitely not doing it for science, and the only thing more laughable is that he's doing it for God. Evan knows that. He's doing it for a check. For money. Close the door. Make the deposit. Screw the lid on. Leave. That's the extent of his commitment to Erin, to Evan, to however many more of them are out there.

Evan isn't as interested in who Bio-Man was before he entered that room. He wants to know who the man is now. Where is he? And does he even care that his deposits are now full-grown people? Evan honestly doesn't give a shit if he does, but he wants him to know.

He *needs* Bio-Man to know.

Evan can't rest until it's figured out.

Charlie Burgers' Great Let Down
(A Short Series of Texts, Mostly Unanswered)

A text from Cheryl on Evan's first night gone: "Hey Evan, did you forget you were scheduled at four today?"

Another from Cheryl later that evening: "Evan, everything okay? It's not like you to No Call, No Show."

The next day, Cheryl again: "Good morning Evan, I hope you're okay. I have you scheduled for tonight through Friday. If you're not planning on coming in. Please just let me know."

Another, later that day from Cheryl: "Okay, Evan. I don't know what's going on. I texted Ro and he said he didn't know either, so I hate to do it, but I'm going to take you off the schedule until further notice. If you want back on, you'll have to meet with me and Kevin first."

Ro: "Hey man, I just heard from Cheryl. Are you skipping out on work? You can at least call and let them know. She's worried."

Finally, a response from Evan, three days later: "I'm so so so sorry, Cheryl. I've been going back and forth to Chicago and my phone kept dying. I'm okay though, just have something going on. Yes, please take me off the schedule for the rest of the week. Do it forever if you have to. I'm so sorry! Please don't hate me!"

There's been a low buzz of excitement humming through my body since meeting Evan. Suddenly, things I haven't wanted to do in months—like, say, attending one of Blaide's concerts—don't sound that bad.

Which is why, here I am, on the sidewalk in front of the venue, doing the predictable looking-at-my-phone-to-distract-from-my-social-anxiety thing. I shoot another quick text to Evan. It's hard to say that he's not being himself since I've only known him for (wow) barely over a month now. But yeah, he definitely doesn't seem like he's been himself lately. He hasn't talked (and oh, god, nor have I asked) about if he's found out any more info from his parents. So maybe that's it.

Evan texts in: "They're playing in a barbershop?"

Me: "Correction: A barbershop/tattoo parlor."

Evan: "Ah, big difference. Nothing I love more than greasy hair and dirty needles. I'm sure it's very classy."

Me: "It actually sorta is. It's one of the nicest places in Langford."

I legit love Lern's Hair & Tattoo Parlour with its original wood flooring, maroon color scheme, early 20th century furniture, old timey photographs from back when people never smiled (relatable!), and Americana flash tattoo art decorating the walls. Everything in the place seems as though it's been run through a LookAtMe filter for "Achingly Cool" or "FOMO" or... "Sepia." Not that I've ever actually gotten my hair done here. Some places are so hip that it's intimidating to even consider, but I've hung out with Blaide here on multiple occasions when he's gotten his hair cut (if you're wondering if Blaide gets one of those slicked back high & tight haircuts that's been co-opted by the perpetually-virgin alt-right, I think you already know the answer).

My phone buzzes.

Evan: "High praise."

Me: "Hey, support small businesses. Especially when they make your town seem like less of a craphole."

Evan: "Are you going to get one?"

Me: "I don't know if you're referring to a haircut or a tattoo, but the answer to both is: no."

Evan: "That's too bad. Do you want one?"

Me: "Yes."

Me: "To both."

Evan: "You should then."

Me: "I can't."

Evan: "Why not?"

It's as good of a question as any. Yet, I don't have a good answer.

Perhaps after seeing the omnipresent ellipsis appear and disappear more than once, Evan texts back in with: "If nothing's stopping you from doing what you want then you probably should."

Evan: "Just sayin."

Me: "I'll start taking your advice when you do."

Me: (winky face emoji)

Me: "Just sayin." (laughing-so-hard-I'm-crying emoji)

The ellipsis bubble appears and disappears twice. My smile fades as it disappears for a third time with no new message. In hell, there's a circle reserved for lesser offenders (say, people who've broken up with their partner by ghosting them) where they're doomed to watch for eternity as their texts are greeted by rapidly appearing then disappearing ellipses bubbles. In a past life, I must've been a jerk to all my boyfriends. That cursed blinking three-dots-bubble pops up then disappears again.

A line of teenage punks starts forming on the sidewalk in front of me. Some of them wear t-shirts for Blaide's old band. Even though it's barely been a couple seconds (and my phone has been in my palm the entire time), I still swipe through to make sure. Nope, no new text from Evan. Maybe he's driving?

Anxiety Brain glances up from its antique fainting couch. "Maybe he died in a car wreck reading your text and your stupid joke was the last thing he ever saw."

Oh, no, you could be right. I should call him.

"Totally. You should totally call him," Anxiety Brain says while munching on Funyuns.

I should.

"Hey, aren't you the girl from RifRaf? You know, the graduation video?" One dude with the same haircut as Blaide asks with a chuckle. "We're all going to dieeeeeee," his friend singsongs in fake autotune.

Ah, there's the reminder that it's still not safe to go outside.

"Tried telling you," Anxiety Brain says with Funyun crumbs spraying out of its mouth.

"Erin." Blaide comes around the corner of the venue, thank God. "We're all hanging out in the Green Room, come with me."

A few of the kids (which honestly, they're maybe two years younger than me) exchange excited looks with each other. The dude with the haircut suddenly forgets whatever shit he was talking.

Truth be told, Blaide is actually kind of a big deal. As much as it sucks to admit, this is another reason I can't bring myself to break up with him. Sure, it's superficial, but hell yeah, I like being with someone who is a big deal even if it's only to (maybe) fifty teenagers in our tri-county area.

"You ready?" Blaide turns to ask me. I look up from my zero-notification phone. Blaide's blue eyes are all-intense like I have anything to do with any of this.

I shrug with every fiber of my being. "Sure."

"I'm just so glad you're here for my comeback show." He leans in to plant a kiss on my lips. "I couldn't do this without you."

Couldn't you though? He always says things like this. Like we're more in love than we actually are. Maybe all artists just go through life faking it like Blaide and his friends do.

They all get to their feet and we shuffle out of the over-glorified broom closet that has a shower curtain serving as a door. Blaide and his band cut ahead of me as I search for a good wall to lean against, somewhere inconspicuous where I can still see. I settle into the glass partition that seperates the tattoo area from the rest of the room. There's not an eruption of applause or anything, but I have to admit there's a little whirr of excitement that pulses through the crowd as the house music fades, the lights dim, and the band takes the stage. Which, really, the stage is just a large maroon rug at the end of the room. Band members and the audience are all on equal footing here, an idea that never fails to move me at least a little bit. Large storefront windows serve as the backdrop for the band. Headlights cutting in from Main Street act as sporadic lighting. Blaide slings his guitar over his muscular frame. A buzz comes from his amp as he flips it on from standby. "We're Open to Oblivion and this is our first show," he says into the mic in his low stage voice (yes, it is sexy but still so lame). A few girls let out a "whoooo" and clap. Blaide nods to Jackson who clicks his drumsticks together four times. Then they launch into their first song, "Liar's Breath" which, you guessed it, despite being an entirely new song for his (mostly) new band, is still about Blaide's ex-girlfriend.

I check my phone again. Nope. Nothing from Evan.

I swipe through my phone to reread my message. After I read it six times, I glance up to see Blaide staring at me as he's singing, and he looks for real pissed that I'm looking at my phone during his new band's first show. For a millisecond, I feel bad before realizing I don't care. Maybe this will push him over the edge. Then he turns away, banging his head as they go into a musical break.

I reread my message to Evan again and yeah, the emojis should've removed any sting in my words. What's his deal?

Anxiety Brain wearing an Open to Oblivion t-shirt asks, "Good point but more importantly, what's *your* deal?"

"You're such a liaarrrrrrrr," Blaide croons into the microphone while his band carries on behind him. A wall of noise barrels over all in its path. "And you're always lying to yourself!"

"You're such a liaarrrrrrrr/Always lying to yourself!"

My phone vibrates in my front jean pocket five consecutive times. I swipe open to reveal a succession of GIFs.

More keep coming in.

There's Andy Dwyer from Parks & Rec doing the "Ooooooh" surprise face with the tight zoom in.

There's the Kristin Wiig "I freaking love surprises"

There's a Tina from Bob's Burgers doing an excited dance.

There's a Lucille Ball kind of recoiling in terror but I guess she's surprised?

There's a Jonah Hill turning from one side to another (I don't know what movie it comes from) screaming in delight.

There's a brown bear puppet with its jaw hanging open as though it just received life-altering news (do puppets get cancer?).

Then to close it out, the most classic GIF of (perhaps) all time, the blinking Caucasian Man GIF.

I push through the crowd. The blaring sound is muffled as the venue door shuts behind.

I fire off a text to Evan: "What's going on?"

"You'll find out soon enough," he texts back.

Instantly, my stomach begins churning.

For some reason, I'm not so sure I'll like this.

Whatever it could be.

Erin & One Thousand ICUs

<u>Chapter Thirty-One</u>

After Blaide's show, I wait outside while he does the whole say-good-bye-to-every-person-in-here routine. Still no word from Evan since his barrage of GIFs three hours ago, but I'm okay, definitely no freaking out here.

I pull up Evan's LookAtMe profile and there's nothing since the post of his melted Orange Dream ice cream from when we met. "It was a good day" reads the caption. I'd ISeeYou this photo a thousand times if I could. Since finding Evan, I've felt less alone. I've felt understood. It's something I haven't really felt since Dad passed away. If I still saw her, Dr. Meera would probably point out that's probably why I freak out so much that I'm going to scare him away. Not that Dad wanted to leave. Quite the opposite really, he fought like hell to stay. Every experimental treatment, every new drug, whatever it took to buy him even a few more days, he gave it a shot, regardless of what anyone else said.

More than (almost) anything, I wish I could just miss him the way I used to. It's like one hand's itching and the other's missing.

Eventually, Blaide comes back, asks me again if I'm ready to leave. I tell him that I am for the second time. He leaves to say "goodbye real quick" to someone else. Twenty more minutes pass. Blaide constantly puts me in this situation. Where either A) I leave here without him making me the jerk or B) I just stay outside waiting for him like a sad orphan puppy.

In either scenario, I'm the loser. Also—

"Also, Evan hasn't replied after his string of GIFs yet either,"

Anxiety Brain cuts in.

I'm done with this.

"I'm leaving," I text Blaide before adding: "I'll catch up with you later."

I drive home blasting Lucy Dacus the whole way. Once there, I head promptly to the medicine cabinet to screw off the lid of the Melatonin and chew two gummies. Then I turn on a *2 Dead Broads* live show video I've already seen and fall asleep in the flashing light.

Until...hours later...I'm woken by my phone vibrating. It's Evan. My heart pounds so hard I can feel it in the walls of my skull.

"Hey," he says, all simple like he's not waking me up in the middle of the night. "I'm outside. We need to talk, and it can't wait."

Erin & The Tilted Axis
Chapter Thirty-Two

The air is that mixture of cool yet still so humid that it's like wading through a swamp on another planet. Sure enough, there's Evan leaning against his car, grinning like he knows a joke I'm not yet in on, which are my least favorite brand of jokes.

I cross the dew-wet grass. Never in my life have I been woken up for something that's good news. At best, it's a tornado alarm. At worst, it's Mom telling me to come downstairs because Dad's getting worse.

This…this is something else.

Evan just keeps smiling. A million white teeth, a wall so bright it could hold back a horde of zombie-vampires. "What's going on?" I ask in a whisper. Ope, there it goes, that question only uncorks the other questions I'm bottling up. "How do you know where I live? How did you get here? Why are you here? Is someone dead? Are you dying? What's going on?"

"Well, I'm going to tell you, but first I'll answer your other questions. You shared your location with me in Hoakie and you left it on. I drove here in the mighty Yaris you see behind me. I have something to tell you. A ton of people are currently dead and many more die every day. That depends on how you view it actually, but to keep it brief, I'll just say we all are all the time. And again, I'm going to tell you."

I can't help but grin. "Proud of yourself?"

"Very much so."

"Okay. Spill it."

"That's a really nice stretch-pant to t-shirt combo you're

currently rocking. Is that a Forever Fifteen shirt you have on? I never pictured you as the boy band type."

"Everyone was a boy band type at some point in their timeline."

"I heard that."

"Most are just too weak to admit it." I cross my arms over my chest, recognizing the ridiculousness of this moment with a smirk. "Okay, so thank you for driving five hours—"

"Six plus. Actually," Evan corrects me. "I came all the way from Chicago."

"Holy crap. Why?"

"We're getting to that."

"Are you?" I ask. "Because so far you've just critiqued my elegant sleepwear."

"Sorry about that."

"No." I shake my head. "You're not."

"You're right. I'm definitely not. But I wanted to come here to say, I firmly believe that you're my sister. Like my for real, blood-relative sister."

It's everything I've wanted to hear Evan say since we met. It feels like when I'd spot my parents' van when kindergarten let out each day and I'd be so happy, sprinting across the grass towards them as they opened the door beaming, always waving, always smiling. I lean forward and wrap my arms around Evan's waist. His t-shirt smells like old car air-conditioning and, ugh, boy sweat.

"There's more though," Evan says, returning my hug.

And the way he says it, hopeful yet hesitant, makes the ground seem less secure beneath my feet. "Oh, yeah?" I take a step back. His hands still rest on my shoulders.

"I think I found our dad too. Our real—well, you know, bio-dad—the donor. I found him. It was fairly easy actually."

"Wait—what?" I back away from underneath his hands.

Evan nods emphatically. "I've been tracking him down like one of those true-crime podcasts you're always listening to. You should be proud—"

"I'm something, that's for sure."

"I've been driving back and forth to the Chicago library, trying to dig up files on Michael Reese Hospital for a while. Then I just started finding last names that showed up consistently on our DN-YAY profiles. One kept coming up the most—Orlasky. Then, I went over to Acquaintances—"

"Okay."

"And started messaging everyone in the greater-Chicago area with that last name. Most ignored me entirely. Probably thinking I wanted to sell them on some pyramid scheme, but yesterday morning, one woman, our third cousin, Mary—with whom we share two second cousins on DN-YAY—messaged me that her first cousin twice removed had a son that used to work at Michael Reese Hospital in the early 2000s. It all lines up. There's a decent chance that guy's our dad!"

"Cool," I say, knowing that the weak timbre of my voice betrays the intended levity of the word. No. No. No. This is not what I wanted. This is like ordering an amazing five-cheese pizza only to have the cook come out and perform an impromptu root canal on you instead.

"I know, right?" Evan's totally not getting it. "Mary's in her sixties, but she was very helpful. She's also pretty deep into figuring out her ancestry and family tree stuff. She gave me his name and where he currently lives. From there I was able to track down where he works, which is what I want to talk to you about."

And with that, the world has officially upended itself (again).

Evan & The Helter Skelter Seltzer

<u>Chapter Thirty-Three</u>

A muted television playing some true crime show lights the living room as Erin leads me into her house. She turns on the lights in her kitchen then eases the dial back seventy-five percent so it's still dim. 3AM can't be greeted with bright lights. Is it really that late? Despite hardly sleeping the last several days, I'm as energized as a tall vibrant energy drink full of chemicals with made-up sounding names that you just know will slowly dissolve your organs if you drink it.

"Do you want something to drink?" Erin asks as I pull out one of the stools along the counter. "Water, almond milk—"

"Sweetened?"

"Unsweetened. It's super gross."

"Pass."

"La Croix? We're an unofficial LC sponsored household, so as such we have coconut, mango, lime, citrus."

"Ehhh, pass on the Devil's Backwash." I fake a dry heave. "Just tap is fine, thanks."

"I too was once lost, but now have been found by the glories of La Croix." Erin pops open a can of the coconut flavor for herself. "You'll come around someday and you will be forever changed." Erin then sets down a glass of water from the Brita filter in front of me.

"Your house is really nice," I say, taking in the high ceiling and wood paneled floors. "Why would you ever want to leave to go to—"

"EIU." Erin hops up on the counter. Her bare feet dangle a good two feet off the ground.

"Yeah, that. Didn't you say you got a full scholarship to the community college around here?"

"I did. A couple a bit further away too." Erin's thin eyebrows pinch together. "I've just seen what happens when people hang around this town too long. It's like they never leave it behind, they never grow beyond it, they never move on. JQUAC—John Quincy Adams College is basically high school with vape breaks."

"And what is it you're going to study?"

"Creative writing," Erin says with a shrug. "It's what my dad always loved."

"Ah." I take a drink. "And you can't do that around here?"

"Sure. But I want to be around people different than me. People from different backgrounds, from different places. I want to experience more from life."

"But isn't that kind of a clichéd thing that small town kids say?" I push back and to be honest, I don't know why I am. There aren't a lot of good times to be a jerk, but I'd bet that one of the absolute worst times is after waking up your new half-sister in the middle of the night to insult both her favorite beverage and her outlook on life. Though also, I respect Erin too much to let her by with lazy platitudes.

Erin takes a drink while giving me the stink-eye. For being so short, I have to say, when Erin stares through your soul, it's downright intimidating. I laugh it off. "Or so says the failed improv performer with little to no plans for his immediate future, am I right?" I flash a grin.

Erin nods without smiling. "So, you found the donor?"

"Maybe. I think so. Yes." I place my hands down on the counter, feeling the coolness of the marble beneath my palms. I'm reminded of Christian. I miss him.

"And…" Erin bobs her head.

"And?" I feign ignorance. I'm pretty good at it.

"Jesus, Evan, and what are you planning to do with the information again?"

"I don't know what Jesus plans to do with it—"

Erin rolls her eyes. "I can't believe you're supposed to be in comedy."

"But yeah, I thought we should go meet him." After hearing myself say the words for the first time, I realize both how scary it is and how bad I want it.

Erin nearly chokes like she just realized she's drinking Charles Manson's bathwater. "I don't think that's a good idea."

"Why not?"

"Because we don't know him. He asked to be an anonymous donor for a reason. Two weeks ago, you didn't believe you came from the donor and now you're ready to track him down?"

"Correction: I already tracked him down. Maybe."

Erin frowns, shaking her head. "This is too much."

"Erin?" An attractive middle-aged woman steps cautiously into the kitchen. She clutches her robe closed, looking from Erin to me. A small black and white cat waits in her shadow.

"Mom." Erin hops from the counter. "This is Evan. Is it okay if he stays tonight?"

Erin's mom pauses, raising a hand to her mouth. Her cheeks flush, before she says, "Of course, of course." She then crosses the linoleum floor to give me a hug, still holding her robe closed with one hand in the process. "I'm Laurie. It's so nice to meet you. Erin's told me so much about you."

"I see now where Erin got her height from." I reach over to return Laurie's hug. Erin rolls her eyes like that's only the millionth time they've heard that one. "You sure I won't be in the way?"

"Not at all." Laurie touches my shoulder. "I'll get you some blankets and clean towels. The bathroom's down the hall and I'll make up the couch for you." With that, Laurie leaves.

"Come on," I say to Erin once Laurie is gone. "Don't you need some answers? Don't you *need* to know who you come from?"

"Nope. I found you. That's enough."

I let out a sigh. I'm good at a lot of things; hiding how I feel is not one of them. "That's fine."

Erin's shoulders slump like an auditioning actor who knows they've lost the part. "When do you want to go?"

"I was thinking...tomorrow morning?"

"I guess we better get some sleep then." Erin takes a long swig of her drink and sets it down. "I'll see you in the morning." Without even offering a hug, she heads upstairs.

"Road trip!" I whisper-yell after her.

Several seconds pass before a meager "yay" escapes from somewhere in the dark.

Erin & Falling to Pieces
Chapter Thirty-Four

Sunlight blinds me as I start the car. My sunglasses drop down from the visor and I can't put them on fast enough. It's 10:37am and for the first time ever, I feel the strong urge to punch Evan right in the middle of his stupid fucking face.

I'm not my best self in the morning.

"Questo Maps says his bar is just about four hours away from here," Evan says as he climbs into the passenger seat. "I'll handle navigational duties. Just get on the interstate and head north-east."

I'm barely listening, and I can't bring myself to look at him out of concern for his own safety. Do we really have to drive out to the middle of nowhere to see the bar that (potential) Bio-Guy owns? I'm sure it's one of those places where some Deer Hunting game beeps erratically from the corner and earworms of America First pop country assault your brain all while you choke down some warmed-over barbecue and soggy French fries. When you grow up in a small town, pretty much all of your "nice" restaurants double as the town bars. They're all the same.

"So, are you excited or what? We're maybe going to find out where—or more accurately who—we come from today," Evan adds.

"Mhhhmmm," is all I can offer over the lip of my travel mug. For once, I actually don't care if he catches the shade intended with the one-word responses and low enthusiasm that I've been throwing his way all morning. Anxiety Brain seems to be sleeping in, so Grump-Ass Erin is the best he's gonna get.

As we near the interstate, I glance over at Evan. He hasn't said anything since my house. Okay, my cappuccino is kicking in. "What do you want to listen to?" I ask.

"This is fine." Evan gestures towards my stereo which is currently playing Alex Lahey.

"Well, what do you normally listen to?"

"Musicals. Soundtracks. That's it, really…" Evan says with no excitement to the windshield. It's like he soaked in my bad vibes or we've traded them off, because no, this isn't what I want to be doing, but if we are going to be doing this, well, then, one of us (like the one that wants to go on this trip in the first place) better be happy about it.

"*Musicals. Soundtracks?*" I take on playful affectation when I parrot his words back to him. It's a real shame that I can only think of *like* two musicals right now and I absolutely refuse to be the noob sister trying to fit in by waxing poetic about how the Hamilton soundtrack has moved me to tears on countless occasions (which I mean, "Wait For It" practically got me through the painfully awkward years of middle school). Which leaves… "So, are you into *Fiddler on the Roof?* 'Match-maker, match-maker, make me a match' and all that?"

Evan glares at me in disgust. "Ugh. No. I hate *Fiddler on the Roof.*"

"What? Why?" I backpedal. "Have you even seen it? It's kind of an older play, way before your—our time."

"Have I even seen it?" Evan gives me the side-eye. "Yeah. Guy chooses the church over his own daughter when she won't marry who he wants her to? Fuck Tevye. Fuck that play."

Dang it. Maybe he'll make us turn around, which wouldn't be so bad actually.

"'Match-Maker' is a banger though." Evan gives a small smile to open the conversation door again just a bit. "'The Bottle Dance' rules too."

I clear my throat. "What other music are you into? Are you secretly a fan of hardcore? Grindcore? Murdercore? Math Rock? Death Metal? Nu-Metal? Country-Rap? What?" Ugh, thank Blaide's crappy local band shows for my extensive knowledge of all the awful sounds human beings can make with their instruments. "Or I know, bad upbeat pop music from animatronic animals?"

"Nice, call back." Evan perks up a bit and sits up straighter in his seat. "Normally, I'd play along, but I have to ask...what exactly is grindcore?"

"Ugh, you really don't want to know."

"It sounds like some kind of sex act."

"You're not entirely wrong if the sex act in question involves two clowns, a chainsaw, a double-bass pedal, and, for some inexplicable reason, a velociraptor."

Evan grins, seemingly relieved that my mood has lightened.

"You didn't answer though," I say as tall fields of grass roll by my window. "What do you like to listen to? Oh, no, you don't like country-rap, do you?"

"Close. Does Patsy Cline count?"

"Umm...I don't think I know who...wait...you mean the lady that sang 'Crazy'? Sure, I guess she has some bars," I say, not knowing if Evan is joking or not.

"Yeah," Evan says in a meeker tone. "She was the only non-Christian singer my mom would play around the house growing up. She's probably still my favorite artist."

"I feel like you think I'm going to make fun of you for this, but if Patsy Cline is really your favorite singer, I think that's awesome."

"I usually just stick with musicals when Ro rides with me. The Book of Mormon is our favorite. My improv group always listens to like loud, basstastic rap stuff to get psyched for shows, which is fine too, but really, nothing gets me more in my feels than hearing 'Fall to Pieces'."

I resist giggling at the image of ultra-hip Evan "getting in his feels" to a song that's older than both of us combined. "So, your one big secret that you've never told anyone is that you love Patsy Cline?"

Evan laughs. "Yep. I've never wrestled with keeping anything else to myself. I've always been an open book my entire life except for one little thing, I freaking love Patsy Cline." Evan tilts his head towards me. "What about you?"

"I don't know. I mean Patsy is fine, I guess, but I'm more of an indie rock kind of girl."

"No, I meant, what's something you've never told anyone else?"

Dang. We're barely on Hour One of the road trip but we've already entered the Reveal Your Deepest Secrets segment.

"Are you sure you're ready for this?" I ask.

Evan nods.

"So, you know how most people have an internal monologue?"

"Yes, I understand how thoughts work, go on."

"Well, I have an internal monologue going like everyone, but I also have another voice that speaks up a lot."

"Ooookay. And is this other voice telling you to—I don't know—drive your devilishly handsome new half-brother to the middle of nowhere to chop him up into little pieces?" Evan raises one eyebrow at me with his lips buttoned tight.

"As a matter of fact…" I'm holding back a smile of my own now. "I hope your affairs are in order." I press the button to lock the doors.

Evan jolts back at the clicking sound. He looks at me with wide eyes, his hair drooping down his forehead. "I was just kidding," he says in faux panic.

"Do you always interrupt people with a joke when they're trying to tell you something real?"

Evan ducks his head. "So…you have an extra voice that sometimes tells you to murder people and…"

"Well, it's worse than that."

"Worse than murder. Got it."

"Not worse than murder, but…" Inhale. I'm already in this far. "It's like this constant source of insecurity. It's actually pretty clever sometimes, but I hate it. I hate it so much and it never stops."

"Sounds like anxiety."

"It is." I jab my finger at Evan with perhaps too much intensity considering I was just joking about, um, murder. "Yes, exactly."

"A lot of people struggle with that," Evan says, though his lack of adding a qualifier such as *I struggle with it too* is painfully obvious.

"Yeah. I know. But I guess with mine…like…have you ever heard the poem, 'Calling a Wolf a Wolf' by Kaveh Akbar?"

Evan shakes his head.

"Well, I wouldn't have heard of it either if it wasn't for my dad. He used to quote it all the time. I can't remember all of it, but it basically says, 'You can give a wolf a name, but that doesn't dull its fangs.'"

"Okay."

"Yeah. So, I've given this voice a name, I call it Anxiety Brain, which I know isn't the cleverest name it could have, but calling it what it is makes the voice less bad…or at least it did…but then that stopped working so I started giving it all these little extra features like body parts…"

"In your mind?"

"Yep, in my mind, I gave it features because like the thought of it being this thing separate from me, that made it less powerful, or at least it did."

"Right."

"So then, without even thinking of why I was doing it, I started giving it like extra accessories like a monocle or a cane, or one time I gave it a top hat—"

"So, Mr. Peanut is your malevolent internal monologue? Sounds nuts."

I laugh at how ridiculous I must sound.

"I'm doing it again." Evan slaps his thigh. "No, I get that. You were trying to protect yourself from your intrusive thoughts. A lot of people do that."

A lot of people do that? Like those that make jokes to keep things from getting serious? I want to say, but don't. "But the point is, none of those things actually weaken it, if anything it seems to be getting stronger."

"Well, does talking about it help? Talking usually helps for most everything."

"I don't know. This is my first time trying. Honestly, and this may sound weird, but being around you seems to help some." I feel myself cringe. Back when I still saw Dr. Meera, she once told me (very kindly, might I add) that I was co-dependent. I knew it was true as soon as she said it, but it still hurt like hell. I'm so needy that I end up clinging to people for the source of all my happiness or I push them away.

Either outcome isn't exactly rewarding.

Evan smiles and relief washes over me. "Well, for what it's worth, I encourage you to keep talking about it. This may be a stretch so hang with me. But in improv, some people treat object work like it's this dumb thing, but it's important to make the negative space you're inhabiting real, because if you don't, then no one else can know what's going on inside your head, and they won't care."

"I think I un—"

"See, what I'm saying is if you don't show—or in your case—talk about what's going on inside your head, then no one can know. It won't be real to them."

"Oh, I got it."

"You sure I don't need to keep explaining?" Evan grins. "Because I'm obviously a master of metaphor over here."

I give a light chuckle.

Evan looks over at me. "You know none of this is your fault, right? You're doing the best you can. It's okay to talk about it or not. You're not crazy. You're not less than anyone else."

Perhaps sensing I'm on the edge of tears, Evan smiles. "Though Anxiety Brain is a bit on the nose. Seems a little sexist too. Have you considered renaming your inner voice, 'The Ruminator'?"

I shake my head with a sniff. "I tried calling it Tucker for a little while. Like imagining the voice as this ultra-conservative cable news show host. That way I wouldn't take it seriously and it couldn't hurt me, but then it just pissed me off all the time instead."

Evan nods instead of laughing. The only sound is the road beneath us.

I wipe my cheek with my wrist. "If you love musicals so much then why isn't that your passion instead of improv?"

"I've done a couple musicals. I love them too. I guess I've never really considered them as like a viable thing I could do." Evan pauses. "I guess improv always felt safer than musicals, like I could hide in plain sight, being whatever I wanted to be because it was so impulsive and free. It was like therapy, you know?"

I nod that I do, even though I don't fully. I wait for Evan to say more. When he doesn't, I pull up some Patsy Cline on my phone and let it play (on shuffle of course). Before too long, Evan's singing along and I'm doing the same. Even if I don't think everything is going to be okay (which I don't), I have to say that in this moment, I feel slightly more optimistic than I have been in a long time. A little more than three hours stand between us and Bio-Man, but who knows, maybe he won't even be there anyway. All I know is right now I'm here in the car, singing along to these old-ass songs with my brother and I feel okay.

I feel okay.

I feel okay.

I feel okay.

And right now, that's enough.

Evan & The Small-Town Kids

Chapter Thirty-Five

Small towns that are little more than gas stations and the same three fast food restaurants, billboards telling me that I'm surely going to hell, and more cornfields than I could ever imagine, blur past my passenger window. Every small town we pass, I can't help but think that there's a whole world there, whole generations of people that wanted to leave but never did, new generations that dream of getting out, but probably never will; all those small-town kids with their big, big plans that will never probably happen. That kind of thought used to always make me so sad, but now that I've met Erin…I don't know. It's nice to imagine there's someone like her in each of these small towns, someone so kind and caring that will either stick around long enough to make the town better or set out on her own path.

It's almost hard to believe we're going to possibly meet our birth father in less than two hours. Something so momentous needs to be shared. I type a long text to Ro before deleting all of it. I pull up the last text I sent him. No response in about a week now.

"I think my best friend hates me," I say to Erin while still looking at my phone screen. It's the first time I've been able to admit it out loud. A part of me hoped it would sound less plausible when I spoke it into existence, but sadly that's not the case.

Erin turns down the Patsy Cline. "Ro? What? No. He's letting you stay in his house, why would he hate you?"

"I know. But he's been on this tour all summer. He hasn't been texting me back like he usually does."

"Well, maybe he's just busy. That could just be *your* anxiety brain trying to tell you things that aren't true. That's how it works." Erin's eyes sparkle with mischievousness. "I don't know if you know this, but *a lot of people* struggle with anxiety, actually."

I wince at my own words echoed back to me. "God, am I always so insufferable?"

Erin tilts her head like she's balancing the thought. "Only most the time."

"Yikes."

"It's okay. I'm just saying, that could be your anxiety telling you that."

"Could be." *But it probably isn't.* I exhale. "But on a more positive note, here's something else I've never told anyone…I hung out with Christian the night I got back from seeing you."

"What?! You're totally burying the lede here, Evan."

"I know. I know." I feel my cheeks warming. "And here's the follow-up. We kissed. Like my first for real kiss."

"You've never kissed anyone before?"

"Well, I've kissed girls."

"Girls don't count as people." Erin sucks her teeth. "Got it."

"That's not what I—"

"Geez, for someone that's supposedly a master of comedy, you can hardly tell when someone is messing with you."

I shake my head with a smile. "Do you always have to crack jokes when someone is trying to tell you something real?"

Erin ducks with a little hand wave that says continue. "Touché."

"So yeah, I've kissed real-life, human girls, several of them in fact. But that with Christian was my first real kiss."

"That's so awesome!" Erin glances over at me with furrowed brows. "Right, that should be awesome."

"It is. It is." I bow my head in concession. "He finally got a phone so we've been texting some. I still don't really know if he likes me or not though."

"I'd say making out with you is a pretty clear indicator that he likes you, though I've definitely been wrong about that before. So why don't you just ask him out, like officially or whatever?"

"I guess I haven't because..." Annnnnd here's where I usually make a joke. I'm resisting the urge, but it's just too strong. "Because my schedule is just too full of eligible bachelors."

Erin furrows her brow. "What is it, two truths and a joke with you? That wasn't even a good one. What's the real reason?"

"I mean...I guess I'm waiting until I'm in a better situation," I say, hoping that now that I've shared a little bit of truth, Erin will let me leave it at that. I'm not exactly a catch right now. I mean I live in my best friend's garage while he's away having the time of his life on the team that I didn't even get picked for. And he may not even be my best friend anymore. And his parents have pretty much said that I need to move soon. And though I told them I did, I don't have a plan about what to do next. And I work at a dorky fast-food place with my fellow directionless co-workers, who were also probably at one time waiting for something to happen. And moving back in with my parents is definitely not happening. And I don't have any plans to go to college. And I honestly don't have much going for me except for...this. My relationship with Erin and going to meet my birth dad, the rare time that I've actually stepped up to make something happen for myself.

I look over at Erin and realize that she hasn't responded yet. Panic covers her face like she just texted the wrong person an insult about *that* person.

"Is—is everything okay?" I ask after a few more seconds of watching her.

"You, uh, didn't say, what town does he work in? The Maybe Bio-Man?"

"Oh. Yeah. Charleston."

"Cool," Erin says with her face pinched tight.

She turns the music back up and we keep driving. Small towns blur by in my peripheral. All those kids with all their dreams. I'm envious of all of them.

Erin & The I'm (Not) Okay, I Promises
<u>Chapter Thirty-Six</u>

Okay. Breathe easy, in through the nose, out through the mouth. All those breathing exercises I could never quite figure out. Still, I do it. Again. Again. Again. I tighten my grip on the steering wheel then let go, my shoulders slumping with the release.

Jesus. What am I going to do?

Yes. That's right, look over and smile at Evan. This is a good song, yes. No. I'm not on the verge of a mental breakdown. Nope. Everything is fine. Just fine, thanks. Charleston has no significance to me as a destination. None whatsoever. I am so *goddamn* happy to be going to a town that has no meaning to me in order to possibly meet the man who spermed (yep, I'm using sperm as a verb now) me into existence. Everything is fine. So fine it may as well be Tom Holland's butt in the Spider-Man suit.

Maybe there's another Charleston in Illinois that is also roughly four hours northeast of my hometown. Why am I so *monumentally* stupid that it took me this long to figure out? Maybe we'll never make it there.

One could hope.

No, no, I don't mean that.

Everything is fine.

Erin & The Go Big Blues
<u>Chapter Thirty-Seven</u>

Sure enough, this is the same exit I pulled off of just four months ago with my mom, back when my dead dad was still at least my dad, back when I still had my valedictorian speech safely ahead of me, motivating me to get through the spring semester without losing my shit, back when we first decided to (ugh) Go Big Blue and claim Eastern Illinois University as my future college home. It's sad how that was just a few months ago. It seems both further and less in the past than that.

Why does heartache have such a way of simultaneously crunching and stretching time?

Evan still hasn't picked up on it though. Surprise! He must not have been paying attention when I told him where I'd be going this fall. Sometimes I wonder if I'm just another member of the audience to him, a blank, faceless audience that will hang on his every word for hours on end. Anxiety Brain stretches out and yawns, "I've been trying to tell you."

Ah, it's barely past two pm. You could've slept in longer if you wanted.

"So much for me not showing up when Evan's around, huh?" Anxiety Brain volleys back.

Yep.

"So much for college being your escape from all this too?" Anxiety Brain cracks its knuckles to really get going. "Good luck focusing on your schoolwork while knowing your REAL dad is right there in your new town."

Well, we don't really know that he's for sure Bio-Man.

"Come on, he definitely is. Maybe you can strike up a relationship with him."

Ugh, please stop.

"No matter where you go on campus, he'll probably always be within a seven-mile radius."

Thanks for that.

"You and Mom could've walked right by him when you visited a few months ago and not even known."

Well aware of that, thanks. And, hey, I don't appreciate you referring to MY mom as Mom.

"She's as much as mine as she is yours. I'm just excited that we get to finally meet Dad," Anxiety Brain says before slinking back into the recesses of my brain.

That's right, bitch, walk away.

"What was that?" Anxiety Brain comes back in.

Nothing.

"So, are you excited?" Evan asks as we pull into the small town of Charleston. Every marquee we pass screams out, "Welcome Summer Students!"

"Mhmmmm," I say through gritted teeth.

We park across the street from "Hitter's," which is (super unfortunately) the name of (possible) Bio-Man's bar. How I (maybe) share the same DNA with someone who would name their sports bar Hitter's in this day and age is as perplexing to me as the fact that we've ended up here in the first place.

The outside is that brown-white brick pattern usually reserved for strip malls. Neon beer lights decorate the windows. The marquee advertises Ladies Night on Wednesdays with half-priced Vegas Bombs (whatever the hell that is).

"So, what do we do now?" I ask Evan, hoping that his answer will be for us to turn around and leave.

"We go inside and eat some lunch." Evan unbuckles his seatbelt and gets out of the car. "Remember, lunch is your favorite."

My body can't be convinced to follow him. For a brief moment, I close my eyes and listen to Fiona settling around me. All the clicks and pops. If only I could just stay here. Maybe I can find the guts to tell Evan that I want to wait out here while he goes in. *You can feel free to tell me absolutely nothing about him,* I would say. *I'll really have no trouble just driving you back, totally unaware of what (possible) Bio-Man looks like. We could even stop for ice cream after.*

Evan taps on my window. "You coming?"

Oh. Eff my life. Of course, I am.

Evan & The Middle-Aged PBR's
<u>Chapter Thirty-Eight</u>

There's a little rainbow triangle in the window of the door. Safe Place for All is written beneath it. Directly below is a far less subtle sign that states: No Assholes Allowed. I tap the sign to show Erin the Pride symbol, my glee probably apparent on my face.

"Don't worry, I'm sure they'll still let you in," Erin says.

By the time her joke hits me, she's already through the door.

The hostess shows us to a corner booth. On the bar & grill scale, Hitter's definitely seems to be more bar than grill. "Not a bad mid-afternoon crowd," I say to Erin as we take our seats, and I mean it, but also, I'm fighting for something, anything to say. She peruses the menu without saying much else while I take the place in. It's actually a pretty cool establishment. Framed film posters line the walls, everything from *Alien* to *Zoolander*. Ro would even be impressed with some of the more obscure titles like *City of God*, *The Lobster*, and *There Will Be Blood*. Of course, there are vintage sports jerseys and stuff, but that's probably more for the clientele than a reflection of the owner's personal taste. An old hip-hop song that my group used to warm up to plays low over the room.

What would life have been like if I was raised by this guy instead of my parents? If he were my dad, I'd probably be more confident—like for real confidence, not the kind I always fake. If he were my dad, I wouldn't have been afraid to apply to some acting programs. If he were my dad, Ro wouldn't be pissed at me for whatever reason. If he were my dad, we'd probably talk about our feelings all the time. He probably would've had a party for me when I came out or he'd say he knew all along and he just wants me to be me. I mean he'd have to be pretty open-minded to own a bar in a college town. Not to mention the rainbow triangle. Who knew one geometric shape of refracted light could make a person so happy?

"Aren't you just so excited?" Maybe if I ask enough times Erin will give me the answer I'm looking for.

"So excited," Erin deadpans behind the shield of her menu.

"I wonder if he's even here," I think out loud. "When I called ahead, they said that he's pretty much always here. Maybe I should ask for him?"

Still nothing to work with from Erin.

"This seems like a pretty cool spot for college kids. Do you see yourself hanging out at a place like this where you go to school?"

No comment from the villager side of the Great Menu Wall.

Then… a man enters the dining room from the kitchen area. He's about six-two with swooped back brownish-blonde hair. He's wearing a vintage faded t-shirt that says *Pabst Blue Ribbon* and form-fitting jeans that don't make him look like he's trying too hard. He's gotta be about mid-forties, which puts him right in the age-range. My throat cinches up.

"Um. Erin." I tap on the table in front of her.

No response.

The man goes behind the counter and says something to one of the dudes who seems like such a regular they may one day retire his bar stool. The dude at the bar laughs.

He's funny! My maybe-dad is funny!

"Erin." I tap on the table again. Come on. How long does it take for her to land on chicken tenders? "Erin."

Still nothing.

The man mixes a drink for a young woman at the end of the bar without asking her what she's drinking. He cracks open a beer for the legendary dude on the soon-to-be-retired bar stool. He wipes down the counter with a white towel. His movements are so refined that I can't help but watch like I'm some nature documentarian crouching in the Outback brush. I can't believe I possibly came from this being who seems so well balanced and has his shit together; he seems so…so…so…goddamn cool. Like he uses the word *goddamn* without it burning his tongue, like he uses it without even thinking about going to hell, like he doesn't even believe that place exists, like he never really considers consequences at all.

As if hearing my thoughts, the man looks up from wiping the bar and catches me looking at him. He smiles and starts walking toward me. "Um…Erin…" I try again.

He's walking right toward me, towards us.

"Erin."

The man that might be my dad is walking right toward me.

"Erin."

He's almost here.

Erin & The Can't Hold Backs

<u>Chapter Thirty-Nine</u>

Tap, tap, tap. "Erin."

Tap, tap, tap. "Um, Erin."

Thankfully, the menu is keeping Evan out of my eyesight because I really might slap the stupid hipster glasses off his stupid hipster face if he keeps it up. It's not like I need to keep looking for chicken strips though. I found them as soon as I picked up the menu. They're almost always in the bottom right corner by the Kids' options.

Tap, tap, tap. "Erin."

"Jesus, Evan!" I slam the menu down.

"Um. Are y'all okay?" The quintessential Standard-Issue-Handsome Man stands at our table, tucking a towel into the back pocket of his jeans. *No.*

"We're fine," I say with the same natural instinct of a bear snatching salmon from a stream. I was born to quickly shut down any unwanted interaction with strangers, especially this particular stranger in this particular place.

"Okay." The guy nods over at Evan. "Your friend was just tapping on the table and staring at me, so I wanted to make sure." He heads back towards the bar. "Brieghlyn should be back with your drinks shortly."

"That was a close one," I say before I finally glance over at Evan. He's pressing into the booth so hard we may have to call the paramedics. At least he finally seems to be on my level. Now we can get the eff out of here. I grab my bag and do the butt-scoot thing us short girls have to do to get out of the booth.

Dad's Random Bits of Unsolicited Advice #29: Don't be afraid to leave an uncomfortable situation. Ever.

"What're you doing?" Evan doesn't peel himself from the booth.

"What do you mean *what am I doing?*" I use my well-honed library voice, but from the way it quivers, I know I'm just moments away from losing my composure. "We came, we saw, dude, let's go."

Brieghlyn comes back with our waters and sets them down. "Are you guys ready to order or…." She glances from Evan to me. Neither of us responds. "I'll come back," she says, flipping her small notebook closed.

Evan just looks at me like he doesn't care if we stay or I go. So, I leave, past the neon lights, past the multiple flat screens replaying the same sports highlights on mute, past the fake-ass slot machines that my (real) dad used to hate so much (he called them an additional tax on the poor), past the obviously hungover frat boys in their wrinkled collared shirts, past the defeated souls here on a Saturday afternoon too tired to even look my way. All the while, I'm too proud to look back, but I hope Evan is following after me.

The "fresh" air doesn't calm me down like I thought it would. If anything, I feel more like crumpling up in a ball in the parking lot than ever. Over there by the shiny motorcycle seems like a decent spot. I could just nuzzle into the parking block, call it my own: This Space Reserved for Mental Breakdowns.

The door squeals open behind me.

"Erin," Evan calls.

I'm so relieved to hear his voice, but I keep walking. Being here and being okay are two ideas that can't coexist. "Erin," Evan says again, coming up alongside me. "What's wrong?"

"Nothing." I can't look him in the eyes, if I do, there's a hundred percent chance of tears. The only thing worse than a sad cry is an angry one and right now I'm two weather fronts merging. "Let's just go. Please."

"No. Seriously, what's wrong?"

I shake my head. "Do you really have to ask that? Do you really not know?" I face him. "I'm going to school here next month, Evan."

Evan narrows his eyes at me. "Ooookay. I must've forgotten. Sorry." Except when he says, "sorry" it feels more like a dagger than an apology.

"I've told you that, more than once actually. It was one of the first things I ever said to you. You'd think someone would remember something like that. I'm starting to wonder if you just check out whenever someone's not talking about you."

"Whoa." Evan stumbles back like I just punched him in the jaw. "So just like that, you're going to leave?"

"Yep."

"Is this just what you do when stuff gets hard, you run away? You know, I'm starting to sense a theme here," Evan smiles like he's joking.

My brain is an old-school computer trying to process too many words at once. My mouth just hangs open like one of those rainbow spiraling beach balls. Then when it comes, it comes like a tidal wave of pop-up windows, eradicating all in its path.

"Wow. Are you kidding me right now? Is this another one of your bad jokes? Because most of the time, I can't even tell. Did you ever think the reason why your friend got picked over you is because you're just not funny? And the reason why he's mad at you is because you're a shitty friend!" I'm yelling. It took me precisely one hour to become a hysterical screaming freshman on my college sidewalk. "I'm sure this whole thing is some sort of late-teenage identity crisis, but it would've been nice, just really *fucking* nice, Evan, if you would've chosen to do something that didn't have to include me. Like, I don't know just asking out Christian or signing up for acting classes at a community college or I don't know, texting your supposed best friend that you're sorry for being a jerk. Any of those things, literally any of those things, would've been better than this."

"Okay." Evan looks to the ground and nods. "I deserve that."

"You knew I didn't want to see him, but you brought me here anyway." My voice loses its edge. My cheeks are hot, so I just know my face is balloon red right now.

"Erin...I..."

"But we saw him, so can we just go?"

I take a step toward my car, but Evan doesn't move.

"We can't just leave," he says without looking at me.

"We don't owe him anything. More importantly, he doesn't owe us anything. He chose to be anonymous for a reason. He has probably forgotten we've ever existed. No, worse, he never even *knew* we existed. And—And! We don't even know if he's for sure the donor in the first place."

"I know. I have to find out. I have to stay."

"Fine." I resume walking to my car. The sun beats on my exposed shoulders with each step across the sticky hot parking lot. Why did I ever wear this stupid dress? The thought of even getting dressed this morning, looking at myself in the mirror, feeling somewhat hopeful that this wouldn't all be a big shit show, it all just makes me want to scream right now. How could I be this dumb again?

I'm eager to hear Evan's footsteps behind me, but they never come. Once I reach my car, I turn back to see him still waiting on the sidewalk where I left him. The sun blares on behind him, making me squint against it, leaving just an outline of Evan, a black space cut out of the blue sky where Evan should be. I wait for him to say something else, like "Sorry I made you come here" or "Please don't leave, I need you here," or "Erin, you're more important than this man, I'm coming with you," but he doesn't say any of that.

"We passed an Amtrak station a couple miles back. You can get a train back to your car," I say then I get in my car and slam the door.

As I pull away, I see Evan in my rearview through the swirl of dust. By the time I reach the end of the block, he turns around and heads back inside Hitter's.

I wonder if it's the last time I'll ever see him.

Evan & The Great Expectations
<u>Chapter Forty</u>

My whole life has been a series of unmet expectations. There's always been some barrier in front of me, some hurdle that I've convinced myself I have to get over in order to be happy. *If I could just come out as my real self to my loved ones, if I could just get out from under my parents' roof, if I could just get on the national improv team, if I could just get out of my hometown, if I could just get a boy to like me, if I could just find my real dad...if I could just...do anything.*

Erin's brake lights flare up at the stop sign at the end of the block. I turn away. I can't stand to watch her disappear.

A different old hip-hop song plays as I reenter the bar. I retake my seat at our table like nothing ever happened. I plan for an excuse that I'll never have to give. Other than me, no one cares—or probably even notices—that Erin left, but playing out the scene occupies my mind, so I lean into it. Erin was right, of course. Why didn't I use my newfound motivation in some sort of positive direction that didn't have to involve her? Then the answer comes to me...

I was too afraid to do anything alone. It explains a lot.

"Everything okay?" Our waitress dips around the corner, glancing from Erin's vacant seat to me.

"Yeah. We're good."

"Ready to order?"

"Oh. Um, no, I think I'm just going to stick with water for now, thanks."

"Great." The waitress leaves.

Erin's empty side mocks me. I pull out my phone and swipe

through to her last message to me. Just yesterday, my barrage of GIFs, everything was so hopeful then. Part of me wishes that she would text me, tell me she's sorry, that she's coming back to get me. Once, I even think I notice the little ellipsis bubbles pop up, but they come and go so quickly that I'm left wondering if I imagined them in the first place like a specter floating just on the periphery of my sightline, bringing a fresh understanding of the term: ghosted.

I could always message her now. Four separate times, I draft out a text asking her to come pick me up, but each time I backspace all the words out. Do I want her to come back because I'm sorry for wanting to stay or because I'm scared of making the next move on my own?

Again, I know the answer. I'm done with making decisions—or rather not making them—because of fear. I made my choice to stay and talk to this dude so that's exactly what I'm going to do.

I get up from the booth and start walking towards him. *Try to think of it as an improv show.* We already got the erratic lighting and braggadocious hip-hop songs. The regulars sitting around the bar may as well be an inattentive audience. I already have the scene suggestion: *Donor kid reaching out to the man who may be his anonymous donor?* Hilarity is bound to ensue.

His back is to me as I take a stool at the bar. Sports highlights play overhead. Players with their names on the backs of their jerseys run across a field, somewhere every one of those players has someone that feels so proud of them, so proud to share that last name.

I clear my throat. Adrenaline rolls down my spine. Here we go…

"Excuse me, is your name Rick?"

Erin & The In-Between

<u>Chapter Forty-One</u>

I'm lost driving around the streets of Charleston. Or perhaps more specifically, I'm lost somewhere between sobbing and screaming, somewhere between wanting to drive ninety-five the whole way home and returning promptly to Hitter's, somewhere between wanting to text Evan "FUCK YOU!" and "I'M SO SORRY," somewhere between wanting to drive until I hit water and wanting to pull over and ask Mom to come pick me up, somewhere between in-control and definitely-not.

Driving around Charleston is strange, like going to an alien planet only to find it looks a lot like earth. Mom and Dad met in college. They always said that's where they made all their real friends. When Mom and I first visited campus here, I couldn't help but imagine myself with my new well-read cool friends, walking down every sidewalk together, laughing, sharing some inside joke that only we know, maybe holding up our one wild friend that had too much to drink, smiles plastered on our faces because we know we're making a core memory. But now as I drive aimlessly down these damned side roads, past all the houses that could perfectly be transplanted in Langford and no one would ever know the difference, I wonder if Evan was right. Leaving my hometown isn't going to solve all my problems. Those bullshit pop-punk platitudes are best left for Blaide and his dumbass friends.

Change isn't going to happen unless I make it.

I keep driving, further out of town, passing through other small towns that are little more than a sign announcing their existence and a gas station serving as their cultural hub. I never plugged my phone into the aux so there's just this fuzz sound on the radio that I don't turn down. The only other sound is the road beneath my tires and the wind throwing itself against Fiona every so often.

There isn't a destination on this planet that sounds good right now.

Think I'll just keep driving into oblivion.

Chapter Forty-Two

Rick holds back one finger to tell me to wait a moment while he takes another Coors Light to the guy posted up by the cash register. My hands leave sweaty palm-turkeys on the bar. I tap the countertop awkwardly, trying to match the beat to the hip-hop song like I'm a natural. Rick wipes his hands on a towel and turns to face me. I hesitate when his eyes settle on me, searching his blue irises, stunned that they match up with mine.

He looks me up and down. "How can I help you?"

All my improv training flies out the window. "Uh, can I get a Sprite?"

Rick arches one eyebrow at me. "Sure." Without breaking eye-contact, he grabs a glass and shoots it full of Sprite. "Now mind telling me what you're really here for? First, you were staring at me from your booth over there. Now, you're asking my name. If you're going to serve me then just grow a pair and do it."

I give an awkward chuckle, thinking he's kidding, but his intense stare doesn't waver. "No, uh, I'm not here to...I just..."

"What then? Did Kat send you? Are you another one of her little boy-toy lawyers? I already told you people I gave her everything."

Learning a lot of things about the man who may be my dad today. Money problems, legal issues, and misogynist tendencies, not great, but still, it's better than being a homophobic hypocrite. "No, uh, my name is Evan Prucasyk." My tongue moves like it's wearing an itchy sweater. "I'm, uh—"

"Hey Rick?" The Dude shouts down the bar. "You got another

of those missionaries there? Want to show'em what we did with the last Choir Boy?"

Rick laughs at the old guy's joke without looking away from me. "Nah, you know we have that Amish village over in Tuscola, they find their way in from time to time. It's just another Amish kid on Rumspringa!" Rick shouts back, several more people join in laughing.

For the first time in a while, I'm on the wrong side of the laughter. Doesn't feel great.

"Hey, we got plenty of Rum-shott-a, why don't you give him some? Put some fuzz on his tennis balls!" The Dude follows up. The whole bar is really yes-and-ing all over me and I have no choice but to sit here like an idiot and take it. It's humiliating.

When the laughter dies down, Rick leans in closer to me. The menacing bite of vodka lingers on his breath. My stomach lurches. "Okay, kid, we're having a little fun. Why don't you just tell me why you're here."

My eyes flick back and forth between his. My mouth hangs open, and…the words aren't coming. Wherever this is going, I can't see it.

"OOOOOOOkay." Rick turns from me with an eye-roll.

"I was born at Michael Reese Hospital," I say to Rick's back.

He stops without turning around.

"My birth father was an anonymous donor," I say, taking one big step off the ledge, knowing well there's no safety net, no Erin, no Ro, no team jumping in at any moment to save the day. I'm on my own.

Rick rubs his jaw with his back still turned.

"I thought you might know something about him," I say.

Rick faces me, his tone unreadable. "Yeah, I might. Meet me out back after my shift is over at eight o'clock."

I nod. "I'll be here."

Erin & The This-Isn't-Happenings
<u>Chapter Forty-Three</u>

Once I get myself good and lost, I begin to fade into a nice dissociative state. Farmlands and cornfields blur by in my peripheral. Green signs label streets and point to towns that only locals know. White noise plays over the radio, blocking out everything else. Every now and then, the rotten smell of roadkill seeps through the vents. Nothing fazes me. Just keep driving, deeper and deeper I sink. Not feeling anything. Not thinking anything. Until...

Fiona begins to slow down in a recognizable fashion. I'm pressing the gas, pressing the gas, and nothing. A chorus of Emergency Lights blow up across the dash like I just gave the wrong answer in a hacky game show. I manage to pull off to the side of the road. The image of Evan and I outside the Cone in Hoakie greets me when I reach for my phone. There's no signal so instead of getting out and walking to find one (like I should), I start reading through old text conversations with Evan. All our little plans and inside jokes, the things that only the two of us understand. A half hour passes, and I haven't accomplished anything.

I squeeze my phone off. I get out and pop the trunk, retrieving my trusty gas can and a hoodie. I grab my half-drank bottle of water from my cup-holder and lock the car doors, clicking the clicker several times just to make sure it's good and locked (wouldn't want anyone to steal my ever-growing collection of discarded straw wrappers in the floorboard). I look to the horizon. The road stretches on forever in either direction.

I pick a path and start walking.

Evan & The Dead Lines

<u>Chapter Forty-Four</u>

The humidity is so unmerciful that it may as well go through a long-drawn-out process to conceive a child and then eighteen years later kick that child out on their ass just for being who they are. So, my sweaty shirt and I decide to stake out in the air-conditioned campus library for a while. Erin should almost be home by now. Reading through our old text threads just bums me out. I'm equal parts pissed at her for leaving me and pissed at myself for letting her.

I pull up her contact and click on it. Straight to voicemail. Try again. Same. What the hell? Is she ignoring my calls? Did I get blocked?! That's so petty. What if I wanted to apologize? What if I truly needed help? It's not like I have phone battery to waste right now and she knows that.

Hope she's happy with the choices she's made.

Erin & The Fucking Fucks
<u>Chapter Forty-Five</u>

Fuck every stupid fucking decision I've ever fucking made in my entire fucking life.

I'm starving. My feet throb. My back aches. My thighs are chafed so bad that all I want is to match with a frozen bag of peas on HookUps so I can then take it out on a nice date, tell it my deepest heart's desires, touch it playfully on the corner when it makes me laugh, later share a milkshake, and then squeeze that bag of peas between my thighs all night long while a mutually agreed upon movie plays quietly in the background (with subtitles on, of course).

It's hard to know how long I've been walking since I've turned off my phone, but, since I'm daydreaming about hooking up with a bag of frozen veggies, it has to be over an hour. I've thrown on my hoodie to help protect my shoulders and neck against the sun (too bad my exposed calves can't say the same). So now your girl is walking tar-hot country roads in a black sweatshirt with the hood pulled up like Michael Myers doing the walk of shame.

Sweat soaks through everything. All I want (besides a frozen bag of peas conjugal visit) is to just get the fucking gas and go home.

"Giving up is always a viable option, you know you're pretty good at that." Anxiety Brain sips from a tall glass of lemonade. "Just lay in the road and wait for a circling pack of vultures to close in."

I'm too exhausted to respond. I turn my phone on to check the signal. Still nothing so I squeeze it back off. I need to conserve as much battery as possible.

A pickup truck whirrs down the road behind me, a cape of dust billowing in its wake. Any hope I had for a ride out of this hell evaporates when the driver slows down. The man behind the steering wheel is all dark thinning hair beneath a camouflage hat and a pair of aviator sunglasses sitting atop a shark smile. "Call it brilliant detective skills, but are you by chance out of gas?" He laughs at his own joke when I don't. "Want a ride?"

"No, thanks."

"You sure? Ride in the back if you want."

"No. I'm good." I resume walking.

"C'mon," he eases off the brake, allowing the truck to keep up with me as I walk. "Heat index is way past triple digits today."

"Nope. No thank you." My heart rate picks up with my pace.

"Closest gas station is still a good three or four miles away." He cocks his head in the direction I'm walking. "At least let me get you a drink of water."

"Nope. I'm good. Thanks." I grip my keys in my hoodie pocket, ready to strike and run if I need to.

"There's a storm rolling in from the south."

"I'll be fine."

"Little girl like you doesn't need to be out here walking alone."

"Thanks for your concern. A friend is coming to get me soon."

"I'm not going to hurt you."

That's not near as reassuring as you think. "No. Thanks. I'm just walking to meet my friend. He's coming to give me a ride."

I can feel his stare more than I see it. The truck continues to idle alongside me. A cornfield stretches to the horizon on my left. Sprinting through it won't be a good time, but that's what I'll do if I hear that truck door open.

"Well, how about I take you to meet him?"

"He'll be here any second now. Thanks."

The man spits on the road. A few more seconds pass. "Suit yourself then." The truck speeds away, spraying me with gravel and exhaust.

Three miles.

Three miles, he said.

I can make that.

Evan & The Fateful Burritos

<u>Chapter Forty-Six</u>

The sun has begun its descent on the western horizon. I wait for the light to change so I can cross the main drag back over to Hitter's. It's still a little early, but I'll find a good spot to wait for Rick. Scattered groups of summer students flow out towards the bars and house parties that border campus. Their laughter and shouted conversations steady the queasiness in my stomach. I can do this.

There's a small line out the front door of Hitter's comprised of cute guys in collared shirts and done-up girls in short skirts. A muscle-bound bald dude with spiraling tattoos down each of his bulging biceps keeps checking their IDs before ushering them inside. Thumping dance music thunders from within Hitter's, peaking each time the door opens.

The side door opens with a boom drawing the attention of everyone in line. "I ain't coming back anyway!" Rick shouts back as he stumbles into the parking lot. The bouncer gets to his feet. Rick spits on the concrete while staring him down. "Don't you try, Justin. I hired you. You owe me." Justin sits down, which Rick must take as a sign to continue. "Prick bastards, I used to own all your asses!" Rick keeps walking backwards.

No. No. His feet start to get tangled up.

Don't do it. Don't do it.

A few dudes in the line cheer as Rick trips over a parking block and bites the dust mid-rant. Justin chuckles with them too. Allegiances be damned. "Where you going, Rick! The night's not even started!" One of the guys in line jeers at him. Rick waves at them from the ground like a clown who knows what he is.

After a moment of hesitation, I hurry over and help Rick to his feet.

"Thanks, buddy," he slurs. It's obvious he doesn't remember me from earlier, but that's okay. All I want is to just ask a couple questions. We don't have to end up pals on Acquaintances or anything.

"Thanks, buddy," Rick says again with his arms around my shoulder. His breath is hot and sticky on the side of my face. A hint of aftershave that smells like leather lurks underneath it. "This is me," he gestures to a motorcycle parked in a handicapped stall.

"Um." I glance back at the line or Justin for help, but they've all moved on with their evening. I successfully shed Rick from my shoulders, leaving him to sway in the parking lot. "I don't think that's a good idea." I scan the surrounding buildings. Then I see it, bright neon lights shining like a beacon through the early summer dusk, BURRITOS AS BIG AS YOUR HEAD. I have to say this moment is as close as I've come to believing in God in a long time.

"Why don't we get something to eat?" I ask him.

"You buying?"

"Sure."

"Well then, I'm in."

Evan & The Potential Puzzle Pieces
<u>Chapter Forty-Seven</u>

The man behind the counter smiles as I enter. "Welcome!"

Then, as quickly as it came, his smile vanishes.

"Hey, Jose!" Rick triumphantly yells as he barges through the door. The man behind the counter scowls in Rick's direction.

"Get me the Large El Paso with a side of nachos." Rick steadies himself with my shoulder, shouting in my ear like we're in a crowded club. "With extra hot sauce, extra sour cream, no pico, and a pop."

I just nod, not wanting to say anything that could encourage Rick, as everything he seems to say and do so far makes me want to curl up into an armadillo ball until he walks away.

I get in line. It's usually hard to tell with places if they're using alliteration because it's an easy sell or if it's very literal, like are the Flying Burrito Brothers actual brothers? I consider sharing this little clever insight with Rick but given how he's eyeing the trashcan like it may be a good place to puke and rally, I decide to let it go. Erin would know where I'm coming from though. So would Ro.

A couple of students wait in front of me. Tidbits of their conversation float back. Brief flickers of what their life must be like here. Talk of summer finals, the impending fall semester, and how Gia's roommate Bianca is so inconsiderate. If Rick wasn't with me, maybe I could appear like one of them, here studying over the summer, a college student with their own rich social life, owning small parts of this campus like everyone else, all while learning new things about themselves, building their own dreams for what life will be like when they leave this place.

When our order is called, I carry our food over to the booth where Rick's slouched against the wall. Rick snatches his burrito off my tray, barely even tearing away the foil before taking a bite. "Hey, Jose! I said no pico!" Rick shouts at the man behind the counter. The man just raises a solitary middle finger while staring Rick down. I try my best to give off *I-Do-Not-Know-This-Man* vibes despite us sharing a table and possibly fifty percent of my DNA.

I watch Rick chow down on his burrito. In a span of less than thirty minutes of *knowing* Rick, I've already went from desperately searching for likenesses to hoping that I don't find any. Sadly, there are plenty—besides the "life in shambles" part—there's his jawline, blue eyes, height, and his full head of light-brown hair. If there are various incarnations of me, based off decisions made for left or right turns at each of the forks ahead, then...Rick is definitely the end of me at one of those.

Rick continues eating without stopping to ask why I wanted to see him or say thanks for the food or, you know, even acknowledge my existence. Natural instincts kick in to just let this scene play out as it would, reacting in subtle ways, nudging the steering wheel bit by bit in the direction I want to go. For a while, this is exactly what I do. After all, I'm hungry and, hey, I got this far. That should be enough right?

It's not though. Aidy is right there in my head, telling me I'm watching again.

"It's cool that your bar has that all-inclusive sticker in its doorway. I'm all for LGBTQ rights too," I say, raising an awkward power fist even though that's not our thing at all.

"Huh?" Rick gawps at me with his mouth full.

"I really like the movie posters in your bar and the music playing too. Did you pick those out?"

"What?" Rick glares at me like I just asked him to name his favorite anime film. "I didn't have anything to do with any of that shit. Keith did. Says it appeals to the hipster college pricks that go there."

"Why'd you name it Hitter's?"

"Was going to name it after a certain World War Two leader but that's not exactly PC." Rick does air quotes.

I nearly choke. Salsa burns my nose.

Rick cracks a smile at his own joke. "Just kidding. Hitter was my name when I ran with my biker buddies. It used to be a place where we all hung out for a while."

I chuckle, more uncomfortable than humored. "So, you own the bar?"

"Used to." Rick thumbs a dollop of sour cream from his cheek before putting it back in his mouth. "Tax problems. Had to sell it to that asshole, Keith. He's probably the one that reported me in the first place."

"Are you worried about not having a job?"

Rick cocks one eyebrow at me. "What're you talking about?"

"You were kicked out tonight."

"Oh." Rick snickers at himself. A flicker of self-awareness that I previously didn't think was possible. He returns to being a person right in front of my eyes. "Shit happens. It was pretty much the end of my shift anyway. I get a little mouthy at the end of my shifts sometimes. I'll be back tomorrow. They always take me back."

"Just like Kat?" I ask, calling back to a name he said at the bar.

Rick stops eating and sits up straighter. "Where do I know you from again?"

It's a 'cops are coming in' type of sobering up. I swallow. "You just mentioned her name before," I say, redirecting the scene back to a more neutral territory.

"Oh." Rick slumps back in his seat again. He eyes me up while scratching his jaw. "No." Rick shakes his head, pointing one long finger at me. "You asked me something earlier at the bar, what was it?"

There's no point in stringing this out any longer. "Did you work at Michael Reese Hospital near Chicago about eighteen years ago?"

"Yeah." Rick holds eye contact with me. "I was an X-Ray technician for a bit after I got my certification, why?"

"When you were working there, did you make any…um…biological donations to the fertility department?"

"I sold some sperm, yeah," Rick says like we're talking about something as mundane as property taxes. "What about it?"

"Well…" Here comes the moment of truth. "According to a DNA site online, we share some of the same relatives, and there's a possibility that I could be your son."

"Hey." Rick leans in across the small table. I don't pull away. I wonder if he's going to put his hand on mine, tell me how this is the moment that he's been waiting for, some sign from a higher power to get his life back on track.

Instead, Rick smacks his lips like he didn't hear anything I just said. Part of me hopes that he didn't. Bitter notes of alcohol still lurk on his breath.

"Can you give me a ride someplace else? There's somewhere I need to go right quick."

As much as every brain cell in my head, every fiber of my being, every natural instinct in my body tells me to follow my grade school anti-drug PSA and "just say NO," I can't.

I have to play this through to the end.

"I didn't drive here," I say. "But I'll order us a RYDE."

Erin & The Edge
<u>Chapter Forty-Eight</u>

When I reach the outer edge of a small town, I check my phone again. One bar. Not enough to stream a movie, but at least it should be enough to call a RYDE. I pull up the map. Loading. Loading. Loading. Loading. C'mon, mother-effer. Loading. Loading. Loading. I shake the thing like that may help. I hold it up to the sky. Loading. Loading. Finally, it comes through. The closest driver is…thirty miles away in Charleston. Great.

I resume walking. I've already made it this far. At least it shouldn't be much further to a gas station. Maybe it'll even be one of those stations with like some super greasy fried chicken or super greasy pizza. All small towns have to have a combo gas-station/quasi-gross restaurant where everything smells and tastes like onion rings and is sure to give you a bellyache. It's in our charter.

"Ah, glad you're still trying to find the bright side," Anxiety Brain says. "That just proves how dumb you are. You're so incredibly dumb. It's stunning that you were smart enough to earn valedictorian, but not smart enough to put gas in your car. You know, the car with the broken gas gauge? Seems like a smart person would've considered that before driving aimlessly into unknown territory."

Fair point. But I've managed to do alright for myself.

"Ehhh, have you though?"

Yeah.

"Have you?"

Yes.

"Have you?"

People like me okay.

"Exactly. People like you the precise minimum amount. You've managed to fool some of them so far, but you'll be exposed when you go to college."

Hey, I got in. That proves I should be there.

"Oh, sure. You know the truth though. Everyone just felt bad for you."

That's not true. I made awesome grades and worked my ass off.

"That's right. You just worked hard. You're not actually smart. That won't work in college."

We'll see. If it doesn't work out at least I'll make some new friends in the process.

"Haha, new friends. Everyone will hate you. They'll see right through to what you are: an annoying little small town try-hard with nothing to say."

No, they won't. I have important things to say.

"Like what? Say one significant thing right now. Go ahead, I'll wait."

Fuck you.

"Bravo, so clever and revolutionary. So much for getting new friends. Blaide will probably dump your ass before you finally get the nerve."

Joke's on you, that still sounds pretty great.

"Oh, it does, does it? Well, enjoy being alone for the rest of your life. No one will ever love you."

That's…not true.

"What are you even going to do when there aren't any more good grades to earn? What will you even be good at then?"

...

"You won't even have the option of getting knocked up and falling into a loveless marriage. You're so ugly, boring, and basic no one will want you."

...

"You can get a nice opioid addiction if you want. I hear those are quite fashionable in small towns nowadays."

...

"The few people who do love you just do so because they have to."

...

"Evan is probably off having the time of his life with *Real* Dad right now. Now that he has that familial connection, he won't need you anymore."

...

"You ran away and let him down anyway."

...

"He was right. That's what you do every time you have the chance."

...

"Running away over doing something brave every time, you're so weak and pathetic. Everyone sees it."

...

"Your dead dad is probably thrilled that he's not actually related to a loser like you. You couldn't even do the last thing he asked you to do. You're such a disappointment."

...

"Your mom would be better off without you around. She could start over. Remarry. Maybe have some sweet step-kids that don't treat her like shit. She wouldn't have to worry about balancing Dead Dad's overdue bills with paying for your stupid college. Without you around, she could be happy again."

...

"You should do all of them a favor and step in front of the next car speeding by. It would be the kindest thing you've ever done for anyone."

...

"Do it."

...

"Do it."

...

"Do it."

...

"Do it."

...

"Do it."

...

"DO IT!"

Evan & The Vapors

<u>Chapter Forty-Nine</u>

The house's address numbers peel off the faded yellow paint. Christmas lights hang from the gutter with a definitely-more-than-just-six-months'-past-due ambiance. Three concrete steps lead up to the front door with weed-filled would-be-flower beds on each side. A TV flickers through the tattered curtains as Rick walks in without knocking. I turn back to the darkened street in time to watch the RYDE driver peel off. All the other houses on the street are dark from either sleep or abandonment. Rick sticks his head back out through the door. "Dude, come on."

The smell of rotting wood and cat litter hits me as I step through the threshold. 1970s wood-paneling covers the living room walls reflecting the images flashing across the TV. Some reality show with people that are so insanely hot that it has infected their brains plays to an empty couch and worn recliner. A light comes from the back of the house, through the kitchen, some further sign of life.

"Hey!" Rick calls to the light. "I'm here. Got a friend with me."

No response. Fear coils tighter in my chest. Something about being called Rick's *friend* does nothing to calm me.

"Hey!" Rick yells again. "My friend wants to meet you!"

I look at Rick with a mixture of no-way and WTF?

Still no answer. Rick steps toward the kitchen, the whole house creaking beneath him like an old ship. "Hey!" Rick calls again.

Finally, there's a sound in response. Someone's retching with the force of a thousand hungover college students. Figures if they're any friends of Rick.

"Oh, no," Rick says with a hint of tenderness in his voice before disappearing into the back without so much a glance in my direction.

It's then that I take in the full scope of the house. My heartbeat begins to slow a little. Pictures of Rick as a Little Leaguer, as a cheerful dragon on Halloween, as a bright-eyed high school graduate, as a college student, as a longhaired motorcyclist, are propped up on the end tables and entertainment center. Crooked frames hang on the wall with seven-year-old toothless Rick grinning out, unafraid of all the life he's yet to live. Judging by the pictures alone, it would appear that Rick's life ended at twenty-eight.

"Um." Rick comes back around the corner, scratching at his neck. "Do you care to sit? It's going to be a minute."

"That's okay," I say without taking a seat. Just beyond the kitchen, I can hear Rick talking to someone with a soft voice. A feeble old lady voice responds back to him. This is his mom's house. We're in Rick's mom's house. Ergo we could be in my grandma's house. This night surely can't get any weirder.

A minute later, Rick creaks back through the house towards me. "She wants to meet you."

As if viewing myself from above, I find my body walking through the house. Floorboards groan beneath my every step like they may give away entirely where I'll fall into whatever sludge is created from decades piled upon decades of regret and spoiled expectations. Passing through the kitchen, Rick stops to pull a Hamm's from the fridge. He cracks it open with one hand. The toilet hisses from the bathroom, the smell of mildewed bathmats. The hallway's so narrow we can't stand side by side. More yellowed photos of Rick hang there, all full of hope and potential.

Then we're standing awkwardly in a small bedroom. Clothes litter the floor. Worn brown carpet shows through in a few places like stepping-stones across a shallow stream. An unmistakable acidic smell emanates from the wastebasket beside her bed.

"Mom," Rick says softly. "I want you to meet your grandson, Ethan—"

"Evan," I correct.

"What Ricky?" His mom sits up in bed as surprised as I am to see me standing in her bedroom. Gray hair sprouts from her head in random patches. She looks from him to me for an answer.

A life of bombing in front of improv audiences has failed to prepare me for this moment. "Test…I took a test."

Rick grimaces at me. "Remember, Mom, when I was working at the hospital. I told you I made some donations to help pay for school?" Rick says and I'm thankful that he at least put it more delicately for his mom than he did at the restaurant. Erin will never believe this. *Hey, you know how you left me on my own to potentially meet our real dad? Well, not only did I meet him, but I also heard way more of his life story than I ever intended, AND I met our dying grandmother. Not to mention, I saw our maybe-dad fall off a curb with his butt-crack hanging out of his too-tight jeans.* If anything, she'll at least feel better about her decision to leave.

"Yes," Rick's mom says, her voice wavering and unsteady, like it may break if she stretches it beyond just a few words at a time. "So, this is…"

"This is Evan. He's your grandson. He's coming to college here in the fall—"

"Wait. I never said that," I try to correct.

"He's super smart and handsome," Rick continues.

"Can't argue there." Weird chuckle.

"And he's got a hot little girlfriend—" Rick keeps going.

"Wait...what?" I say before it hits me. *Oh, god please don't let him mean...*

"Both of them came into my bar earlier today and Evan introduced himself. Seems like he takes after his old man, huh?" For the first time, since leaning on me in order to stay upright, Rick puts his arm around me. "He's really got his life together."

If only.

"What about Aubrey?" His mom asks.

Rick waves her off. "Anyways, I thought you two should meet."

"Oh. Okay," his mom says with her gaze set on Rick.

"Nice to meet you." I give a little wave, relieved that this painful exchange is over. If Evan from six weeks ago could get a flashforward ahead to this moment, he would be so incredibly confused. I step toward the door before Rick puts his hand on my shoulder to stop me.

"I gotta go look for something real quick, Mom. Evan's gonna stay here to talk to you, okay?" Rick nods at me and then steps into the bathroom around the corner. Through the wall, it sounds like Rick is spraying a firehose in there.

"I like your house," I say to block out the sound of Rick peeing. "All the pictures of Rick...that's really cool."

Rick's mom smacks her lips in response. Thirty seconds pass. The humidifier in the corner of the room warbles like it's out of water. The unrelenting stream in the bathroom finally stops. The whole house shudders with the flush of the toilet. Then Rick steps from the bathroom, glaring at me before he heads into another part of the house.

"Do you like watching TV?" I ask Rick's mom. "I—I saw it on in the front room when we came in."

Rick's mom just looks at me with tired, watery eyes that are the same color as mine.

"I like watching TV," I answer my own question when she doesn't say anything. She's recoiling from me like a disgusted audience. I don't blame her.

"Do you like musicals? Most people from your generation tend to. In fact, my friend Ro sometimes says I have more in common with grandmas than I do with people my own age." The sound of furniture being moved comes from the other part of the house. Muffled curses leak through the walls. "Which isn't meant as a slight to people your age by any means. It's just a...just a funny observation." Sweat beads on my forehead.

She doesn't say anything.

"Um...do you have a cat? I thought I smelled...um...I love cats. Or...well...I like them okay." I scratch my neck. "My family's cat, Bridgette, didn't really like me much. But then again, none of them really did." I offer a weak smile.

Rick's mom just stares at me blankly. Table legs scrape against linoleum. I can hear Rick muttering to himself through the paper-thin walls.

"How long have you lived here?" I shift my weight from one foot to the other. A cat-clock on her dresser stares at me with dead eyes, the hands permanently stuck at 4:35. I swear the floor is tilting beneath me.

"A while," Rick's mom answers in a high, reedy voice as she looks at me with mild concern. The humidifier gurgles aggressively.

Sweat drips down my back. It's suffocating in here. I glance toward the hallway. A faint rectangle of light on the brown carpet. The toilet continues hissing. "Almost done," Rick calls from the front room. His shadow imposes its dark figure against the hallway wall.

Rick's mom is staring at me when I turn back around. "Um." I pick up her humidifier, unplugging it from the wall. "Do you want me to fill this?"

Rick's mom slowly nods for me to go on. I take the two steps to the bathroom. I shut the door behind me, but it drifts open. I shut it again only for it to drift open again. Rick's shadow passes, stopping briefly in front of the door. I shut it for a third time and slide the pin lock in place. It holds this time. My hair is slick with sweat. I turn on the cold water and palm it over my face. Then I straighten back up, banging my head on the medicine cabinet door that hangs open. Empty pill bottles fall out and skitter around the sink. I quickly put them back.

Then I stand at the sink, washing my hands with the tiny shard of soap left in the dish. From the other side of the wall, I can hear Rick murmuring to his mom in a soft tone. I wonder if he found whatever he was looking for. A big paper McDonald's cup sits on the top of the sink. I use it to fill the humidifier.

When I step into the hallway Rick's sitting at his mom's side, holding a washcloth to her forehead. Rick scowls at me. "What were you doing in there?"

My cheeks burn. "Sorry."

"What's that for?" Rick juts his chin at the dripping humidifier.

I take it over and plug it back in. "Sounded like it was out of water." The humidifier begins coughing up a more productive flow of vapors. I can feel Rick's stare on my back. "Hope this helps some," I say to his mom.

"Go wait in the front room," Rick snaps. "We're almost done here."

I head through the kitchen. Trash overflows the can. Old soup cans and fast-food wrappers spill onto the floor. I pick it all up the best I can and consider taking the trash out for—I can't think of her as my grandma. For now, and ever, she will only ever be known as Rick's mom.

Then I notice a baby picture underneath a State Farm magnet on the fridge. It's dated for eight years ago. Below it, there's another picture of a four-year-old girl splashing in puddles with big yellow boots on. I pull it from the fridge and hold it up for closer inspection. Could this be…my baby sister?

"Hey!"

I jump, dropping the photograph on the floor.

"Put that back where you found it." Rick points at me with his non-beer hand. Whatever kindness Rick had in his eyes while talking to his mom is long gone.

"Yeah." I bend over to get it only to drop it again. I snatch it up, hastily placing it underneath the magnet only to have it float down to the ground for a third time. "Sorry." I repeat the process and make sure that it stays this time.

Rick stares me down as he drains his beer. "Let's go."

I start towards the living room door, but Rick doesn't move out of my way. He puts his shoulder into me as he walks towards the fridge for another two beers. Rick pops open one and takes a long swig. Wiping his mouth with the back of his hand, he raises one eyebrow at me. "Alright, now let's go. Son."

A chill descends down my back. If ever there was a scene that needed to be abruptly ended, it's this one. "Actually. Since you're home now and everything." I thumb over my shoulder towards the door. "I'm just going to catch a RYDE back to my car."

Rick steps toward me. The floor screeches the score of a horror movie beneath him. "You said you didn't have your car here."

"Yeah." I chuckle though I know my eyes convey my fear. "I mean I'm just going to catch a RYDE back to my friend."

"Well, that's convenient. I need a ride back to my bike." Rick drains the rest of his first beer and then opens the other. "Let's go," he slaps me hard on the shoulder and pushes past me toward the front door.

Erin & The Hidden Powers

Chapter Fifty

I close my eyes, anchoring myself to the shoulder of the road. A burst of air hits me as the car whooshes by. Once it's safe in the distance, I resume walking. Yellow gas-station lights provide hope less than a mile away. Unfortunately, Anxiety Brain won't shut up.

"Big surprise you've wimped out on following through with something else."

. . .

"Dying now is pretty much the only way to ensure that you're remembered fondly. You've peaked. You'd have a line clear around the funeral home, longer than Dead Dad's even. Madison and all your half-friends would make a big show of how much they mourned you. Blaide would finally dedicate a full album of songs to you. You're better as a memory than in reality anyway."

. . .

"If you did it now, everyone would see it as an accident even."

. . .

"It's predestined really."

. . .

"So why wait?"

. . .

"I mean if you think you're so sad and alone now, just wait until all your loved ones finally give up on you. Just wait until all your friends move onto better and more interesting people. Just wait until you're old when you've wasted all your potential and privilege to amount to absolutely nothing."

...

"I can only imagine what you'll feel like doing then."

...

"It will be so tragic and pitiful, really."

...

"See? It's inevitable. May as well get it over with."

All I can do is put one foot in front of the other. I just need to keep moving forward. Get gas, a Gatorade, and something to eat. I can make it there.

"Keep setting yourself up for disappointment, sweetie."

Grounding myself in the moment would just make things worse. So would most the other advice Dr. Meera used to give me. I sing Camp Cope songs in my head to block out the thoughts.

"You'll never create anything as meaningful as a song."

But they don't quite do the trick.

"Even Blaide can write a song. He's too good for you."

I think about VideoChatting Blaide. He'd probably help me feel better.

"Very brave. I don't know why anyone would ever call you co-dependent."

But I'm almost there. I can do this. I can make it.

A few folks come and go from the Casey's gas station, the sound of slamming truck doors and engines starting. The smell of gasoline and wet concrete. I head straight inside. The air-conditioner blasts my sweaty clothes, sending a shiver through my shoulders. I grab two Red Gatorades (I only call sports drinks by their color, thank you), a slice of cheese pizza, and a Kit-Kat. "Out of gas?" The dude behind the register nods at my gas can.

"Yep."

"That sucks."

"You said it." I swipe my card and head outside to sit on the curb. I plug my phone charger into the outside outlet by the air compressor. Then, I nearly drain my Red Gatorade with one drink. My second polishes it off. If there were a video-game-character energy bar hanging over my head, it would transition from a blinking red to a healthier orange. I start in on my pizza. Not thinking about anything. For the moment, all is quiet in my head. Not currently hating myself. Not currently living unwell. Not currently burning in hell. People continue to walk by like I'm not even here. Thank you for not noticing me.

A memory comes back to me. Ten or eleven years old, riding in the backseat of our old black Dodge Caravan. Mom sat in the passenger seat. Dad drove.

"What superpower would you want if you could have any?" I leaned up between them to ask.

Dad twisted his face up in serious thought. "I'd want to be able to freeze time. Like everyone else in the world would freeze and time would stop, while I could keep on writing or reading all the books I want, maybe I would work out some even. Maybe. Also, the calories I eat then don't count. And then when I'm ready, time could pick up again."

"Well, if your calories don't count, then any burned calories from working out shouldn't count either," Mom cracked.

"Ah, good point. I wouldn't bother with jogging then, but at least

I'd have time to finally binge-watch all forty seasons of *The Simpsons*." Dad smiled over at Mom. "What superpower would you want?"

Mom tapped her finger to her lips. "I like the freezing time idea, but I would want to improve on that some by being able to move back in my life to any specific point in time so I could let a day play out exactly like it happened the first time all over again."

"Good answer." Dad placed his hand on Mom's before calling back to me, "What about you, Air-Bear?"

"I'd want to make multiples of myself. Like just hundreds of me so I could be everywhere, learning everything at once, being everything to everyone."

"My girl, we are the same." Dad caught my eyes in the rearview. "You've thought of this before."

"Sounds exhausting," Mom said.

Dad chuckled. "You said it."

"That or I'd want to be invisible so no one would ever see me."

Mom and Dad cracked up laughing and I shrank back into my seat, never understanding until now why they thought my answers were so funny.

When I finish eating, I fill up my small gas can. Anxiety Brain remains quiet, but I know he'll be back any second. I look to the empty road. Storm clouds flicker in the distance like a lighter struggling to strike. I walk towards them. My phone now has a signal and just enough battery to (hopefully) last the walk back. I pull up Blaide's contact and tap it for a VideoChat.

"Babe, what's up?" Blaide's handsome face fills up my phone screen (seriously, who looks good on VideoChat?). "We're just practicing."

"Cool. Do you, um, have a minute?"

"Sure." Blaide speaks off screen to the guys and starts walking outside. "Where are you?"

"About thirty miles away from Charleston, I think."

"Oh." Blaide's face goes orange beneath a streetlight. "Was it some sort of early college check-in or…" Blaide asks with more curiosity than jealousy.

For some reason, I still feel like lying rather than saying *well, my long-lost half-brother and I came up here to meet our Bio-Man but then I chickened out and left him there. Then I drove on and on until I ran out of gas.*

In the end that is exactly what I say though, and then some.

Dad's Random Bits of Unsolicited Advice #59: When you can't take anymore words, you need to let some out.

"Wow," Blaide says when I finish. "That must've been like—"

"So shitty of me?" I shrug and look away. "Yeah, I know."

"No." Blaide's eyes soften. "Really hard. I was going to say that must've been really hard. All of this, the whole summer, the whole year really, everything you've been through. All of it must've been so damn hard. That's why I always tried my best to distract you."

"Wow, I bet you realllly feel like shit now huh?" Anxiety Brain returns to say. "No way you can do this now."

I blink away tears. "What?"

"I don't know. I just hoped by talking about stupid band stuff, it would, I don't know, distract you. Or at least, get you back to the old-you since you've been so distant lately."

"That's really sweet." I clear my throat as I pass beneath another streetlight. "But I...as hard as it's all been, that isn't what I wanted."

"What do you mean?"

"I want to talk about this stuff," I say with a half-laugh. "I want to talk about it all the time. I want to talk about my dad, about freaking out at graduation, about pulling away from my friends, about not being able to talk with my mom, about finding out I came from a test tube. I want to talk about all of it."

"Oh." Blaide nods. "I'm sorry we didn't then."

"Me too."

"You could've just said something."

"I know."

"I would've listened."

With a sniff, I teeter my hand and smile, hoping to break the tension. "Ehhhh, would you have though?"

Blaide sighs. The glimmer is fading from his eyes. "I really love you, Erin."

"I... really like you, Blaide. I do."

I pause. He knows what's coming next.

You'll be alone forever. You can't do this.

I can. It's time. I inhale sharply like I'm preparing to rip off a Band-Aid. "But I don't think we should be together anymore," I say.

"Okay." Blaide looks away and bites his lip. "I understand."

"I—I'm sorry to do this over VideoChat. I know it's not ideal, but I just can't go on pretending anymore. You...you always talk about me like I'm someone else, like we're this great love story, and it's just not true. But you will have that someday. I hope you know that. You'll find someone that makes you feel that way. Neither of you will have to fake it. It'll just come naturally."

Blaide looks back at the screen with tears in his blue eyes. "Thanks." He clears his throat. "So, um, listen, the band's starting back up again. I better go."

"Okay. Bye, Blaide."

"Bye, Erin."

After our call ends, a few memories take the stage for their final bow: the day last summer when Blaide was just a crush and I chased him around my yard, trying to dowse him with a water bottle after he put his cold hand on my neck, our first kiss out in the porch swing, the mosquitos ate us alive but we didn't care, and the first time I got to ride in his car on a warm fall day with the windows down, my left hand in Blaide's and my right hand gliding on the wind. For the first time in a long time, I don't feel guilt or regret or despair when letting go of someone.

I feel…peace.

My phone's pretty much dead now and there'll be no service soon anyway. Still, only two miles stand between my car and me. When I make it there, I'm going back for Evan.

And nothing is going to stop me.

Rick sits on the concrete front porch, drinking the last of his second beer. I'm a few feet away in the overgrown grass acting like I'm tapping into my phone for a RYDE. My face is poised and calm while my mind spins. There's no bold choice to be made here. What can I do?

"They coming?" Rick asks from the stoop.

"Yeah, any minute," I say, though the truth is no. No, they're not. Climbing back in a RYDE and riding back to Hitter's with Rick is the last thing I want to do. I could take off running down the street. Get a safe distance away; call a RYDE to the train station from there. But that doesn't seem possible. One common misconception that people have about me is that I'm athletic since I'm tall. The truth is the last time I ran anywhere was for a skit at one of our shows when I pretended to be a rollerblader named Zeke. Even just sprinting across the stage left me winded. I look up and catch Rick staring at me. He rips a massive burp without breaking eye contact as though he can read my thoughts and he's unimpressed.

Rick gets up and starts toward me. "Hey, can I borrow your phone?" Rick smiles with his hand out. "Just gotta make a call real quick."

"Um." I glance down the street. Almost on cue, the last lit streetlight burns out. The universe does speak in metaphors but the only thing it's trying to tell you is *"you're on your own, pal."*

"My battery is almost dead," I say, which isn't even a lie.

"Oh. It'll just be a quick call." Rick takes another step in my direction with his non-beer hand still outstretched. "I just gotta call my buddy, Smoothy, let him know I'm going to swing by later."

Something tells me that Smoothy isn't named because of his love for tasty-yet-healthy fruit drinks. I look over my shoulder down the dark, empty street again.

"Who you looking for? We both know you didn't call for that RYDE. How about I just call Smoothy to come pick me up and you can go your own way?" Rick shrugs like he could care less one way or the other.

I'm out of excuses and options. Without a second thought, I tap to share my location with Erin before handing my phone to Rick. "Keep it short please."

"Sure thing." Rick snatches it away and immediately walks away with his back to me. Rick punches in a number. Hushed murmurs follow. Rick shoots a glare over his shoulder as though he knows I'm eavesdropping.

A few seconds pass, then a few more. A minute. Just when I think I may actually start to get up the nerve to ask Rick to get off the phone, he hangs up and saunters over to me. "You know, I was thinking…" Rick points at me with my phone. "You seem like a pretty well-off kid—"

"Haha, no. I live in a garage and work fast food. I'm as poor as it gets."

"Worse than us?" Rick raises his eyebrows at me as he takes another glug from his can.

"Well…"

"Didn't think so. Why don't you help us out a little bit?" Rick steps towards me. "You came all this way to meet me, to meet us, and as you can see your grandma isn't doing okay."

I take a couple steps backward. Every bad decision I've ever made has joined together and gained sentience against me. "I don't really have anything."

Headlights shine down the street. My heart leaps at this small semblance that life exists beyond this front lawn. But then it just as quickly does a free fall down onto my guts. "Oh, here's our ride." A Crown Victoria screeches to a stop in front of us. Rick opens the door, ushering me into the middle of the long bench seat.

"After you," Rick says, still holding my phone. "Smoothy's just going to give us a ride back to the bar so I can get my bike and you can meet up with your girlfriend."

When I hesitate, Rick smiles like a wolf. "Come on, I was just fucking with you about that money stuff. Just my twisted sense of humor, right, Smooth?" Rick bends down to look at Smoothy, a large bald man with a dark gnarly beard covering the lower half of his face. Poorly drawn tattoos snake down each of Smoothy's massive arms. Smoothy gives Rick a slight nod.

The dead-end street offers no outlets. The only decisions I can make, the only places I can take this scene all end badly.

"The backseat is full of shit," Smoothy says, his voice higher than I expect it to be. I turn to see that; yes, indeed, the backseat is full of bicycle wheels, greasy tools, tarps, dirty clothes, and all sorts of things.

"You gotta ride bitch then." Rick slaps me hard on the shoulder, and before I realize it, he's pushing in beside me and pinning me against the man named Smoothy that smells of body odor and weed.

For the first time in months, I just want to go home.

Erin & The Maybe This Times
Chapter Fifty-Two

Dad always said that I never let him down, that there wasn't a moment in my life when I wasn't making him proud, but I don't believe that. I disappointed him in life plenty of times, like when he'd be so excited to play me one of his old emo records and I'd let out a groan or when I listed off my reasons for no longer loving Harry Potter even though we bonded over it when I was nine. Those things are bad enough, but I think part of what tore me up so bad after failing to give the commencement speech is the fact that I had managed to fail him in death (again).

Dad never asked much of me. Even in his last days, when I'd sit by his bedside, holding his hand while we both pretended to watch whatever Dad Movie was playing in the background, when I kept asking what I could do for him, he'd always just pat my hand and say, "This is plenty, Air-Bear." Mom and I would always have to guess when he wanted Gatorade (Blue, of course) or something to eat, dreading the end of whatever movie was playing since we knew that would start a new round of "What Does Dad Want to Watch?" The only thing he ever asked of me was to deliver his eulogy. I said I would. Condensing down all my memories of him, his true essence, his Random Bits of Unsolicited Advice, brought me a new sense of purpose in his last days. I truly believed I could do it.

When the time came though, I couldn't do it. Watching his friends, acquaintances, and family members I didn't remember fill up the room, knowing that I was going to stand in front of his casket and talk about his life, it was just too overwhelming. I sprinted out of the funeral home and found a parking block to hyperventilate on until Mom found me. The commencement speech was supposed to be my way to make up for that, my way to finally let the world know my dad was this amazing (mostly) overlooked person. When I failed at that too, I thought there would be no way to ever make it up to him.

Walking back to my car to go pick up Evan helps me feel better though. Like *if* (and we're talking big *if* here) Dad could see me now, he'd be proud that I'm doing the right thing.

Dad's Random Bits of Unsolicited Advice #44: The bravest thing you can say is "sorry."

Dad's Random Bits of Unsolicited Advice #28: Be brave, be kind (or at least try).

That's what I'm doing. I'm trying.

Fiona shimmers ahead in the distance like a dutiful stallion waiting patiently right where I left her. I jog ahead, the gas swirling in its container. The rain finally starts. Tentative at first, but its pace quickens even with mine. I start filling the tank as the drops sting my skin.

Once inside, I plug my phone in the charger and try calling Evan's phone, but it goes straight to voicemail. Leaving a rambling lunatic message would just make it worse. He's probably having too much fun with (possible) Bio-Man anyway. I can see Evan now playing pool (or darts?), getting uninvited cliché life advice like: "always trust your gut," probably having the time of his life.

That's okay. I can see all that. I can handle all that now.

Heavy raindrops pelt my windshield. Lightning cracks the sky in two. I'm going to find Evan and tell him I'm sorry.

I'm not going to let him let me go.

"He definitely hates you now," Anxiety Brain comes back.

"All you've ever done is lie to me. I'm not listening to you."

"Good luck with that." Anxiety Brain crows. "Evan doesn't want anything to do with you now. He's not going to forgive you."

"I don't care. I'm going to try."

Twenty miles outside of Charleston, my phone picks up another bar of service and buzzes with a new notification.

"Evan Prucasyk is now sharing his location with you."

Evan & The Withdrawing Wombats
<u>Chapter Fifty-Three</u>

"Isn't Hitter's…um…back in town?" I'm squished between the man I possibly came from and his distinguished colleague, Smoothy, in an old car with no seatbelts.

"Don't worry about it," Rick says with a cigarette clenched between his lips.

"Can we at least crack a window?" I peel my thighs from the vinyl seat. My left arm is lodged into Smoothy's damp armpit. I pull away but it only sends me further into Rick. "It's pretty warm."

"Windows don't work," Smoothy answers in his high pitch.

"We'll be there soon enough." Rick exhales a wall of smoke, stinging my eyes.

"And where is *there* exactly?" I ask and though neither of them answers, I don't need to hear it to know that wherever "there" is, it isn't good. If only I had any valuable skills to get me out of this. Maybe my dad was right when he tried to get me to take Taekwondo when I was seven. Or when he tried to take me hunting when I was twelve to "toughen me up." There's only one thing I got…

Can I get a suggestion from the audience, please?

Heart condition.

Okay. Heart condition. We can work with that.

Heart condition. Heart condition. Heart. Condition.

"Mm." I clutch the front of my damp shirt and start panting. My cheeks are hot. Thankfully, the current conditions make this easy to fake. "My…heart…I need…to—"

"What the fuck you going on about?" Rick barks out the side of his mouth. "There ain't nothing wrong with you. You're just being a pussy."

Ah, I only had to know my bio-dad for four hours for him to call me that. Must be some kind of record. My real dad never even got there, aloud at least. Still, I have a show to do here. I just need one of them to buy in.

"My...heart," I say again, pulling at the front of my shirt. Sweat starts down my forehead. "I have a...condition. Coronary Artery Disease."

"Bullshit," Rick says, which is technically correct. Smoothy hasn't said anything yet so there's still hope.

My hair is damp with sweat. "Pull over...we need to...pull..." I plead heavy breaths.

We pass beneath a couple of streetlights. Their light distorts and smears across the streaked windshield. A few signs of life show from the homes that line the street, the flicker of a screen, the soft light of a lamp dampened by the shades, the low thunder rumble of trashcans being pulled to the street, I'll take it. I continue muttering in half-sentences and gasps for air, really committing to the scene, there's more at stake here than getting a laugh or bowing to silence.

Neither Rick nor Smoothy say much. The fact that I haven't been told to "shut the hell up" or called a name again is a small victory in itself. "Just drop me off at the closest Emergency Room...or...just leave me here and I'll call an ambulance."

Smoothy shifts in the driver's seat. His tattooed knuckles relax their grip on the steering wheel. My heightened improv senses pick up that he's weighing the pro's and con's. Is it worth it to steal twenty bucks and a phone off a kid only to have him die in your car?

"Hitter..." Smoothy starts. "What's the plan here? I can't go back to jail, man."

"Just keep driving. I didn't find enough at Mom's," Rick sneers. "Besides, he's faking it. Clover's expecting payment and I'm not giving up my bike. The kid has money somewhere. If he won't give us his ATM numbers the easy way, then we'll find some way to get them."

Smoothy does as he's told while I continue writhing in the front seat, each movement becoming more futile than the last. It's like that time I mimicked a wombat coming down from meth for one of our shows, I'm just thrashing and falling over myself, and no one is having a good time, especially not me. I don't even know what comes next, but I do have a few questions like: Um, who is Clover? Is he lucky? I doubt it. Why does Rick owe him money? And what happens when they find out I have a negative balance in my bank account? The panic attack begins to set in more aggressively and for real this time.

Orange and yellow lights blur and swirl around me as we continue down the street. Smoke, humidity, and evaporated sweat fill my lungs. My skin feels clammy, cold, hot, all at the same time. The reality of the moment continues to pull me further into myself where all I can do is consider each individual symptom as I fall down into the black well.

Mimicking a bad German narrator: *Flailing and writhing, the desperate wombat tries to kick his unhealthy addiction, knowing well that the cure for the pain is in the pain.*

Until...the car veers to the right and starts to slow down. Rick and Smoothy argue back and forth. Something about "what the hell are you doing? We're almost there" and "this is on you, not me" and "I ain't going back to jail for your ass" and "Clover's gonna kill me" and "your ass can get out too if you want." And then I'm jerked from the car. I crash onto the hot pavement. Pain shoots through my shoulder. Someone forcefully rifles through my pockets, taking my wallet. I close my eyes tight, hoping this is as bad as it gets. A car door slams. My eyes stay closed. My body's still clenched. It's not over until it's over.

My phone crashes on the pavement beside me. "You're lucky, you little shit," Rick scoffs. Then another car door slams.

Exhaust blasts me in the face and gravel skitters past me as the Crown Vic speeds off. For a while, I lay on my back, watching the storm close in.

I'm alive.

Flash of lightning.

I'm alive.

The rain starts pouring.

I'm alive.

Erin & The Emergency Wig
Chapter Fifty-Four

The storm follows me to Charleston. The dark clouds I hoped to leave behind are now directly overhead. Like Blaide's drummer clicking his drumsticks together to announce the start of their set, a crack of thunder splinters the sky in the distance, unleashing a torrent of rain more ungodly and threatening than any music created by my (now) ex-boyfriend. Much more concerning though is that Evan's location disappeared five minutes ago.

Fiona's wipers can't keep pace with the sheets of rain so I'm driving down a bumpy, gravel road on the outskirts of Charleston, hunched over the steering wheel, knuckles white, hoping to not get swept off into the ditch by the pounding water. Evan's last shared location was somewhere around here. There aren't many possible reasons why Evan could be out here. There are even fewer *good* ones.

Visibility comes and goes in one-second intervals. All I see is the road, trees, and rain. Road, trees, and rain. Road, trees, and rain. Road, trees, and—holy shit!

I swerve to avoid a dude walking near the shoulder of the road with his head down. He's wearing khaki shorts and a bright plaid button-up just like…I slam my car in park and run out into the rain, not even bothering to shut my door.

He's looking at the ground as I approach. I stop in my tracks ten feet away. "Evan! I'm sorry!"

He looks up. His face is splotchy and red. "Don't say that to me."

I hesitantly step closer to him, not caring how drenched I am. "I know. You have every right to be mad. I'm sorry for leaving you. I never should have. I was just scared. I didn't want to meet him." I give a pained laugh. "Honestly, I think I was scared I would actually end up liking him. Like what if he was really cool or—"

"Stop." Evan shakes his head. "Just stop."

"Evan. Please believe me." I'm reaching out for him, but he won't come closer. "I'm sorry. And I'll do whatever I can, for however long it takes to make it up to you. I promise. I'll—"

Evan closes the gap between us and throws his arms around me. His chest heaves where I lay my head. "You have nothing to apologize for. I'm the jerk. I should've never left you for... for him."

"It's okay." I hug him tighter. "It's all okay now."

Evan shakes as I hold him.

The rain washes over us.

"We should probably go, huh?" He holds me at arm's length as the downpour continues. "I promise I'll tell you everything soon. It's been a long terrible night. But I'm so happy you're here. I don't deserve you."

I nod, knowing that Evan's shitty day most definitely beats mine, not that it's a competition or even matters now. We're both winners in the Shitty Days Sweepstakes or we're both losers. Whatever we both are, we're the same. We start back towards my car as the rain onslaught continues. A memory hits me.

"Oh!" I shout, running ahead of Evan. "I got just the thing!"

I throw open the backdoors, digging through the pile of clothes, until I find it. "Yes!" I throw the old thing over my head and sprint back to Evan, rain pouring down my face. "Emergency Wig," I shout with the ridiculous purple thing over my head.

Evan bows with his arms outstretched. "All Hail, Emergency Wig!"

Then, we're back in the car, laughing and dripping wet. I hand Evan a towel from the backseat to dry off with. "So, what's the story with Emergency Wig?" he asks as we start towards home. "Let me guess, your dad was a former drag queen and used it to make you smile?"

"Oh, I wish," I say, still rocking it like no big deal. "Actually, it was my mom's thing. My dad had the worst temper. Like he was almost always annoyingly kind, but then, other times, he would lose his temper over silly things, like waiting thirty-five minutes for a table when the hostess told us it would be fifteen or if he took a wrong turn when he was trying to get somewhere. So, my mom..." My throat seizes up at the thought of her. "Mom used to keep the wig on hand to throw on her head whenever Dad started getting pissed off and it would instantly make him laugh. She's done it for me a few times too...though not in a while."

"I wish I grew up with your family," Evan says wistfully.

"Me too," I say, reaching over for his hand. "But you're my family now and that's enough."

August

We found a way out.

Evan & The Come Up

<u>Chapter Fifty-Five</u>

Once I've condensed my many piles of dirty clothes into a more manageable single pile and packed up my assorted hair products, hygiene items, and tangle of charger cables, it looks like I was never here at all. Though I've been putting it off for days, the whole process takes maybe ten minutes. I fall back onto the couch that's been my bed for the last three months. Dim early evening light cheats through the dusty garage windows. Mr. Holloway's push-mower buzzes in the distance as the Cricket Orchestra begins stretching their strings for their opening number. Meanwhile, my heart beats fast and loud in my chest, not from packing up my meager belongings, but because I heard Ro get back at least thirty minutes ago.

In the old days, Ro would've come to see me before he went into the house to see his parents even. These aren't the old days though. So, I'm pacing the garage floor, running my thumb over the smooth porcelain angel I stole from my parents. I stop in my tracks as a new text comes in from Christian. We finalize our road trip plans for tomorrow. It helps me feel a little better, but that feeling soon passes when Christian's ten-minute break is up. Erin's out with her mom tonight so that leaves me to work on my old laptop while I wait for Ro. By the time I look up again, it's night out. Mr. Holloway's mower gave up who knows how long ago, and the Cricket Orchestra is midway through their raucous set.

Right when I begin to reconcile that maybe Ro isn't going to come out at all, the door creaks open before shutting with a bang. "Hey," Ro says meekly, stepping into the light, hands shoved into his pockets.

"Hey," I reply, trying not to be taken aback by how different he looks. It's always weird when you get used to someone existing more in your head than they do in real life. "New haircut?"

"Yep." Ro nods. He looks in my direction without making eye contact. "New glasses?"

"Uh, yeah."

"Cheryl told me you've worked your last shift at CB's. What's up with that?" His tone stays flat, without its usual warmth.

I watch him for a beat. My bottom lip quivers over the apology I want to say. Then I consider launching into an elaborate joke about Weird Allan and I starting an illegal fight club in the storage room after hours, but instead I just tell Ro the truth, all of it. I tell him more about Erin, about the multiple fights with my parents, about finally learning that my dad isn't my bio-dad, about how I skipped out on a couple shifts so I could track down the donor, about how we did find my bio-father, about how I sold out Erin and got in a huge fight with her just so I could meet that man, about how that dude tried to use his sick mother to extort me for money and when that didn't work, he and some high-voiced knuckle-tatted guy named Smoothy mugged me. I tell Ro how Erin came back for me. I tell him about Christian. Then...

"I missed you all summer," I say to Ro when I finish catching him up.

Ro meets my eyes and nods but doesn't say anything.

My chest tightens like a bee sting. "I'm sorry I didn't come to your going away party. I'm sorry I wasn't more supportive of you like you were for me. I'm sorry I check out when things aren't about me. I'm sorry

I'm not better, but I'm going to try. I'm trying." Most my life I've avoided apologies like a Bible study led by Marjorie Taylor Greene, but now that I've leaned into it, I feel a massive weight slide off my shoulders.

Ro nods again, the damage still apparent in his eyes. He clears his throat. "I appreciate that. But you know what honestly hurt the worst?"

Blood rushes to my ears. I shake my head.

Ro sighs. "What hurt the worst is that you would ever think that I just made the team because I'm a minority."

Hearing this hits like a punch to the gut. "What? I wouldn't ever...I didn't—"

Ro holds up one hand. His mouth a straight line. "I know *you* didn't say it. I did, as an obvious bit. But when I joked that I probably just made the team because they needed another brown person, you didn't disagree or even laugh, you just sat there."

"I'm sorry, Ro. You're right. I guess I just thought that was so far from the truth that I didn't even need to dignify it with a response. I'm just so stuck in my head, so used to you helping me feel better all the time, that I don't ever think about helping you." I give a half-laugh. "That's not how it should be though."

"Exactly." Ro nods sternly, a rock-solid impersonation of his dad. "So...Ashanti told me you all put on a pretty good show last night at the High Watt?" This time, his tone has lifted some, but not all the way.

"No. First tell me about your shows. Seems like you all were killing it all summer long. Tell me everything."

Ro gives me a city-by-city breakdown of his summer of shows, all the people he met, the drunken pool parties in rich kid neighborhoods, the late night diners, the hookups, and, more importantly, the best skits they pulled off. As Ro talks, the ice begins to melt away from our relationship. A rush of adrenaline courses down my shoulders as the thaw settles in.

"So, what're you going to do now?" Ro gestures at my stuff packed up.

"Well…I kinda did something." I tap the spacebar and spin my laptop around for him to see.

Ro's face lights up in disbelief.

"I start next week. It's this little theater school outside Chicago. I signed up for their acting and improv classes. Despite being pissed at me for missing some shifts, Cheryl helped me get set up with a new job. And I found an apartment to rent nearby." I bite my lip before moving onto the next part. "There's also a counselor there that I'm going to start seeing for my mental health stuff. Whether they like it or not, I'm still on my parents' insurance so they'll be footing the bill."

"Evan, this…" Ro shakes his head. "This is really awesome. I'm proud of you."

Without hesitation, I move to my best friend and wrap him up in a massive hug. "I'm proud of you," I tell him. "You've done so many incredible things."

Ro lets go of me. "Wait…what about tomorrow?" He wrinkles up his forehead at all my stuff packed up. "You said you start next week. Did a talking goat convince your parents to take you back in the meantime?"

"It would take a talking goat, a burning bush, a plague of locusts, and the threat of being reduced to a pillar of salt for that to happen, but no, Erin has this birthday thing tomorrow so Christian was going to drive me down for it. I'm going to stay with her for a couple days before taking the train back up here." I run my hands over my knees. "Would you maybe want to come too? I'd really like for you to meet her."

"No. I got plans to meet up with Tony."

"Ah, that's alright then."

Ro breaks up laughing. "Whew. This summer made you way too serious. Of course, I want to go, man. I can't wait to meet Erin *and* Christian. There is one thing though…"

"What's that?" My eyebrow does its natural arch.

"DN-YAY, seriously?" Ro cracks. "That's the best name they could come up with?"

"Hey, you're the one that got me to do it after you saw that documentary." I push his shoulder. "Remember, *don't you want to see if you're secretly a prince or related to someone famous?*"

"You're right. You're right. I mean, at least it's better than Chromo-Home." Ro shrugs.

I wince. "Oooh, that seems homophobic somehow, but I'm not sure."

Ro looks at me in shock with his mouth a perfect O until I let a smile show through. Then he grins too. "I'm just saying, they might as well have called it 22&You," Ro says.

We keep going on and on, except instead of riffing into oblivion, I laugh at every genius line Ro delivers. We lose ourselves in the game, never knowing what the other one is going to say next, not knowing how all the ever-expanding scenes in front of us are going to play out, but ready to take part in them all the same.

Erin & The Simple Truths
<u>Chapter Fifty-Six</u>

It's nicer here than I imagined. A gentle breeze peels through the trees nearly overpowering the dry August heat. My hands tremble. Deep breath. Let it out. Now is a good time to start.

"One day, we're all going to die, and there's an immense pressure on each of us to be extraordinary, to be the most popular, the richest, the smartest, the best, to be world changers in the little time we have. I think for a lot of us, there's this underlying belief that recognition, that being seen by as many people as possible, will make us more tangible, proving our existence, thus making our eventual death more palatable. I know this because I've been doing this for most of my seventeen years. What I've found is that no achievement is ever enough. Sure, someone could look at that as 'staying hungry' or some other kind of sports drink slogan metaphor, but when I really start to look at the underlying reasons for my quest for greatness, they're usually much sadder and lonelier than I would care to admit. Making stuff, setting a goal and chasing after it, it allows me to fool myself for months at a time that I'm actually *never* going to die." I pause and glance up at my mom.

She wipes her cheek, nodding for me to continue.

I look back down at my paper. My hands are steady now. "I used to watch endless videos of famous people delivering commencement speeches, soaking in their wisdom, hoping that if I took enough from them, maybe one day I could be rich, famous, relevant like them. In doing that, I totally missed the point. The smartest man I ever met lived under the same roof as me for most of my entire life. He wasn't rich. He wasn't a genius. He wasn't universally adored or even known. He dedicated countless hours to writing, in his words, 'bad science-fiction novels that no one ever saw any point in publishing.' He was insecure and jealous of others. He was unsure of his own talent. He was brave and unafraid of failure. He was human through and through. He told me once, 'Life is endlessly complicated. Find a few simple truths to guide you through. Challenge them. Fight for them. Allow them space to grow so you can do the same.'" I stop there.

I look at Mom with my hair blowing in my face. "Okay, so you get the gist of where I was going."

"I want to hear how it ends," she says with a grin, her smile lines on full display.

"I've rewritten the end since then."

"Well, good, let's hear it then."

I reflect her smile as I return to my speech. "Life's not just about how much you can desperately accomplish in the numbered days you're given. It's about finding your people, those that fill you up rather than drain you, and holding onto them with all you got. I believe that if you do that, you'll find yourself in the process by digging in, finding those parts of you that make you proud to be who you are, those parts of yourself that make your people love you, cultivate those parts, build them up. There will likely be parts of yourself that you don't like as much—find out why that is, challenge those parts, interrogate them, either become comfortable with their existence or erase them entirely. Through that process, you'll likely find your purpose. That's what makes living life not just more bearable, but also joyful."

I stop again, glancing to Dad's headstone, his name with the dates below it next to Mom's without any yet. The carved granite doesn't offer any advice and though it's shiny, it doesn't come close to reflecting any of the light I saw in his eyes. In an odd way, the absence of him here makes me more hopeful. Like maybe he really did pass on to a better place when he died. I look to the blue sky and continue, "Now I know, all this is easier said than done, but at least it's a road map. At least we know where to start. I may spend my entire life working through these things, but I feel like it will lead to a happier existence so that's what I'm going to do. If somewhere along the way, I find this not to be true anymore for me…then I'll grow and move beyond it. Maybe that's the point of this big beautiful complicated mess we're in called life. Find your people. Find yourself. Find your purpose. I'm lucky I've found the first part. I'm working on the second. And I have no clue what the third is yet, but that's okay. I'm excited to find out. Thank you."

Mom claps silently and comes toward me, wrapping me up in a tight hug. There's nothing about this place that makes me miss Dad any less, but with Mom's arms around me, it's kind of like when I used to catch them hugging in the kitchen when I was a little kid and I'd burrow in between the two of them so I'd be in the middle, just smooshed in by all that love. It's not as good as that, of course.

It's something different, something new.

After a couple minutes, I head back to the car to give Mom a moment alone up there. I watch as she straightens up his flowers and Windexes bird poop from the headstone. I can see her mouth moving as though she's talking to him. It feels too personal, so I look away.

A half hour later, Mom opens the driver's side door and scoots in. "Sorry, time got away from me. You okay?"

"Yeah. I am. You?"

"Honestly, this is the best I've felt in months."

"Me too," I say simply, thankful that Mom isn't going on about how good my speech was or how proud Dad would be. She knows I know those things and for the first time, I really do.

We make small talk for a couple miles. Mainly just talking about Mom's new job working at a children's shelter in downtown Langford. "Some people help others because of this great altruistic motivation. Me? I do it because helping people heal, helps me heal."

I shrug. "That's as good a reason as any."

"You don't think it's selfish?" Mom asks half-joking. "Isn't it a little 'hey-look-at-me' selfies-in-the-soup-kitchen kind of thing?"

"Maybe you're just being honest with yourself where those 'altruistic' a-holes are carrying on with their savior complexes."

Mom cackles. "Ah, I see your appointments with Dr. Meera are wearing off on you…just let me ask, how often will you be coming home again? Just for the appointments, of course."

"At least once a month. Strictly for my appointments, of course." After Evan's whole Bio-Man debacle, I couldn't stand to be within a five-mile radius of that dude, so I relocated to a junior college only an hour away. It's far enough away that I get out of Langford, but still close enough that I can come home to see Mom when I want. Bonus points that they still honored my academic scholarship so yay, no crippling student loan debt.

"Good." Mom reaches over and gives my hand a squeeze. "Erin, can I ask you something?"

"Of course."

"You mentioned that you're still searching for purpose, have you decided what you want to study in college? Still going with creative writing?"

"No, I think I've found something better for me. They have a great psychology program. I want to take a couple of classes to see where they lead." This is the first time I've said this out loud to anyone. Hearing the words leave my mouth feels good.

Mom nods to the windshield. "That sounds perfect for you."

"Is it weird that I'm looking forward to a family get-together for once?" I ask as we round our corner.

"That's what it's like when you've found your people," Mom says with the glimmer of a smile. "A really smart person said that once, I think."

Noonie and Poppy's car (grandparents on my mom's side from California) is already parked out in front of our house. I sprint across the grass to hug them. "My dear, what did you do to your hair?" Noonie asks as she reciprocates my hug.

"It's awesome isn't it?" Mom comes up behind me to hug Noonie next. "I just love the purple."

We lead them inside to finish getting ready before everyone else shows up. The Happy Birthday Erin! banner hangs from one side of the dining room wall to the other. Purple and yellow streamers billow from the doorway. The doorbell rings as my Aunt Val and Uncle John come in. I give them hugs and try not to be disappointed that Evan isn't here yet.

No intrusive voice shoves its way into my head to suggest that he won't be coming at all. I am past that (for now) though not far enough that its absence goes unnoticed, nor far enough that I've even begun to let my guard down. Some battles I'll fight my entire life.

I sneak off to Dad's office as a few more family members trickle in. From down the hall, I overhear my Uncle Todd saying they hoped to come to my congratulations party back in May. I sit down at Dad's desk, imagining him sitting here trying to type one of his several failed manuscripts. I pull out the keyboard to find the corner of a Post-It sticking out from under it. I quickly snatch it up. There are several more stuck behind it in a series.

Dad's Random Bits of Unsolicited Advice #101: Erin, I used to think adults had everything figured out. By now, you've learned that's far from the truth. I've gotten to live forty-six years. They've been (mostly) good years. Still, I can't tell you how many nights I wasted, worrying endlessly about some stupid thing I said in passing to a casual acquaintance that I don't even like. I can't tell you how many moments I wasn't present for because I was reliving some awkward, embarrassing moment from my awkward, embarrassing past (there are a lot!). I've often felt like the walking punchline to a joke that everyone else knew, but I never got to hear. I hope you never feel that. But if you do, I hope these little reminders I've left will guide you through. Oh, please forgive me if they've been overbearing or condescending. If anything, these Post-It's have been as much for me as they've been for you. I don't have it all (or anything really) figured out. There's a lot I don't know (so much!!!) but what I do know is that your mother and you made my life more enjoyable than I ever imagined. Thank you for that. Thank you for loving me. Thank you for each and every beautiful, wonderful, messy moment. Being sick hasn't granted me much wisdom (screw every movie that taught me that would be the case), but it has shown me that as my days dwindle down, I find myself not caring at all about the stupid things I've said or done, or if some dude I went to high school with still thinks I'm a loser because I never got published, all I care about is you and your mother. That's it. You both are all the good things. Nothing else matters. Sure, it's a bullshit dying man's platitude, but as a bullshit dying man, I gotta tell you, it really feels true. I'm so incredibly proud of you not because of what you've accomplished, but because of who you are. I always will be. I love you, Dad.

"Thanks," I say out loud to the room. Unlike the cemetery, this room, here at his desk, this is where I feel him more than anywhere else. "I'm proud of you too." I wait a minute as though he might respond.

The door creaks open seemingly on its own.

Chevy the Cat bumps his head through. "Meep," he gives his little squeaky noise.

A chorus of Hello's comes through from the living room. Evan's bright voice is among them. "Thanks for letting me know they're here." I give Chevy a little pat as I bound through.

I launch into a hug when I see Evan. "Oh, my God, I love it!" He says when he sees my hair. Introductions are made. "This is my brother, Evan," I say to my relatives with full confidence. Having already heard the story several times in the last couple of weeks, they all take it in stride (Uncle Todd included). Evan introduces me to Ro and Christian. We eat, tell stories, and everyone blends in together so naturally, it's almost hard to imagine it being any other way. Madison doesn't show up because she wasn't invited. No one asks where she is, same for Blaide. Everyone who matters is here. My people.

Evan, Ro, Christian, and I are sitting out on the back patio. Mosquito candles flicker around us as the sun merges with the horizon in a blend of purple, pink, and orange.

Evan and Christian sit side-by-side, casually holding hands, occasionally sharing in a small joke or conversation that only they know.

"This has to be mind-blowing, right?" Ro leans forward to me. "Like how many of you could there be?"

I shake my head. "Honestly, don't have a clue."

Ro cocks an eyebrow at me. "Have you seen that Vince Vaughn movie?"

"Dodgeball?" I scrunch up my face with a tilt of my head. I know where Ro's going with this, but I like playing coy. "My ex unfortunately showed me that one."

"No, the one where he's a…" Ro trails off like he's unsure of the exact terminology he should use when referring to our (once) anonymous donor. It's so sweet and earnest that of course we have to mess with him.

"Ro." Evan puts his hand on Ro's shoulder. "I appreciate your sensitivity over this very private matter. But for the record, we prefer the term Jizz-Volunteer."

"Or Splooge-Benefactor," I add.

"Or Semen-Philanthropist," Evan says next.

"Or Patron of the Seed." Christian steeples his hands together and bows.

"Or Commissioner of the—██████!" I yell the three-letter alliterative proudly, knowing that I just threw down the gauntlet of dirty words. Being a short (mostly) cute girl has its advantages; one of them is that no one ever expects you to say the filthiest thing.

All of them fall over each other in laughter. Ro starts laughing so hard he launches into a coughing fit. "Okay, okay, okay." Ro holds up his hand in surrender. "So, in that movie where he plays a…ahem…Commissioner of C—I can't even say it." Ro shakes his head. "Anyways, he finds out that he has an insane amount of donor kids. Do you guys think you have like five hundred siblings out there?"

"Ro, I know you love crappy movies, but this is a whole new level, why would you ever see that movie?" Evan asks in mock offense. "That dude is like a million years old and he hasn't been funny in at least that long, if ever."

"Hey, man, it was on streaming, seemed dumb so I gave it a shot. And let me tell you, it *was* indeed dumb as hell," Ro counters. "But back to the point, do you guys think there are more of you out there?"

Evan looks to me. "There would have to be, right?"

"Our own extended universe," I say with a grin.

"I like that." Evan smiles warmly. "Just think of all the stories. How many could there be?"

"I think I read online that most donors are capped at like twenty-four donations," I say.

"Wait." Christian leans in with a wry smile. "How exactly are these donors 'capped' exactly?"

Ro nods in approval. "I like him." Ro taps Evan's knee.

Just then my phone vibrates in my pocket. "Holy crap!" I shout as I look at the screen. "Oh my, Evan…did you get this same notification?"

"What? From DN-YAY? A new match? No way." Evan starts fumbling for his phone.

Ro and Christian exchange a glance.

Evan hurriedly swipes open his phone before looking at me with disappointment. "I didn't get anything. This is a new phone. What's it say? Who is it? Where're they from? Brother or sister?"

"You just…you've got to see this." I shake my head. "I don't believe it."

Evan leaps up to look at my phone. I can barely hold back my smile.

"Oh…you jerk!" Evan yells in disbelief.

"What? I just can't believe those deals." I turn over my phone to show the rest of them my Spam Email from Applebee's. "How could those tasty appetizers be any cheaper?"

Our laughter echoes into the night. Honestly, I don't know how many more of us are out there in the world, just carrying on with their lives, unaware of our existence. We could walk by them on the street, stand behind them in line at Target, or flip them off in traffic. They could be the man in the next viral video cussing out a helpless barista or the person in the next feel-good LookAtMe post about starting a creative non-profit to fight homelessness.

They could be anyone, anywhere.

Maybe they'll find their way to us in the end or maybe they won't. Maybe we'll find them.

Our constellation will be forever evolving.

Each star above is a possibility.

A Song of Thanks Sung by a Hack (Part Two)

Our Extended Universe is loosely based on the experience of my wonderful wife and best friend Stacy finding her (almost) equally wonderful brother, Ethan, through a DNA match website. All the parts about them meeting the donor and him being an awful dude are made up, etc. etc. But the shock of them each discovering later in their lives that they're donor conceived, the impact that had on their identities, and the comfort they found in each other is all entirely real. It was a running joke for a while that I should write a book based on their story. Like all good on-going bits, that "joke" held a lot of truth to it, and eventually, while in the midst of a global pandemic, led to some brainstorming / several bad drafts, until eventually now, here you are holding this book in your hands. So, with all that said, thank you to Stacy and Ethan for encouraging and trusting me to tell your story while providing so many of your own insights, details, and character preferences. Though giving you both just a compound "thanks" like that isn't sufficient, so please allow me to thank you both individually as well.

Stacy, every day I wake up hoping to make you proud and to help you feel seen, heard, and valued, so if that's the only thing I accomplish with this book, that's more than enough. I love you, Stacy. Thank you for letting me see myself.

Ethan, I'm so thankful not only for the close friendship you share with Stacy, but to have you as a beloved uncle to our kids, as the sharer of adventures, sing-alongs + countless inside jokes, and as a true brother and friend of my own. Thank you, Ethan.

Thank you to my editor, Evan Fisher, for their thoughtful observations, keen typo-finding / grammar correcting eyes, and for making so many helpful suggestions for how I could better achieve the goals of a given scene. Thank you, Evan. Here's to creating more books together in the future.

Thank you to Major Rich for helping me with early revisions of this novel, for once fatefully texting me about how the Purge extended movie universe could be so much more interesting, for taking me to my first improv show in Chicago, for giving me his improv books to help round out that world a bit more here, and for being such a great friend. Thank you, Major.

Thank you to Romann` Frost, the estate of Joe Burgess, and, again, Major for letting me into the world of their improv groups. Hanging out in the iO lobby bar, seeing the interactions between the team members after the shows, learning the terms, witnessing the play-by-play breakdowns of so many hilarious scenes that were soon forgotten, and the joyful reenactment of failed scenes that I will remember forever, all of that unbridled creativity made a profound impact on me and I hope that came through at least a little bit here in this book. Thank you.

Thank you to Sierra Porritt, Jonathon Brooks, Kalinda KC Schreiber, and Tracy Marchini for being early readers of Our Extended Universe, for giving insightful notes of what needed to be improved on while also letting me know when I hit the mark. Thank you all for helping me become a better writer and believing I could do it.

Thank you to Allison Staulcup for letting me use her brilliant band name, Pizza4Sluts, for Evan's improv team name. If you enjoy stunning songwriting and lyrics that are so funny they break your heart, be sure to check out Pizza4Sluts wherever you stream music.

Thank you to Sarah Baldwin for the beautiful cover design and book layout. Thank you to Tyler Chance and Romann` Frost for providing illustrations for the OEU zine. Thank you to Joshua Clifton and the Honey Gold Records folks for helping me put this book out.

Thank you to so many friends that always ask about what I'm writing next, always encouraging me to continue doing this and whatever creative avenue I want to pursue. I started naming some of you and it took up a whole page and I still worried I left someone off. Thank you.

Thank you to my sister, Vanessa, and the whole Durfee crew, Kris, Alicia, Weslyn, and Theo. I'm sure you all appreciate the humor of having the word Sluts just a couple paragraphs above your names.

Thank you to my Dad, Mark Johns, for all the bits of unsolicited advice he imparted to me over the years, for always telling me he's proud of me, and for always legitimately believing I'm capable of doing anything. It was that belief that always made me feel like I could achieve anything too. Even if I never came remotely close to making the NBA.

Thank you, Ezra, Eli, and Ewan just for being who you are.

Thank you to Diane & Steve Bailey for teaching me so many things, chief among those lessons being that family means more than just what you're born into. You both teach us that every single day.

Thank you to everyone who has taken time to read OEU or anything else I've written. This is a small operation so thank you so much for leaving reviews online and sharing this stuff with others. Thank you.

About the Author

Dane Johns is an independent writer, musician, and social worker living in beautiful southern Illinois with his wife, Stacy, and their three children. His debut novel, The Futile, was released in April 2022 via Honey Gold Records and is available now wherever books are sold online. Our Extended Universe is his second novel.